"We need to get out of these wet garments."

～⌒♋⌒～

Mercy shivered, her skin prickling with goose-flesh, not only from the wet chill, but from her own suggestion. But what choice had she? They both needed to get warm.

She reminded herself that if she'd trusted him enough to save her from drowning, then she could trust him enough to be naked in front of him.

Along with that thought came another shiver that sent her body trembling. Before she could reach for the ties of her soft green blouse, his hands were there, trying to force the stubborn, wet strings apart.

With curiosity, her glance shifted to his chest. His wet tan shirt was plastered to it. He had a nice chest, thick and solid with muscle, and she wondered if, like his hands, it bore battle scars. His shoulders were wide as was his neck, and she realized then the size of him.

He caught her gaze and she started, though certainly not because he caught her examining him. No, it was his strikingly dark eyes and the intensity of his look. And his words.

"I'll have you free of these stubborn ties soon, I promise."

By Donna Fletcher

ATTENTION: ORGANIZATIONS AND CORPORATIONS
Most Avon Books paperbacks are available at special quantity discounts for bulk purchases for sales promotions, premiums, or fund raising. For information, please call or write:

Special Markets Department, HarperCollins Publishers, 10 East 53rd Street, New York, New York 10022-5299. Telephone: (212) 207-7528.   Fax: (212) 207-7222.

DonnaFletcher

Bound TO A Warrior

AVON
An Imprint of HarperCollinsPublishers

This is a work of fiction. Names, characters, places, and incidents are products of the author's imagination or are used fictitiously and are not to be construed as real. Any resemblance to actual events, locales, organizations, or persons, living or dead, is entirely coincidental.

AVON BOOKS
An Imprint of HarperCollins*Publishers*
10 East 53rd Street
New York, New York 10022-5299

Copyright © 2010 by Donna Fletcher
ISBN 978-0-06-193471-1
www.avonromance.com

First Avon Books paperback printing: September 2010

Avon Trademark Reg. U.S. Pat. Off. and in Other Countries, Marca Registrada, Hecho en U.S.A.
HarperCollins® is a registered trademark of HarperCollins Publishers.

Printed in the U.S.A.

10 9 8 7 6 5 4 3 2 1

*When summer touches winter and the snow descends
the reign of the false King begins to end.
Four warriors ride together and then divide
among them the true king hides.
When he meets death on his own
that is when he reclaims his throne.*

A SEER'S PROPHECY

Chapter 1

Scotland Highlands, 1005

Duncan tumbled down hard onto the woman. He lay sprawled across her, hoping he had not hurt her. She was a bit of a thing that a good wind would blow away, but in the short time he had been shackled to her, he had come to realize that she was a strong one, a survivor.

He rolled off her, and with a slip of his arm around her narrow waist, took her along with him as he got to his feet. Her slim hand grasped hold of his arm until she found strong footing and then she let go. The strength of her grip shouldn't have surprised him, but her slim body led one to believe her weak.

"Move it!" one of the soldiers yelled and gave the woman a rough jab in the back with his sword handle.

She stumbled forward and this time grabbed hold of his arm. And he did, the strength of his rock-hard muscles alone enough to steady her and keep them from repeating the act.

A tentative smile told him that while she was appreciative, she was also hesitant to rely on him. Unfortunately, she had no choice. They were shackled at the wrists with iron cuffs and a connecting chain that didn't allow for much distance from one another.

Even in their dire circumstances he couldn't help but appreciate her lovely features. Though her round face was dusted with dirt there was no hiding her beauty; bewitching sapphire blue eyes that sparkled more brilliantly than the gem itself were framed by long, curled, black lashes. And no amount of grime could hide the luster of her waist length, raven black hair. Her garments were that of a peasant, and yet he had noticed that her hands showed no signs of hard toil.

He couldn't help but wonder who this woman was that he was chained to.

"I fear they mean us harm," she whispered.

It was the first words she had spoken to him since their ordeal had begun hours ago, and while he agreed, his thoughts lingered more on her low, sultry voice than their present situation. He almost laughed. How could he focus more on his attraction to her than their problem? He wisely contained his humor, but could not do the same with his thoughts.

"I agree," he said.

"Is there nothing we can do?" she asked.

He tapped at her iron cuff. "This could present a problem."

"I'm not afraid to fight."

While he admired her courage, it was obvious that she had never tasted battle, and he didn't believe she would have the stomach for what must be done if they were to attempt an escape.

As if she understood his doubt, she said, "I have more gumption than it may appear, and the odds are even, two of them to two of us. Besides—"

Her lovely blue eyes glazed over with tears, though she didn't shed a one.

"What choice do we have? They most certainly intend to kill us."

She was intelligent as well and no doubt wondered why they had been singled out from the group of captives the king's men had gathered along their route home. He hadn't given any reason to arrest him, though more than likely it had something to do with the prophecy many believed was soon to be fulfilled. He fit the age of the man prophesized to be the true king of Scotland, who would soon return and claim the throne that was rightfully his. As for the woman, her handsome features were reason enough for the king's men to arrest her and give as a gift to the king for his entertainment.

She was right. They truly did have no choice but to attempt an escape.

"Hurry along with you," the one soldier ordered, jabbing Duncan in the back.

"We must be quick if we are to do anything," she murmured, "for they hurry us to our deaths."

"Follow my lead," he whispered and she nodded.

Duncan knew that he had to strike at both men almost simultaneously if they were to succeed. Otherwise one would have enough time to strike and it wouldn't be him who the soldier targeted.

The two soldiers grew more impatient, shoving at the shackled pair and causing them to stumble. Duncan worried about making a move, his apprehension more for the woman's safety. If he were on his own, he would have been free by now. But being chained to the woman made escape that much harder.

He could almost hear his three childhood friends, Reeve, Bryce and Trey laughing at him, since they had all declared that they would never let a woman shackle them. Memories of the three brought to mind the mission he was on, a mission that couldn't fail. He had no choice; he had to survive.

The men kept urging them forward, though this time it was the tips of their swords jabbing at their backs that kept them moving rapidly. That was when Duncan knew without a shred of doubt that something wasn't right.

He did his best to prevent them from falling again by keeping a hand to her arm, and he was glad he did. They suddenly broke through the thicket of woods to a small clearing and Duncan grabbed quick hold of the woman just before she almost tumbled off the edge of a cliff.

The soldiers laughed and one said, "You'll be going over dead or meeting death soon."

Duncan silently cursed himself for not acting sooner.

"Choose," the other soldier said. "A sword through you to send you over or—" He laughed as the other man joined in. "Or jump. It's death that will be greeting you either way."

"But we want to be fair and let you choose," the heavier of the two said with a snicker.

Duncan gave a glance over the edge. It was a long, deep drop to the turbulent river below that would either swallow you up or spit you out. On his own he'd have a chance; a slim one, but a chance. Two shackled together, one a mere wisp of a woman, was not good odds.

"Figured it out, have you?" the one asked with a grin.

Duncan wanted to strangle the man. The woman obviously understood his snide remark, since he could feel her body tremble beside him. However, once again he had to admire her courage, though he was beginning to believe it was more tenacity, for she took firm hold of his hand and raised her chin.

"I'm ready."

The two soldiers snorted with laughter, but Duncan realized that she was letting him know that she could do this. She was ready to survive.

Duncan, knowing a slim chance was better than no chance at all, bowed his head to the two men who continued to snicker. He then hooked his arm around the woman's slim waist and yanked her hard against him. Strange that at a moment like this when death could be a hair's breath away he should notice that she molded so perfectly to his body, almost as if she had been created for him and him alone. It made him want to protect her even more and pray that they would survive.

"Hold on and don't let go," he ordered and without hesitation he stepped off the edge, keeping his arms wrapped tightly around her.

She buried her face against his chest as he continued to keep her pressed against him. They tumbled for what seemed like forever to their deaths, or would it be to the rescuing arms of the river?

They hit the water feet first and submerged to a good depth. He released his hold on her and gestured toward the surface, and then he immediately began swimming in that direction. She followed his lead, her slender arms pumping as fast as she could, though unable to match his mighty strokes.

Her effort, while valiant, hampered his attempts. And he soon wrapped his arm around her waist and with one hand swam to the surface. She gasped for breath and sputtered and coughed while he kept an arm around her waist and managed to easily regain control of his breathing.

The cliff was a sheer wall of rock from river to sky and it appeared to travel horizontally for as far as he could see, leaving no river bank they could swim to.

They had no choice but to keep swimming.

The woman seemed to struggle and he yelled to her, "Easy or you'll sink us."

Her head disappeared beneath the rough water and he yanked her up.

She sputtered and struggled to speak until finally she spit out, "I can't swim."

Duncan quickly wrapped his right shackled arm, taking her left shackled one with him, beneath her breast, leaving his left arm free to keep swimming. He couldn't believe that she had the audacity to jump off that cliff knowing that she couldn't swim. Or had she trusted him enough to save her?

Finally he spotted a small section of riverbank and swam toward it. He feared that the strong current would rush them right past it, and to his surprise, as he reached for a rock jutting out from the shore, the woman did so as well.

Her extra effort helped sustain their hold there, giving Duncan a chance to catch a good breath. He then managed to get them both to shore where they collapsed on the muddy bank.

While summer was in its waning days, the nights grew chilled, especially this far north in the Highlands. They would need to get a fire going and get dried or else a fever was sure to finish what the river had started.

"We need to get moving," Duncan said and stood, though was prevented from rising all the way since the woman didn't follow.

She sat up, giving slack to the chain so that he could straighten some, and she placed her hand to her chest.

He was amazed at the way her creamy wet skin sparkled from her dunk in the river and her blue eyes were a more brilliant blue, if that was possible. Damn, but he couldn't believe he continued to be captivated by her after she almost drowned him.

She patted her chest and barely managed to say, "Mercy."

He was surprised that she begged when she had shown such bravery. "I know you're probably exhausted from your ordeal, but this is no time for rest."

She shook her head and patted her chest again. "Mercy. My name is Mercy."

He went down on his haunches with a twinge of guilt for having doubted her courage, and with a smile introduced himself. "Duncan. Duncan MacAlpin."

"Thank you, Duncan MacAlpin, for saving my life."

"Haven't saved us yet," he said. "We need to find a safe place to get a fire going and get dried, or death will get us after all."

"Do you think they believe us dead?"

"Those two idiots were certain you would drown me."

"I realized that and knew then we had a chance," she said.

"But you can't swim. And how did you know I could?"

"I saw the way you looked over the edge. I realized you believed there was a chance, though it was a slim one with us chained together."

"You trusted me, a stranger?" he asked.

"I believed it was wiser to do so—"she held up her shackled wrist"—since I truly had little choice."

"Another matter that needs remedying."

She shivered.

Duncan gave a quick glance to the sky. "Night is a few hours off and we need to be settled well before then."

"Need we worry about them making certain we're dead?" she asked as he helped her stand.

Duncan shook his head. "I doubt they'll bother to search for us, but the king's men are everywhere. We must avoid them, especially since we have the king's property."

Her eyes turned wide with apprehension.

He smiled and shook his wrist, rattling the chain. "He may want these back for other prisoners."

She smiled while wringing the water out of her long black hair, and once again he was struck by her beauty. The distraction, though it was more attraction, annoyed him and without thinking he turned and abruptly walked away.

The quick yank of the chain had her falling against him and he turned just as she fell into his arms. And damn if she didn't feel good even soaking wet and damn if he wasn't staring straight at her two luscious, full breasts.

He should have felt guilty and he did; not for staring at her breasts, but for forgetting they were joined together and causing her to fall into his arms. A place he didn't mind her being, though not like this.

"I'm sorry," he said. "Being chained is going to take some getting used to."

"Yes, in more ways than one," she said with a slight blush.

Only then did he begin to realize the many ramifications of being tied together.

"We need to free ourselves," he said.

"I couldn't agree more," she said. "Do you think it will be soon?"

"That's hard to say."

She suddenly looked defeated, but he wouldn't make the mistake again in believing that she was easily giving up, as he realized the problem.

"You need private time," he said.

"Desperately," she begged.

"The best I can do is turn away and let you have the time you need and—" He shook his head. "You'll need to do the same for me."

"All right," she agreed quickly. "But I need that time now. Right now."

They walked a ways into the woods, and after finding a good spot, he turned his back, stretching his arm out behind him. He knew this could not be easy for her, and yet she had managed to get through dire circumstances without crumbling, weeping uncontrollably or surrendering.

Mercy was quite a woman.

"Your turn," she said, and gave him the same privacy.

"We just might make it through this," he said as they were on their way.

Near dusk he began to change his mind. The temperature had dropped more than he had expected and while normally it wouldn't cause a problem, with their garments being wet it chilled them to the bone.

They found a spot by a cropping of rocks that provided good shelter and they both gathered twigs, fallen branches and what dried leaves they could to start a fire.

Duncan had one going in no time and they both snuggled close to it, not only to get warm but to dry their garments.

"You must be hungry," he said, recalling what little if any food the soldiers had given them.

"I had a nibble of bread early this morning."

"Why a nibble?" he asked. "A slice was passed to each person."

"There was a young lad . . ." She didn't finish.

That she would share her food with a starving lad spoke much about her nature, though she hadn't shared, she had surrendered it. "It's too late for me to hunt," he said, disappointed since he was hungry himself.

"Tomorrow is soon enough."

"You have the most agreeable nature," he said.

She laughed. "Truly I don't."

"You'll have to prove that to me."

A shiver accompanied her laugh.

"This fire isn't drying our garments fast enough," he

said concerned. "In the meantime we're getting more chilled."

"There's not much else we can do."

There was something they could do, though he warned himself it wouldn't be easy since he found her so damn attractive. But it could very well save their lives. And if not it would be a lovely way to die. He rolled his eyes to the heaven and couldn't believe what he was about to say. He never got to say it, because she did.

"We need to get out of these wet garments."

Chapter 2

Mercy shivered, her skin prickling with gooseflesh, not only from the wet chill, but from her own suggestion. But what choice had she? They both needed to get warm and they couldn't do that by remaining in sopping wet garments.

She had to remind herself that if she had trusted him enough to save her from drowning, then she could trust him enough to be naked in front of him.

Along with that thought came another shiver that sent her body trembling. Before she could reach for the ties of her soft green blouse, his hands were there, trying to force the stubborn, wet strings apart.

His hands were large and far from delicate. They bore the scars of a warrior used to battle, some faded with time, some more pronounced, and one or two bright with the color of more recently healing wounds. His scars and their predicament made her wonder about this stranger who had been so suddenly thrust into her life and bound to her with no present means of separation.

With curiosity, her glance shifted to his chest. His wet tan shirt was plastered to it. He had a nice chest, thick and solid with muscle, and she wondered if, like his hands, it bore battle scars. His shoulders were wide as was his neck and she realized then the size of him.

He was a big Highlander, a good inch, maybe two, over six feet. Next to her meager four inches over five feet she was a bit of a thing. With his sizable width and height, she could easily take cover behind him and not be seen.

While he continued to diligently work on her ties, her inquisitiveness turned too potent to ignore, so she took the opportunity to peruse the rest of him. His long hair was dark and because it was wet she wasn't certain of the color, deep brown or black?

He caught her gaze then and she startled, though certainly not because he caught her examining him. No, it was his strikingly dark eyes and the intensity of his look that made her realize that he truly was concerned for her well-being. And his words confirmed what she felt.

"I'll have you free of these stubborn ties soon, I promise," he said and his eyes quickly shifted to where his hands continued to work.

He spoke with such conviction, his voice a deep rumble like that of the faint thunder that rolls across the land preceding a storm, that she had no doubt he would do just that.

Her glance remained fixed on his face.

Handsome?

Not in the usual sense. His nose had a slight crook, his lips a visible scar tucked in the right corner of his mouth giving him a perpetual half frown. His brow was clear of wrinkles, though not the arch between his eyes. Did he frown more than smile?

Just as she decided that his weathered complexion enhanced his wildly rugged features, he yanked her blouse over her head.

She stood stunned, the cold air slapping her breasts like a dash of cold water and she felt her nipples harden even more than they already had. She was fully exposed and she cursed herself for not having slipped on her shift yesterday morning when she had unexpectedly found herself on the run. And while she wanted to wrap her arms protectively across her breasts, she didn't want to appear vulnerable or a coward.

He shook his head and held up their joined arms. "The garment goes no further."

She kept her eyes on his and was relieved his remained focused on hers. "Your shirt will fair no better. When we settle for the night, we'll need to somehow spread them out to dry."

He nodded, while his hands busily worked to free his black and red plaid. Without hesitation he dropped it to the ground and then stripped off his shirt to let it join hers trapped by the shackle.

"Let's get your skirt off," he said and she thought she saw him wince. "Then we can spread our garments near the campfire."

There was that rumble of his voice again and for some reason it soothed her. But then she had always favored the sound of faint thunder. It preceded a storm that brought with it the much necessary and life-sustaining rain that nourished the crops and replenished rain barrels.

Was that why his voice soothed her? He had arrived as unexpectedly as a storm sometimes does. Would he help nourish and sustain her life? So far he had. And would their separation end as abruptly as some storms do?

She slipped out of her skirt, her thoughts occupied, leaving her a little less apprehensive. Until she realized that they were standing quite naked in front of each other.

They spoke not a word and kept their eyes locked. It was almost as if they were afraid to let their gazes stray, until finally Mercy found the courage to speak.

"We should set the garments to dry."

He nodded. "We should."

And yet they stood there not moving, until once again Mercy made the first move, though she didn't plan it. She visibly shivered.

Duncan immediately wrapped his arm around her, bringing their naked bodies flat up against each other. He quickly and steadily ran his hands up and down her back, massaging every inch of her cold flesh.

She stiffened when their chilled skin first met. Never mind that she had never been naked in front of a man, she had never been touched so familiarly by a man. And though she was not comfortable being in such an intimate position with a stranger, her body began to respond to his touch.

Warmth began to spread not only over her limbs, but began to creep inside. She found herself snuggling closer against him, aching for more of the heat he provided. Her body and insides kept growing warmer and she felt ever more relieved, when suddenly she realized how selfish of her not to do the same for him.

Her arm slipped around his back, the movement so much less painful now that a fair amount of warmth had been restored. His skin was cold and she shivered for him before she began to massage his back with one hand as rapidly and methodically as he did hers. She didn't know when she had rested her head on his chest. It was there, so close and she was so tired.

But she didn't stop rubbing warmth into him, nor did he to her.

"Mercy."

His gentle whisper had her eyes fluttering open.

When had she closed them? Her hand was no longer at his back. It was tucked between their chests.

Her eyes sprang wide and she stared up at him.

"You fell asleep," he said, "and I think that would be best for us both."

She nodded, agreeing, though she was disinclined to leave the warmth of his body. However, their wet garments did need their attention.

"We'll hurry and get done with it," he said and reluctantly she stepped away.

His absence caused a blast of cold night air to hit her warmed body and sent an uncontrollable tremble through her.

He reached out, grabbed hold of her and brought her into the warmth and safety of his arms once again. "We need to do this fast and settle next to the fire for the night."

She nodded, knowing he was right and anxious to be done with it, for then she would remain in the heat of his arms for the whole night.

They set to work, her thoughts no longer on the cold, or their nakedness, but on the task at hand. First, they arranged a sizable bed of leaves for a sleeping pallet. Then she helped him spread their clothes around the fire.

"Branches," he said.

She scrunched her brow, not understanding.

"We'll use them as a blanket."

She nodded and followed him.

They didn't go far from the fire and he ordered her to stand back as far as the chain would allow. She watched as he reached up and easily broke a large branch from a towering evergreen. He turned to break another and her glance fell on the muscles hunching in his back as he broke the branch with one forceful snap.

She noticed then that though wide, his waist narrowed just enough to define the sheer beauty of his form and his backside rounded thick and firm, while long muscled legs followed, completing the mighty size of him.

He turned and she had a clear view of him. Thick,

tight muscles were everywhere. There was no doubt he was a strong warrior and a generously endowed man.

With no more time, nor wise to dally in such thoughts, she bent along with him to help with the branches and together they dragged them to the campfire.

"We'll need to stay wrapped around each other," he said as they both lowered themselves to the leaf pallet.

She nodded and didn't hesitate to accept the invitation of his outspread arms. She snuggled against him. And then working together they spread the two wet garments beyond the shackles. They had made certain the garments would be close to the campfire in hopes that by morning they would be dry.

Duncan then reached for the branches on the ground beside him and covered them, the leaves a bit prickly against their skin. He draped his legs over hers, forcing her closer against him. She didn't object. She needed his heat as surely as he needed hers.

She wasn't surprised when after a few minutes she felt him grow large against her and she raised her head from the crook of his shoulder to look up at him.

"He has a mind of his own when I have a beautiful woman in my arms," he said with that rumbling tone that was growing familiar and comfortable to her. "Don't worry. I won't let him bother you."

She couldn't help but smile. "Thank you for the compliment and for your chivalry."

Laughter tickled her ear. "Chivalry only goes so far, so we need to get this chain off fast."

While he teased, she also knew he warned and he was right. They couldn't remain shackled long. After all, he was a man and a man had needs, as her mother had often explained in more detail than she had cared to hear.

But then her mother's needs had been just as ravenous as a man's and had been the cause of her own tragic downfall. Unfortunately, with her mother's downfall came Mercy's.

"Perhaps tomorrow we'll come across a croft where we can seek help," she suggested.

"We'll need to be careful. The farmers will fear retaliation from the king's men if they help those in chains."

"I didn't think of that," she said. "What then do we do?"

"We'll scout the area and see what we can find. If it doesn't look safe we'll need to make it to my people."

"How far is that?"

"A week's travel without any incidents," he said.

"A week?" she asked apprehensively.

He smiled a half-smile. "I'll behave if you will."

While the one corner of his mouth turned up in a smile, the scar in the other corner appeared a constant frown as if he continued to warn, and she would do well to remember that there were two sides to their dilemma.

"I'll do my best," she said with her own gentle smile.

"Then don't fancy me with that lovely smile, or I'll be begging for mercy."

The twinkle in his devilishly dark eyes had her chuckling.

"That's even worse," he said, sounding wounded. "A laugh that tempts the soul itself."

"What of chivalry?" she bantered playfully.

He brought his lips close to hers and whispered. "Ah, what of it? It would be more chivalrous of me to kiss you and couple with you throughout the night, generating all the heat we need to survive."

If she hadn't caught the glint of humor in his dark eyes, she might have been frightened that he would take advantage of their situation. But he teased, and she wondered if it was simply to see how she would respond, or perhaps he thought he could convince her to agree to an outlandish appeal.

"I'm astounded at what you would sacrifice for chivalry," she said with feigned sincerity. "But it would behoove me to see you forfeit so much, thus I decline your generous offer."

He laughed. "Do I get a kiss for at least trying?"

She pecked his cheek lightly.

"Mercy, Mercy," he said continuing to laugh. "One of these days I'm going to have to teach you how to kiss as a reward for saving your life."

"When we are safe, our chain gone, I promise I will reward you with a kiss."

"I will hold you to that promise," he said adamantly.

"I have no doubt you will," she said and settled her head back in the crook of his shoulder.

He in turn wrapped her more tightly in his arms.

With their long ordeal finally behind them, sleep was fast claiming them. But it wasn't worries or fears of what they had yet to face that occupied their thoughts and dwelled in their dreams, but rather the promise of a kiss.

He had every intention of collecting it. It was clear she had every intention of keeping her promise, but what nagged and surprised him was that while he wished to be free of the chain that bound them, they now had another good reason to free themselves.

They both wanted to taste that kiss.

Chapter 3

Dampness remained at the ends of Duncan's plaid and at the hem of his shirt, but mostly his garments were dry. And glad of it he was, since he slipped into them as soon as his eyes cleared of sleep.

Mercy was too tempting a morsel to remain beside her naked and not want to do more than just keep her warm. He had fought his carnal urges like a stoic warrior throughout the night. It wasn't an easy battle, especially when she had tucked her free hand in places that provided the most warmth.

It hadn't been bad when she had tucked it between their stomachs, but when her hand had begun to drift toward a more heated, sensitive area, he knew he was in trouble. He had reluctantly grabbed her roving hand just before it could . . .

He didn't want to think of what could have happened. It had taken all of his skill as an honorable warrior to do it, for he would have liked nothing better than to let her slim fingers settle around him.

He had kept hold of her hand for a time, the campfire's light casting a golden glow on her creamy skin. He noticed that while her hands had a few scratches, they bore no signs of toil. That would make her a member of the gentry or nobility, but why would one of such class be a prisoner of the king's men?

It was a question that had haunted his thoughts during his near sleepless night and he knew would continue to plague him until he had an answer.

He finished fastening his worn wool plaid of no distinguishable colors. To all it represented him as a wandering warrior with no allegiance to any particular clan and that was how he wanted it.

When he finally settled his glance on Mercy, he had hoped she would be fully clothed, but she wore only her blouse, which she had slipped on just before he had his shirt. He had been so intent on getting his plaid on, he hadn't realized that she required two hands to help get her skirt on.

"Sorry," he said apologetically. "Next time you dress first."

Her eyes widened, his assumption that there would be another time they would be naked together obviously upsetting her.

He shook his head. "Though the situation probably will not arise again."

He felt disappointed at the thought, and she looked relieved?

He helped her into her skirt with some regret, taking

a quick, last glance at her creamy smooth skin and her slim limbs, not to mention the tiny patch of curly black hair between her legs that tempted the hell out of him. Her lovely naked vision would not leave his head for a long time, no matter how hard he chased it away.

"We must find food," he said needing to get his thoughts on something less tempting.

"I must admit. I am starving," Mercy said.

He helped her sit so that they both could slip on their boots they had left by the campfire to dry.

"My stomach has been grumbling since before dawn," he said.

"You didn't sleep well?" she asked as he assisted her to stand.

"Well enough." He certainly wasn't about to tell her that her constant shifting and snuggling had been the cause for his fitful sleep.

"I had a wonderful sleep," she admitted. "I am refreshed and ready to meet the day. Where do we find food?"

She was right about being refreshed. Her smooth skin glowed with a renewed rigor and her deep blue eyes sparkled with determination. She looked even more beautiful today than she had yesterday.

Why that made him grumpy he couldn't say, and he sounded curt when he didn't intend to. "We need to get moving."

Surprisingly, she wasn't offended by his terse response or perhaps she simply ignored it. "I agree. The king's soldiers could be searching for us."

His tone turned civil. "We'll find something to appease our stomachs until tonight. Then we'll camp early and hunt for a hare or two."

Mercy licked her lips. "I look forward to it."

Wet, shiny and plump.

"I'm ready."

"So am I." He had to smile, though he didn't admit it wasn't food he was thinking about. Those lips of hers were luscious and he wouldn't mind tasting them.

They walked for a couple of hours, the sun bright and, fortunately for them, the last breath of summer in the air. But that could change tomorrow this far north in the Highlands. They would do best to get to their destination as soon as possible.

Duncan wondered how his three friends had fared in their mission. They had all worked hard to get to this point in time and their success or failure would be Scotland's success or failure.

He nearly stumbled when he was suddenly yanked to a halt.

"I'm sorry," Mercy said with a sincerity that had him shake his head.

"Don't worry about it. It isn't easy being chained to someone."

"Shackles aren't the only things that chain people," she said and turned to walk away, then stopped and turned back. "I'd like to pick some sprigs of heather."

"We can't dally," he reminded, though followed her.

She didn't. She hastily claimed two sprigs, one dropping to the ground as she tucked the other in her hair behind her ear.

Duncan quickly snatched it off the ground, the sweet scent drifting across his nostrils. She reached for it as he moved to tuck it alongside the other sprig and their hands met. They stilled for a moment, and while Duncan knew it would be wise to surrender the small blossom to her, he didn't.

He placed the sprig beside the other one, running his fingers lightly along the tip of her ear as he finished.

"It suits you," he said.

Did he imagine that her breath caught before she spoke? Had his breath caught as well? How strange that such a simple act could cause breathlessness.

"How silly of me," she said. "Our lives are in danger and I stop to pick heather."

He took a solid hold of her hand, though the chain already held them firm. "Nonsense. It is good that you think to do the things you normally would. It makes our dire situation seem less dismal, and besides the heather looks lovely in your hair."

She smiled and released her grip on his fingers, though kept them laced gently around his. "I will miss your compliments when we part."

Not two full days spent with her and the idea that they would part somehow troubled him.

Enough foolish thoughts, he had a mission to accomplish.

"We best pick up our pace," he advised strongly.

"Yes, I agree," she said with a nod.

They did just that and traveled a good distance before they came upon a croft. They remained hidden behind a boulder on the edge of a field where the crop had already been harvested, nor ravaged by the king's soldiers, a common occurrence. It seemed the king felt fit to issue an edict that his soldiers were to be fed regardless of farmers and their families' needs.

After watching for near an hour, it appeared that an older man and woman were the only occupants.

"If we ask them for help, will we not be placing them in harm's way?" Mercy asked with concern.

"They are in harm's way regardless. The soldiers will torture them for answers either way, and they will die because of it either way. The king cares not for his people, only for filling his own belly and coffers."

"What do we do?"

"Our burden would be lighter without this chain," he said.

"Then it is tools we look for?"

He nodded.

It didn't take them long to make their way to the open stable area as soon as they determined no one was in sight. If they were to find anything helpful it would be there. They remained as quiet as they could, though Duncan grew annoyed when their search results produced not a single thing.

"How can he tend his horses when he has no tools?" Duncan said with an irritated whisper.

"My exact question to the king's soldiers this morning."

Duncan and Mercy spun around and came face to face with a man, not near as old as they had surmised, but rather aged by hardship. Gray mingled with thick black hair and worry lines dug deep across his brow and down around his eyes and more heavily around his mouth. And yet the rolled up sleeves of his tan linen shirt showed arms thick with muscles and a broad chest that stretched the worn fabric.

"I'm Bailey," The man offered his hand and as Duncan took it, the man said, "I prefer not to know who you are."

"It is better that you don't," Duncan said as their hands locked in a strong grip.

"I wish I could offer you the hospitality of my home, but ever since I spotted you, my wife has grown concerned for our safety."

"You knew we were hiding?" Mercy asked, surprised.

Duncan answered for him. "You're a tracker."

Bailey shook his head vigorously. "I am no more than a simple farmer."

Duncan didn't argue. The man was obviously more than simply a farmer, but he could understand why he wouldn't want anyone, especially the king, to know of any special skills he possessed. He could very well be forced into the king's service.

"I can provide you with food," Bailey said.

"Can you spare it?" Duncan asked.

"For those in need, food can always be spared. Wait here. I'll return in a moment."

Once Bailey was out of sight, Mercy turned to Duncan. "The soldiers are looking for us, aren't they?"

He saw worry on her face and he couldn't say he didn't feel the same. "It would be the most logical reason why all the tools are gone."

"They believe keeping us shackled will slow us down," she confirmed. "But that would have to mean they believe us still alive." She shook her head. "How could they know that?"

"They may not know," Duncan said. "They just may not be taking any chances."

"One of you must be—"

Mercy gave a little yelp and instinctively slipped into the crook of Duncan's arm, which he immediately slipped around her as they both turned to face Bailey.

"Sorry," Bailey apologized. "I didn't mean to frighten you."

"You're light on your feet," Duncan said.

"Old habit," Bailey confessed.

"Not a bad one to have," Duncan said.

Bailey held out a sack. "There's bread and cheese and a blanket. The Highlands get cold at night."

"What about you and your wife?" Duncan asked, his arm remaining protectively around Mercy.

"We'll be leaving here soon enough," he admitted. "It

won't take the soldiers long to pick up your tracks and trace them back here. My wife, Kate, will give birth in about five months and I want her and our child safe."

"I'm so sorry that it is because of us you are forced to leave your home," Mercy said.

Bailey sneered. "It's not our home. The king claims everything. I but work for his pleasure."

"What will you do?" Mercy asked anxiously.

"I intend to go find the true king of Scotland and join his battle to restore him to his rightful power, so that my land will be mine."

"Some believe the seer's prophecy that the true king will soon return nothing but myth. You believe otherwise?" Mercy asked.

"I have to believe, or else there is no future for my wife and unborn child," Bailey said.

Duncan reached out his hand. "We wish you well and we are grateful for your help. May your journey be swift and safe, my friend."

"I have no doubt it will be," Bailey said.

Duncan took Mercy's hand and they both hurried off, neither commenting on Bailey's unfinished remark.

One of you must—

They kept silent, though each thought over what Bailey intended to say.

One of you must be mighty important for the King to be searching so hard for you.

Chapter 4

They walked for another hour before they settled in the safety of a thick grove of oaks. Mercy eagerly accepted the hunk of bread and cheese Duncan offered her before taking any for himself.

While there were questions she wished to ask him, she was just too hungry to waste time on talk. And though she knew her empty stomach would want more than Duncan had given her, she also knew they would need to be careful with the sparse amount they had.

Though she hadn't voiced her thought, Duncan agreed. "While hunger still gnaws at me, it would be wise for us to conserve."

Mercy nodded. "At least it is good to have a little, and we're lucky that Bailey's wife bakes such delicious bread."

"It is good." Duncan smiled. "Or we're too hungry to notice."

Mercy laughed. "You are a humorous one."

Duncan dusted his fingers. "A smile shared is far better than a frown given."

"You're a poetic philosopher as well."

"What do you know of poetic philosophers?" he asked. "Only in a family of means would you find an educated daughter, or wife?"

"I am neither," she responded quickly. "I was simply raised by a mother who took great care to educate herself and wished the same for her daughter." She brushed her hands. "We should go."

His hesitation warned her that he pondered her explanation, while she preferred he not give it thought. It was better he knew nothing about her, better she took her leave as soon as she was free of him.

Her only problem was . . . where did she go once she was on her own?

"You frown," he said. "Something troubles you?"

"Only the soldiers that follow us," she said, confident it was no lie.

He stood, bringing her along with him. "No doubt the soldiers will pick up our trail somewhere and follow soon enough."

She shivered at the thought. She had no want to die. Her mother's foolishness had marked them enemy of the king, thereby sentencing them to death, when truly she had known nothing of her mother's devious plans.

"You're chilled?"

Mercy shook the fretful musings from her head as she answered him. "No. Not on this lovely warm day.

It is fear of capture that sends a shiver through me."

He smiled again, though her glance was drawn to the scar at the right side of his mouth. She did something unexpected then. She couldn't say why, or even that she was aware of what she was doing until her fingers touched the thin, barely visible scar that ran from the corner of his mouth to his chin, leaving the everlasting frown, so foreign to his nature.

"How did you get this?" she asked, her finger trailing along the thin line. She suddenly realized how inappropriate was her behavior and looked up into his eyes, ready to apologize, but his intense dark glare froze her silent.

What did she see in them that frightened her? An anger that could kill? A fierce hatred that demanded revenge? Whatever it was, she wanted no part of it.

"It's not for you to know," he said.

"I'm sorry," she said almost shivering again, only this time from the icy coldness in his voice.

"We need to go."

She simply nodded and followed quietly alongside him. Until this moment she'd had no fear of Duncan. And even now it wasn't that she feared him as much as feared what he was capable of, since for the first time she caught a glimpse of the fierce Highlander warrior within him.

They kept a steady pace, exchanging not a single word. Even when fatigue crept up Mercy's legs she pushed on, and when her feet protested in pain, she ignored them. She knew she had no other choice. Right now her life depended on her stamina.

He stopped abruptly and she swayed unsteadily. His hand slipped quickly around her waist, pulling her near so that she would not tumble them to the ground.

She almost collapsed against him, exhaustion ready to claim every limb and muscle of her body. But instead, she struggled to keep a steadfast hold of herself.

"Night will claim the land soon enough," he said. "We need to find a safe place and settle in."

"Food?" she asked hungry and thirsty.

"I think we should avoid a fire tonight, in case the soldiers are near."

She had thought the same, but hoped differently, though was grateful they had been wise enough to conserve what little food they had.

Mercy nodded while disappointment settled heavily over her, and without thinking, she rested her weary head to his chest. Though it was thick with taut muscle, it served as a comfortable pillow and his woodsy scent was more pleasing than potent.

"My chest will gladly pillow your head anytime, after we're settled for the night."

Her head shot up, and she smiled, catching the glint of humor in his eyes. She patted his chest. "And a good pillow it is."

"It's yours as long as you need it."

She realized he offered more than his chest as a pillow. He was offering her comfort and protection, and it gave her a sense of safety, if only for their time together.

A sudden gust of wind swirled around them, stirring

leaves and her skirt, and startled them into moving.

"There's a stream nearby," Duncan said. "We'll make camp not far from it."

Mercy wanted to run to it, drink until she burst and then soak her aching feet. Instead, she kept her pace steady alongside Duncan. And before she knew it they were there, and for a moment she was so overwhelmed with relief that she almost cried. Almost, but didn't.

Tears were something her mother had taught her to control. She had told Mercy that tears could help or hinder a woman, and she needed to know when it was wise to hold her tears and when it was beneficial to let them fall. So Mercy had gained control over them and could cry at will, or halt a tear from ever staining her face.

Mercy was relieved that Duncan didn't stop but went straight to the stream. She followed when he went down on his knees and cupped his one hand to drink from the clear cold water.

She did the same, refilling her cupped hand time and again. She quenched her thirst before him and saw how he struggled to keep a good amount of water in his cupped hand. She realized why she had no difficulty and he had. She had use of her right hand, while his right hand was shackled to her left one.

Of course for her it would not have mattered for she was just as skilled with her left hand as her right. Another aptitude her mother taught her, insisting that one never knew when another skilled hand would be needed. And a talent, she warned her daughter, that would be best kept a secret.

"Perhaps an extra hand would help," she said extending their joined ones.

"You sure you've had enough?"

"For now," she said, appreciative of his thoughtfulness.

The refreshing water dribbled down his mouth and onto his shirt, but that didn't stop him from assuaging his thirst. And she couldn't blame him. She had never been so thirsty in her life, nor had she ever been hungry until these past three days.

Life had changed for her in one split moment and she had yet to fully grasp the enormity of it. There were too many questions she had no answers to, and certainly too many problems with no solutions. For the moment she could only focus on staying alive; the rest would have to wait.

When he finished, he turned to her. "I noticed your gait changed a couple of hours ago. Do your feet pain you?"

This Highlander noticed more than she realized. She would need to be careful.

"Yes, they do, and I would like nothing more than to slip my boots off and sooth my aching feet in the stream."

"I'll join you," he said and yanked his boots off.

Mercy, however, winced when she tried to remove her boots.

"You're not used to walking, are you?" he asked.

"Not long distances without a chance to rest," she admitted.

Duncan took hold of her ankle. "This may hurt, but bear the pain. Sound carries too far in the woods."

Mercy nodded and squeezed not only her lips tightly closed, but her eyes as well.

Duncan was quick about it, and she opened damp eyes caused by the stinging pain to survey the damage. As she suspected, patches of skin had been rubbed raw here and there, the most painful being the small toe on her right foot.

To have a man, truly a stranger, take hold of her ankle was an act of intimacy and much too improper, or so she had been instructed. She almost laughed at the thought, for just last night she had slept naked in this man's arms and had been glad for it.

Besides, this large Highlander had a tender touch she favored.

Duncan cradled her ankle in the palm of his hand, while he examined her injuries. "These will need to be tended, or you'll not travel well tomorrow. "

He traded one ankle for the other and winced. "This tiny toe is the worst. A good soaking will clean it off." He glanced at her with a grimace. "It's going to hurt when the cold water rushes over them."

"What's a bit more pain before they numb?" she asked with a weak laugh.

"Pain is pain, long or short; it's still felt, still suffered,"

Duncan said and one by one he carefully placed her sore feet in the cool stream.

The harsh sting clouded her eyes with tears, though not a one fell. It took only a few moments before the throbbing pain faded, and she sighed with relief.

"You should have told me you were in pain."

"There was nothing you could have done, and we couldn't stop." She nodded toward his unblemished feet. "Your feet are accustomed to strenuous hikes?"

"I've walked a good portion of the Highlands."

"Where are you from in the Highlands?" she asked, curious to know more about him.

"Not far from here," he said. "And where do you call home?"

Since he wasn't forthcoming with answers, she purposely kept her response vague. "We're far past my home."

"Where is it you'll be going when you're free of me?"

His question jolted her. How was it that in such a short time she had grown accustomed to having this man by her side? And the thought of not seeing him ever again, while a foolish musing, actually disturbed her.

"As far away from here as possible," she admitted with a degree of sorrow. "And you? Where will you go?"

"I will remain with my family and friends and tend to my duties."

She would have liked to know more, but a crunch of leaves had them both anxiously scurrying to their feet.

Two squirrels in play tumbled along the ground and

then raced up a tree to jump from branch to branch until they were out of sight.

"We need to find shelter," Duncan said as he turned, snatched up his boots, tugged them on and then reached for hers and the sack of food.

She took them from him, but before she could slip them on, he startled her by scooping her up into his arms and settling her firmly against him.

"You'll stay off those feet," he said as if he just passed an edict.

Authoritative tones did not rankle Mercy, as she knew well how to deal with them. Besides, the prospect of not having to walk another step was just too appealing to deny. But there was one thing he forgot.

"That means you'll be doing the same," she said, rattling the chain.

"Damn," he mumbled and abruptly stopped.

While annoyance sparked his dark eyes, worry was quick to wrinkle the arch between his eyes. It embedded itself deep. That he could feel such concern for her had Mercy wishing that she could reach up and caress his worries away.

She did with words what she couldn't do with a touch. "Your thoughtfulness touches my heart and I truly appreciate it, but let us get done with what we must and then we both can rest my weary feet."

He smiled. "You are a rare beauty in more ways than one."

She sighed a bit dramatically. "I'll never grow tired of your compliments."

"I'll never stop giving them."

Her heart gave a little ache, for his compliments would stop when finally they separated. She silently chastised herself. Hadn't she been taught to rely on no one, particularly a man? She had to keep her wits about her if she were to survive.

"We best get settled," she said reluctantly, since she found comfort and safety in his arms.

She noticed that he released her hesitantly, but then perhaps it was the warmth of their bodies he unwillingly surrendered.

They decided on a secluded spot in a grove of shrub. They suffered a few scratches to gain entrance, but the protection it offered was worth the small wounds. They made quick work of putting together a bed of leaves; and while both were beginning to feel the chill of the setting sun, neither was willing to build a campfire and tempt being caught.

When night completely claimed dominance over the day, they sat on the bed, the worn, warm wool blanket wrapped snugly around them, and enjoyed the remainder of the food. It wasn't much, but it was a feast to them.

"It took such little time for the soldiers to discover that we survived," she said with concern. "Do you think it will delay our journey to your home?"

Duncan nodded, swallowing the last piece of his

portion of cheese. "No doubt. We'll need to stay off the well-traveled roads, but my main concern is that the soldiers have stopped at most of the farms in the area, robbing them of the tools that can set us free."

"I never thought of that," she admitted.

"And news travels fast in these parts. It will be known soon enough that Bailey and his wife left their farm in fear of their lives for helping us."

"Which means no one will want to offer us assistance."

"It's not that they don't want to," Duncan said. "They're just too afraid of the consequences."

"So we're on our own," she said and handed him her last piece of bread. "I'm not hungry anymore."

He took it, though he didn't eat it. He held it to her lips. "If we both are to survive, we both must remain strong and that takes nourishment. Eat."

Though her stomach no longer yearned for food, she did as he asked, for he was right. She had to fortify her body when possible, since there was no telling when next they would eat.

A chilly crispness filled the night air, though Mercy wasn't as cold as last night, but then she had been naked, her clothes soaking wet. And tonight they even had a blanket to help keep them warm.

She didn't stop to think whether they would snuggle together for warmth once again, it seemed to be expected. Once stretched out on the pallet of leaves they nestled together in each other's arms with the comfort of old lovers reunited.

"Much warmer than last night," Duncan said, "even without a fire."

"And our stomachs are at least somewhat satisfied," she added. "So it seems that our lot has improved."

His arm tightened around her. "For now, but our journey is far from over."

She nestled her cheek against his chest, the familiar scent comforting. "We work well together, therefore, we will do well together."

He rested his cheek on the top of her head. "We make a good pair."

Mercy laid in silence listening to Duncan's steady breathing while sleep crept over her. His words danced in her thoughts and she smiled.

They did make a good pair. How sad that they would have to part.

Chapter 5

Duncan woke early the next day, and though he would have much preferred to let Mercy remain comfortably snuggled in his arms, he knew he couldn't. He had to get her feet bandaged and they had to get moving. There was no telling where the soldiers were by now, or if a larger contingent was sent to track them. Besides, not being able to travel the main roads would surely hamper their progress.

He hesitated a moment more, lingering in the warmth of her body pressed so intimately against his. They might not be naked this time, but that didn't stop him from remembering the swell and curves of her enticing body. He would not at all mind coupling with her.

He silently cursed his own tempting thoughts that instantly turned him hard. And he didn't favor Mercy waking to his arousal pressed against her. They had enough to concern themselves with, without her needing to worry that he'd take advantage of her. Not that he wanted to take advantage of her. He rather hoped it would be a mutual coupling.

Stop thinking about it, you fool!

That's right, he silently berated himself. *Keep it up and—*

He shook his head, taking his own words the wrong way and making him harder than ever. There was only one way out of this.

He pulled away from Mercy abruptly saying, "Wake up. We need to get started."

Startled, Mercy bolted up, hurriedly rubbing sleep out of her eyes. "What's wrong?"

"Nothing," he said curtly. "We just need to be on our way. No telling how many soldiers are on our trail."

She yawned, rolled her shoulders and winced. "I miss a soft mattress."

"Lucky you are that you once had one. I've had no more than a pallet."

For a moment she appeared a bit anxious, but recovered quickly. "Nothing lasts forever."

"What of love?" he asked.

"What of it?"

"Love lasts forever."

Again she startled, though didn't recover as quickly. "You truly believe that?"

"Don't you?"

She shrugged. "Men love when it's convenient for them."

"Not all men."

"You have never told a woman you loved her for the sake of the moment?" she asked.

"No. Never," he answered tersely. "There is only one woman I will pledge my love to and that is the woman I take as my wife. She will be my partner, my lover, my mate for life. I will love no other but her, and she will love no other but me."

"Then she will certainly be a lucky woman," Mercy said.

"And I will be a lucky man."

She leaned forward, closer to him, nervously chewing at her bottom lip as if she was uncertain to reveal something, so he was rather disappointed when she said, "You're right. We better get going."

"I'll tend your feet," he said, reaching for the sack that had held their food.

Mercy took the sack from him and began tearing off a strip. "I can manage it myself."

He would have protested, but she looked determined and there was no time to argue. They truly did need to get started.

When she finished, he noticed that she winced when she slipped her boots on and it bothered him to know that the day's journey might prove painful for her.

She held up the sack. "I just took some off the top edge. This way the sack is still useful to us."

Duncan snatched the blanket up, folded it, then shoved it in the sack. "How are your feet?"

"They will do fine."

He had to smile at her determination. "You'll let me know if they become too painful."

She was about to respond when an unfamiliar noise startled them both. Duncan motioned for her to remain silent and she nodded.

Suddenly a hare hopped into their lair so fast that Mercy would have screeched if Duncan hadn't clamped his hand over her mouth. He cautioned silence with wide eyes and a shake of his head. For an animal to scurry in fright could mean only one thing . . . something chased it.

"You fool, you missed it," a male voice chastised.

"It's around here somewhere. I'll get it," said the other man with gruff irritation.

"It's long gone and I'm long hungry," the other fellow complained. "Now let's do what I said and get us some fish to fill our empty bellies."

Duncan removed his hand from Mercy's mouth and leaned forward to peer through the brushes as best he could without stirring them. The hare remained where he had landed as if he sensed it was a safe spot.

"I'm telling you the two are dead," the one said. "I don't know why we have to waste time looking for dead people."

"You want to tell the king that?"

The man must have shaken his head since the one fellow spoke again.

"Fine. Then let's get our bellies fed."

"No need to hurry," the man complained. "The dead ones aren't going anywhere."

Their footfalls finally faded to nothing, but Duncan and Mercy, along with the hare, remained perfectly still and silent. None of them wanted to take the chance of being caught. Finally, the hare made the first move, hopping off.

Still, Duncan chose to whisper. "We need to move fast and quietly."

Mercy nodded.

"Stay extra close so that the chain does not make noise," he said.

Watching every step they took, Duncan and Mercy left the protective covering of the bushes and quietly made their way in the woods, opposite from where the two soldiers had gone.

It was at least three hours before either of them spoke. And it was with a quick nod to the heavens that Duncan said, "A storm brews."

"Then we best pick up the pace," Mercy said, doing just that.

Duncan matched her new rhythm, having thought the same himself. But then the will to survive could certainly produce parallel thoughts. Or was it that they were similar in nature, thus thought alike?

How odd that they should work so well as a pair when they barely knew each other. Normally, it took time to get to know one another and yet it seemed that Mercy and he were far from strangers, or even acquaintances. They were more like old friends who long understood each other. And yet he knew little about her.

The thought had him asking, "Will your family search for you?"

"The last of my family is gone."

He almost halted in his tracks, but caught himself and kept his pace. "If you have no family, where will you go?"

"I have friends," she said.

He noticed her response held a hint of hesitation. Assuming her situation was more precarious than she admitted, he offered her a safety net.

"You are welcome to remain with my people as long as you'd like."

"That's kind of you, and while I may rest my weary feet for a few days, I will no doubt soon be on my way."

He smiled and said, "As you wish."

However, he had no intention of letting her take her leave on her own. A beautiful woman just wouldn't be safe traveling alone and for some reason he felt her safety his responsibility.

A crack of thunder had them both stopping abruptly and casting anxious glances to the heavens.

"It won't be long before the rain starts," Mercy said.

Duncan was conflicted. He wanted desperately to forge ahead regardless of the weather, gaining as much ground as they could. He doubted the storm would stop the soldiers, which would make travel even more dangerous for him and Mercy.

He knew their chance of survival would increase the

closer they got to his home. Sentinels were kept posted on the far perimeters of the land just for that reason, to make certain that approaching clansmen reached home safely.

"You don't want to stop, do you?" Mercy asked.

He voiced his concern. "I doubt the soldiers will stop."

"Then we can't."

"We'll get soaked again," he said.

"That doesn't matter," she said. "We keep going and dry out when we can."

He grinned. "I wouldn't mind you naked in my arms again."

"Enjoy it while you can, Highlander, nothing lasts forever."

He surprised himself when without forethought, he slipped his arm around her waist and drew her up against him, settling his mouth close to hers.

"Love," he whispered. "Love lasts forever."

A startling crack of thunder should have broken them apart, but it didn't. They remained pressed against each other, their eyes locked and their lips so close that one small pucker, and they would kiss.

It wasn't the first falling raindrop, but a few fat ones that finely separated them and had them quickly resuming their journey. They kept ahead of the storm for a distance until the heavy rain caught up with them and in no time they were both soaked through.

It didn't stop them though, they kept going, their clothes

soaked to their skin, their hair dripping with rain. Duncan glanced her way now and again and wondered if perhaps the torturous ordeal would bring her to tears. But when he looked, he couldn't tell if she was crying, since rain was falling continuously down her face.

It wasn't until several hours later when the storm grew worse, the wind howling and whipping around them so severely that Duncan tucked Mercy in the corner of his arm and bent his body partially over her to protect her from the ruthless squall, then decided they had no choice but to stop.

They were lucky to stumble upon a small cave. It was barely big enough for the both of them, but at least it offered shelter from the storm.

"We need a fire," Mercy said, shivering.

Duncan was already looking to see if the cave had anything else to offer them, and he smiled when he saw enough small broken branches to serve well as kindling. He didn't have to say a word to her; she must have followed his glance as they bent together and began picking up the wood to start a fire.

They kept the campfire near the mouth of the cave, though far enough back so that the rain and wind wouldn't disturb it. As soon as Duncan got the fire going, he removed the blanket from the wet sack and with Mercy's help spread it nearby to dry. Then they huddled together in front of the flames.

"We made good distance until we were forced to stop," Mercy said and quick as a wink slipped her blouse over her head and twisted the rainwater out of it. "Hurry and do the same," she urged. "We'll hold my blouse and your shirt by the fire and hopefully they might dry enough for us to put them back on tonight.

He didn't protest, especially since he worried that if her full, bouncy breasts and those tight hard nipples stared at him for the entire evening, he would do something regrettably foolish.

Duncan followed her leave in rubbing himself dry with his free hand, at least the top part of him. He had yet to remove his plaid and actually didn't want to. While the wet wool dampened his desires, it certainly couldn't keep entire control of it. And every time she leaned over closer to the fire, her breasts swinging loose and free in front of her, he ached to reach out and cup one in his hand.

He could almost feel the mound resting heavily in his hand and then all he'd have to do is run his thumb over that taut nipple and –

"Watch out!" she yelled and yanked their chained wrists back. "Wet or not, you near singed your shirt on the flames."

She stirred restless. "We best shed the rest of our wet garments."

"That's going to be a problem."

"Why?"

He was blunt. "I want nothing more right now than to lower you to the ground and couple with you."

Chapter 6

⁓ ⟨ᏭᏭ⟩ ⁓

Mercy froze, her mouth agape, staring at Duncan.
"That's not going to happen."

Duncan shook his head, running his fingers through
his long hair and squeezing the water out the ends before
he asked, "Why?"

She didn't know how to respond and floundered in an
attempt to supply an adequate answer.

"I could understand if you believed in love," he said
with a casual shrug. "But since you don't, why not enjoy
a good toss when you can get it?"

Again she couldn't find the right words and she
wondered was it because she didn't know herself? If
love remained in question for her, whatever was she
waiting for?

"Your silence confirms that you have no answer." He
reached out and ran a gentle finger along the side of her
face. "It also tells me that you probably have never been
intimate with a man and you're simply frightened of the

first time. I promise you that you would enjoy me nestled between your legs."

Mercy brushed his hand away, his once tender touch now feeling more like a branding iron. She had no intentions of being like her mother, branded by a man and subjected to his whim.

"Why is no concern of yours," she snapped.

"Besides being courageous, you're feisty. I like that."

She reached out and poked his bare chest. It was solid and made her realize that wit was called for rather than anger. "And I like that you're chivalrous."

"You're forever going to remind me of that, aren't you?"

"As often as necessary," she said with a smile.

"If you should change your mind—"

"I shall let you know."

"How?" he asked with a teasing glint.

"Why, I shall simply tell you, of course."

"You'll tell me that you want to couple with me," he said as if confirming her response. "You will say it clearly so it could not be misunderstood."

Mercy took a step closer to him, though not close enough that they should touch. She then reached out and did what she had seen her mother do time and again to the man who had kept her. She caressed his lips with the tip of her finger over and over and over again as she said, "I want you, Duncan. I want you now."

Mercy only intended it as a demonstration.

Duncan took it differently.

She was in his arms and his lips on hers before she had a chance to react and by then she realized she liked the taste of him. His kiss wasn't hungry, sloppy or hurried and he didn't grope her. His arm remained taut around her waist while his lips simply took command.

And though she had never been kissed, it didn't matter. She did what came naturally to her and tasted him with all the enthusiasm of a novice ready and willing to learn. And she didn't want to stop. She wanted to go on tasting him, until a tingle started between her legs and she felt the urge to press closer, more intimately against him. She knew then she had to stop, or soon passion would take command and the choice would not be hers. And hadn't her mother told her endlessly that when a woman controlled the passion, she controlled the man? Right now, at this moment, she needed to be in control.

Reluctantly, she broke away from him, her lips lingering for one last moment on his before she took a step back.

"That is how you shall know I want you," she said a bit breathless and trying to ignore his flaring nostrils and heaving chest.

He looked about to speak and then, as if thinking better, shut his mouth tightly.

"Perhaps we should leave our remaining garments on to dry," she suggested.

He nodded, turned toward the fire and continued to remain silent.

She chose to do the same.

She suddenly realized she was still bare-breasted and wished to slip her blouse back on. But it was too wet, as was her skirt. She needed to get her garments dried and with hours yet before nightfall, it was possible that her blouse could dry. Then she could slip it on and her skirt off, leaving her long blouse to provide cover.

She moved to gain distance, forgetting they were attached, and yanked him along with her. He stumbled, though righted himself without touching her, and then in unison they sat before the fire.

Where once she felt comfortable with him, she now was apprehensive. She blamed it on the kiss. The kiss had changed things between them. How or why, she wasn't sure. She only knew that things were now different.

A twinge in her foot reminded her that she had not attended to her sore feet, and she quickly set to the task, besides her boots needed drying. The wet leather gave her a bit of a struggle and after her effort produced a grunt and a groan, Duncan reached out and took command.

He pushed her hands away and with a gentle yank had her boots off in no time. He did the same to his own and placed both hers and his near the heat of the fire. He then turned and slipped his hand around her ankle and lifted it to rest on his crossed legs.

"I can see—"

A quick raise and snap of his hand had her protest dying on her lips. Now was not a good time to argue with him, so she let him have his way.

He was gentle as he unwrapped the swath of cloth she had used to protect her blistered toe. He examined it, raising her leg to get a better look. When he was done he did the same to her other foot.

She thought him done, since he draped the strips of cloth over the boots. And with her feet more chilled than aching, she wanted to warm them by the fire. But when she started to slide her feet off his legs, his hand quickly stopped them. Then without a word he began to rub the warmth back into one.

She never expected his large hands to be so nimble. He massaged her sole with deep, thrusting strokes, chasing the chill from her feet. Then he tenderly worked heat into her toes, taking his time until each one glowed pink. After finishing the one foot, he worked on the other. And she simply sat with her eyes closed and enjoyed as the heat spread from her feet up along her body.

Somewhere in her head she was reminding herself that she should be more concerned with making certain her blouse dried, but convinced herself that her feet were just as important.

Suddenly she recalled her naked breasts and the consequences of not seeing that her blouse dried. It meant sleeping completely naked in Duncan's arms again. And after their kiss, she didn't think that was a wise idea.

He stopped just as she opened her eyes, and she was relieved that no comment was necessary. She stretched her feet out far enough so that the fire's heat would continue to keep them warm. She then fussed with arranging her blouse as best as possible to dry, hoping he would follow her lead. Gratefully he did, and they once again settled quietly in silence.

She didn't care for the uncomfortable silence between them. She missed the ease in which they had talked with one another and the sense of safety she had felt with him. The kiss had simply ruined everything, but yet . . .

She couldn't deny that she favored his kiss, unexpected as it was and with no sense of expectation; it had been a memorable experience. And if she was honest with herself, one she wouldn't mind experiencing again.

Stop being foolish, Mercy.

Her mother's sharp warning rang clear in her head. She had expected it; even though her mother was dead, her lessons had been drilled too deeply for Mercy to ever forget. Her mother would expect her to use Duncan for what she could get from him and then be done with him. After all, he was not a man of means or power and thereby worthless to the likes of her mother.

But if he could keep her safe and provide a safe haven until she could find better, then her mother would advise her to do whatever was necessary, and that included coupling with him.

Her mother had warned Mercy not to waste her time on love—that it was a grievous condition that brought only pain and suffering. She recalled the rare few times she heard her mother crying. She had been young and her mother's sobs had ripped at her small heart and she wanted to comfort her, but when she had tried, her mother yelled that this was what loving a man did to you and don't be foolish enough to ever let it happen.

And so she was left confused about love and men. Her mother told her not to worry, since she would see that a generous marriage arrangement was made for her. However, her mother had made a foolish and costly decision, and now Mercy was on her own.

"We will need to find food in the morning."

Mercy was so relieved that Duncan had broken the silence. Being alone with her thoughts didn't help, since it made her realize the true precariousness of her situation.

"It would be nice if we could catch a fish or two, but that would require a fire to cook them," she said disappointed.

"There are farms throughout this area. We're bound to come across one soon."

"The tenants may fear helping us."

"Or they may be as kind as Bailey and his wife. And if not we'll survive on the last of the fall berries and apples, if we can find them. Then when we arrive at my home, Mara will have a feast prepared."

He spoke the woman's name with such fondness and glee that Mercy couldn't help but ask, "You love this woman?"

With a broad smile and a glint of joy in his eyes, he said, "With all my heart and I have since I was born."

Strangely, she felt a pang of relief. "She's your mother."

Duncan shook his head. "My mother died giving birth to me and my father died shortly after in battle. With no other family left to care for me, Mara and her husband Carmag took me in and raised me as their own along with their son Trey, who is but a year younger than my twenty and seven years."

"So Trey is like a brother to you."

Duncan nodded. "So are Reeve and Bryce, who arrived at Mara and Carmag's doorstep one cold snowy night. Bryce was barely five years and Reeve just four years and they clung to each other for a good week until they finally realized they had found a good, safe home."

"They're brothers?" she asked happy that she was learning more about Duncan and relieved she was feeling comfortable with him once again.

"No. They met along the road after their farms had been destroyed and their parents killed."

"Clan war?' Mercy asked.

"If the clans aren't battling themselves, they're battling those who wish to claim sovereignty over Scotland."

"But it is being whispered that the true king will return soon and his reign will bring peace," she said.

"Many hope and pray that it is true," he said and reached his hand out to feel his shirt. "Almost dry."

Mercy eagerly felt her blouse. "Mine is dry. Now I can put it on and take my skirt off and leave it to dry."

Duncan stood along with her. She wasn't surprised that he turned his head away while she removed her skirt and maneuvered herself into her blouse. Then she quickly spread her skirt out to dry.

She let him know he could turn around with a quick, "All done."

His dark eyes took in all of her much too slowly and lingered much too long in certain areas. And while the linen blouse provided sufficient covering, she also realized it tantalized. Her mother taught her that a single revealing garment could entice a man more than if a woman stood naked before him.

"You should know by now that I'm extremely attracted to you and that kiss we shared makes me want to sample more of you."

She felt a nibble of the same, but it would be unwise to let him know that now. He would assume that she was willing, when actually she was curious. And curiosity could be a dangerous thing.

"And presently, I wish *only* for the safety and warmth of your arms," she said.

"Does that mean you will still keep your promise of that kiss when we are free?"

She smiled. "A promise is a promise."

"Then I promise you the safety and warmth of my arms for as long as you need them." He grinned. "No matter how difficult it is for me."

She laughed softly. "You are an honorable man, Highlander."

"There you go forever reminding me."

"I don't think you need reminding. I believe it is your nature. It is simply who you are."

"Keep that thought strong," he said, his hand going to his waist. "Since I'm about to take this annoying wet wool plaid off and stand naked in front of you."

Chapter 7

"You're not even going to turn away?" Duncan asked as he unwrapped his plaid.

"There's no need," Mercy said. "I have nothing to fear from you. You gave your word."

Duncan let his plaid drop and wondered if he should have considered more carefully what he had been agreeing to. She was a delectable morsel that tempted his appetite and challenged his civility. She was quite unique and he enjoyed her company, even though it had been forced on him.

And he was trying to keep his mind off the fact that she looked deliciously appetizing in nothing more than her blouse. Her creamy skin glistened like the early morning dew on flower petals and he knew it felt just as smooth, and damn if that didn't make him itch to touch her.

To keep his hands busy he slipped his shirt on, not caring it was still damp and not caring that it didn't fully cover him. They had been naked before in front of each other and no doubt would be naked again before their journey was done.

He felt no unease as he turned and took her hand and eased them down to sit.

He wasn't surprised when she snuggled against his side. Even with the fire, there was still a chill in the small cave.

He kept hold of her hand giving it a slight squeeze as if reassuring her.

She rested her head on his shoulder in return.

And again they sat in silence.

The storm abated just before they snuggled beneath the dried blanket, and wrapped in each other's arms, fell asleep.

The early morning brought with it a crisp chill and Duncan insisted that Mercy use the blanket to keep warm. She fashioned it into a shawl and they were soon on their way.

The day's priority was food. They had to find something if they hoped to keep up the strength to continue their rushed pace. Already his stomach was grumbling loudly and he thought he heard Mercy's give a protest or two. And while he wished to remain on a steady course, he felt it was wise for them to veer off so that the soldiers would find it harder to track them.

Mercy made no objections when he started them up a hill. She removed her shawl, shoved it into the sack and twisting the top, tucked it partially in her waistband. Then she kept pace with him as they climbed the hill, though he had to grab hold of her a few times and prevent her from sending them tumbling.

They stopped at the top to catch their breaths and take in the view and they both smiled. Tucked in a grove of trees not far from a stream was smoke billowing from a chimney, which meant a cottage.

"Food," they echoed.

They descended faster than they had climbed, though they approached the small farm with caution. The last crop had been harvested from the small field and the ground prepared for winter's rest, but a few flowering plants still grew in a garden patch beside the cottage. A neatly stacked pile of wood sat to the side of the front door and a rough hewn bench sat on the other side.

Not seeing anyone about, they waited from their perch at the edge of the woods. Duncan kept hold of her hand; not only did it alleviate the burden of the heavy chain, but it helped them work more in unison, not to mention that he had grown accustomed to holding her hand. Her small, delicate one fit so perfectly in his large calloused hand, like she belonged there and always had. And for the moment that's where he intended to keep it.

He peered past the foliage, focusing on the cottage and its quiet surroundings. He didn't want to take a chance and approach before determining how many occupied the place, and if there was a chance that anyone posed a threat.

"You're welcome in my home."

Duncan immediately swung Mercy protectively behind him as they swerved around, forcing her against his back. He almost shook his head in dismay that he had allowed this woman to sneak up on them. A mass of white curly hair was piled on top of her head with several curls falling around her aged face. Her broad smile deepened her many wrinkles, though showed a fine set of teeth. Her wide, bright green eyes held the inquisitiveness of a child rather than a crone, and she was as petite as Mercy, though slimmer. And she wore a dark blue skirt, white blouse and pale green vest, belted at her thin waist.

"I'm Dolca, welcome to my home," she said and with a slow gait walked past them.

They followed, Duncan impressed by her soft, barely detectable footfalls.

"I'm sorry, but I have no sufficient tools to remove those shackles. I depend on my neighbors to help me with certain tasks, though I can provide you with food and drink."

Duncan looked to see Mercy smiling happily and he realized he was grinning himself. Finally they would have a substantial meal.

"My place is secluded enough that not many cross its path. You should be safe enough for now."

Duncan listened, realizing that the woman was sharp in mind and observation for one her age. She had probably observed them in the woods and saw that they were chained together and surmised they were no threat unless . . .

"Have soldiers past this way?" he asked.

"They take an opposite route from you, or so neighboring farmers tell me." Dolca pushed the front door open. "Come in, sit and let me feed you."

Duncan sensed that the woman posed no threat, so he didn't hesitate to let Mercy precede him into the cottage.

A welcoming warmth and scrumptious scent greeted them. A multitude of crocks sat bunched together on various sized chests and bunches of dried plants hung from roof rafters. A single bed rested against the side wall and a solid wooden table and two chairs sat before the fireplace that consumed the whole back wall, a black cauldron hung on the hook, its contents bubbling and the smell divine.

"Sit. Sit," Dolca urged. "You must be starving."

Duncan didn't need to be told again, nor did Mercy. They quickly moved the two chairs close enough for them to sit.

Dolca brought two loaves of freshly baked bread to the table and made quick work of scooping out the middles, placing the discarded bread in a bowl in front of them. Then she took each bread trench to the cauldron and filled it with the delicious stew.

Duncan and Mercy were quick to grab for the broken pieces of bread and use them to scoop up the tasty fish stew.

Dolca poured them cider from a jug and placed a bowl of apples on the table. Duncan didn't have to ask for more stew, Dolca was quick to replenish his bread trench as soon as it was near empty and she did the same for Mercy.

"You are more than generous to us," Duncan said between mouthfuls.

"You are in need. It would distress me not to offer you help," Dolca said.

"Still, you place yourself in danger by helping us."

Dolca smiled and for a moment she looked much younger than her advanced years. "Not so. True danger for me would be *not* to help the innocent, but enough of me," she said with the wave of her hand. "You are both welcome to spend the night if you wish."

Mercy immediately turned pleading eyes to Duncan. "What say you?"

While a solid roof over their heads and good food to fill their bellies tempted, it wasn't a wise choice. It could give the soldiers time to realize they followed a false trail and retrace their steps, leading them right to Dolca's door.

Duncan voiced his concerns regrettably, not wanting to disappointment Mercy, but having no choice. "A brief reprieve would be welcome, but any longer would be unwise."

Mercy didn't object or argue. He didn't think she would. And while they laced fingers often enough for good reason, he hadn't expected her to lock her fingers with his.

It was an innocent response and yet so intimate, for

it represented the trust she had in him and he suddenly swelled with immense pleasure, though passion had nothing to do with it. Not that he didn't think much too often about bedding her, but surprisingly this time his pleasure centered on the comfort of a simple touch, and that he had never experienced with any woman . . . and he very much liked it.

"At least rest for a bit and let me tend to your sore feet," Dolca said, turning to Mercy.

"Is my discomfort that noticeable?" Mercy asked.

But it was Duncan who spoke. "You should have told me you were in pain."

"There was nothing you could have done, and I refuse to allow my sore feet to slow us down."

"You are a stubborn one," he snapped, angry with himself for not noticing.

"Stubbornness is sometimes necessary," she said, though not defensively, but rather matter-of-factly.

"And it *is* necessary, if you two are to survive," Dolca said. "There is talk that the king searches frantically for someone."

"Who?" Mercy asked anxiously.

"Some surmise it is the true king," Dolca said.

Duncan realized that Mercy had squeezed his hand hard when she had asked who, as if in fear, then her grip relaxed when Dolca answered. Had she expected a different answer?

"The king is a fool if he believes the Highlanders will not protect their own," Dolca said. "Old, young, fit or not, Highlanders will protect the true king and see him on the throne."

"If the seer's prediction is true, why has the true king not yet made himself known?" Mercy asked.

"He is wise to keep his identity secret," Dolca explained. "He would be in grave danger otherwise. When it is time, he will step forward and lead his people. Until then the present king will do anything to protect his reign, and that includes killing innocent Highlanders."

"A good reason for us to take our leave sooner rather than later," Duncan said, knowing no one was safe from the king's men, not even an old woman.

"Don't worry about me," Dolca said with a smile. "I plan on being around to see the rightful king take the throne."

It didn't take long for Dolca to tend Mercy's blistered feet and Duncan was pleased to see the relief on her face.

"They feel better already," Mercy said after slipping on her boots and turning to Duncan. "You best be careful, or you'll not be able to match my pace."

He laughed and shook his head. "Not likely."

"Why don't you two sit by the fire and rest a bit, while I gather a sack of food for you to take with you," Dolca said.

"Can't we help?" Mercy offered.

Dolca grinned. "Chained as you are, you'd be more hindrance than help."

"Is there anything we can do for you?" Duncan asked, wishing to repay her kindness."

Dolca nodded. "Survive."

Duncan worried about the trail he planned to take. It was a route he had traveled many times and one he favored. It allowed him time alone, time to think and time to appreciate the beauty of his homeland. He loved the mist that capped the mountains and drifted down into the valleys. He loved the way the land dressed for the different seasons and watching the wildlife at play. Most of all he loved the peacefulness that pervaded his soul when he walked amongst nature. This was his home. This would be his children's home. And he would gladly give his life to protect it.

While he was accustomed to the treacheries of hill walking, he feared Mercy wasn't. And there were many hills to traverse and slopes that could prove not only difficult, but tiring. Did she have the stamina to conquer them?

There were alternative routes, but more than likely the soldiers were covering them. Not familiar with the treacherous hill terrain in this area, the soldiers were more likely to avoid it, giving him and Mercy a better chance of reaching their destination safely.

So far Mercy had proven herself a determined one, but the land could sometimes be unforgiving and only brute strength and endless willpower could combat it.

He glanced at Mercy from the corner of his eye. Since leaving Dolca's a couple of hours ago she hadn't spoken a word and he wondered what occupied her thoughts. He knew little about her, almost nothing, though in another sense he felt he knew her well.

If he voiced his concern to her, she would no doubt tell him that she was up to the task. Signs, however, had warned him otherwise, her feet quickly blistering, her hands not a callous or scar on them, her gracious manner when speaking with others. It was obvious to him that she had to be part of the gentry. What he wished he knew was what had happened that she had lost her status?

"Let's stop a moment," he said, slowing his steps.

"We haven't been walking that long," she said in protest, halting her steps.

"I know." He took her hand and her slim fingers quickly closed around his as he led her to sit with him on a large flat boulder. "We need to talk."

"About?" she asked, relaxing against him.

Strange how he expected that of her; he would have thought it odd if she hadn't rested against him. He hastily cleared his thoughts and answered, "The terrain we're about to face can at times be uncompromising."

"This whole ordeal has been uncompromising from the start, but what choice do we have? We do what must be done." She smiled at him. "I will do my best not to slow us down."

"This way will take more time."

"But it is safer, isn't it?"

He nodded. "It is not a guaranteed safety and we may reach a point where we cross paths with the soldiers, but by then we should be on my land and there will be others to help us."

"Then it's the path we must take." She took the sack from him, reached in and brought out two apples. "To fortify us."

He took one from her and for a few moments they sat and enjoyed a small repast and then once again were on their way.

By late afternoon gray skies had moved in overhead and Duncan feared another storm was brewing. The weather seemed to be at odds with him reaching home. They could stop now, though he preferred to climb the next hill before they stopped for the night.

He looked to Mercy keeping a good gait beside him. As was her way, she had not uttered one complaint, but he could see the tiredness creeping over her lovely face and hear it in her mounting sighs.

He took hold of her hand and she slowed and glanced up at him.

"Do you think you can make one more hill before we stop for the night?" he asked, nodding toward the distance ahead.

She gave a look and chuckled. "That little thing? We'll be over it in no time."

He admired her courage, knowing her feet and legs must be protesting, and he smiled. "Then we will rest and feast."

"That's reason enough to conquer that hill."

With hands remaining clasped, they made it to the hill in no time and were soon starting up the steep slope. It was easy at first and Duncan believed as Mercy had suggested, they'd be over it fast enough.

But halfway up, the terrain changed. It turned rocky, making footing more difficult and dangerous, and costing more effort on their part. A few times he and Mercy had almost lost their footing and he was quick to keep a tight hold on her.

They slowed their pace and climbed more carefully, finding it necessary to hold more tightly to rocks and sturdy branches as they climbed.

"A bit more and we're there," he encouraged and she nodded, her breathing too labored to speak.

Anxious to reach the top only a few feet away, Duncan gave a push forward, grabbing a jutting rock and finding another good rock to plant his foot on, when suddenly both rocks gave way under his weight. He reached out frantically, trying to grab onto something, anything, but whatever he touched crumbled in his hand. With nothing to latch onto, he went plummeting backward and Mercy went with him.

Chapter 8

~~~~

Mercy couldn't avoid the dirt and stones that rained over her. She wanted to glance up at Duncan, just a step or two ahead of her, to see what was wrong, but it was impossible with the falling debris.

Then with a sudden shock she was violently wrenched away from the hillside and found herself tumbling down the rocky terrain. Duncan swiftly grabbed her around the waist and yanked her against him. He shoved her face against his chest and wrapped his solid body tightly around her. She clung to him just as tightly as they tumbled over and over and over; rocks, stones and sticks jabbing them everywhere.

It seemed an endless fall when finally they reached the bottom, rolled and slammed into a tree trunk. Mercy was too stunned and frightened to speak. She wanted nothing more than to remain in the protection of Duncan's strong arms.

"Are you all right?" he asked with an anxious breath.

"I think—" Her breath caught and she fought to regain it.

"Easy, Mercy, easy," he urged, his hand soothing along her back.

She tried too hard to breath and she was soon grasping for breath.

Duncan sat up taking her with him, his arms remaining steady around her. "Calm down, lass," he said softly. "You're all right. I'm here."

She gasped a couple more times, though his reassuring words soothed her, and then she was finally able to calm herself and breathe easily.

"That's it," he encouraged. "You're doing well."

Once Mercy fully reclaimed control, she felt foolish. Lord, she had jumped off a high cliff shackled to a stranger and landed in deep water when she couldn't even swim, and she had not felt the intense fear that she had a moment ago.

She was even more embarrassed when she shuddered uncontrollably.

Duncan drew her gently against him. She was quick to rest her head to his chest, quick to admit how wonderfully comforting his hard muscles felt and quick to appreciate the soothing rhythm of his strong, rapid heartbeat.

"I lost my hold and my footing," he said, blaming himself.

"You kept hold of me though." Another shudder racked her body.

His arms tightened around her. "Since we're already

shackled together it was the wisest action to take."

She shook her head, though it remained resting against his chest. "No, you didn't have time to think, only react. And it was to protect me."

He slipped his finger under her chin and with a little tug had her looking up at him. "Know well, Mercy, that I will protect you whether or not we are shackled together. I will always be there for you."

"Your chivalry is showing again," she smiled softly.

"That is your fault," he teased.

"How so?"

"You constantly put me in situations where I have no other choice."

"I'm not the only one who puts us there," she reminded with a poke to his chest and he winced.

"You're hurt," she said sitting up, her hands rushing to spread open his shirt. She grimaced as soon as she caught sight of a large bruise beginning to form on the side of his chest just below his nipple. And it looked as if it deepened in color as she stared at it.

She reached out and with delicate strokes ran her fingers over the darkening wound, accidentally brushing his nipple with her inquisitive touch.

He jerked, his body stiffening and she was quick to apologize. "I'm sorry. I didn't mean to hurt you."

He took her hand in his and eased it away. "Better to leave it to mend."

"You will rest," she ordered and moved away only to wince herself.

She immediately pulled up her blouse to search for the painful spot. She cupped her full breast, flinching as she squeezed and forced her plump bosom up so that she could examine the damage beneath.

"Does it look bad?" she asked, unable to see all of it.

His hand reached out, but retreated before he touched the tender spot. "It's not that large and the color has yet to deepen."

She let the blouse fall back in place and turned a worried glance on him. "Do you have pain elsewhere?"

"I'm fine," he reassured her and reached to pick a few twigs from her dark hair. "And you?"

She tended to him as naturally as he did her, brushing dirt and debris off his shoulders and plucking twigs from the ends of his long hair before answering, "A throb in my ankle, that's all."

With quick and deft hands, he lifted her skirt.

Though he assumed privileges meant only for a husband, that was the way of things for the moment. She had no choice. She hadn't had a choice since she had taken the plunge off the cliff with him. That day that decision had not only physically bound them together, but had also forced them to start sharing some privileges meant only for husband and wife. So here she sat allowing him to lift her skirt and not at all upset by it.

"It doesn't look bad. A small abrasion, that's all," Duncan said.

She smiled with relief. Happy that it is was nothing that would slow them down.

"Then let's conquer that hill and be done with it," she said, though hesitant to stand. "That is, if you feel up to it."

He grabbed her elbow and hoisted them both up. "There you go challenging me again."

"Are you up to it?" she asked.

He leaned his brow against hers. "I'm always up to it, woman."

"Then let's see how much fortitude you have." She turned toward the hill, but he grabbed her arm and she looked back at him.

"I'm thinking I may need some incentive."

A twinkle danced in his dark eyes, but the jut of his chin warned that he was serious.

"And what would give you the impetus to climb?" she asked curiously.

"A kiss."

"I've already promised you a kiss when we are free of our chains," she reminded. "And you have kissed me once already."

"True enough," he agreed with a nod, "but this time I want to kiss you with permission."

Mercy was fast to detect the danger in that situation, and yet her first thought was that she had very much enjoyed their first kiss and longed for another. And so she answered without sparing it anymore thought.

"Then you may kiss me."

His eyes rounded, as if he didn't believe her. "You promise?"

"You have my word," she said. "You may kiss me once we finish the climb."

He shook his head and grinned. "No, not when we finish the climb. I want to kiss you when and where I choose."

"But—"

"No buts," he interrupted. "You gave your word for the kiss and no more. Now it is in my hands."

"But—"

His raised hand warded off her protest. "No. It's done."

"I want a warning—" She just wasn't fast enough. He interrupted her again.

"No. A promise is a promise and the promise is a kiss, no more."

"That's not fair," she complained.

He laughed and tweaked her chin. "All's fair when it comes to kissing."

Mercy wanted to argue with him, but she knew it was senseless, she'd get nowhere. She had given her word and there was nothing she could do about it. Nothing but wait for him to kiss her and the prospect fluttered her stomach.

Her hand hurried to rest in the spot that continued to flutter wildly in hopes of somehow stopping it.

"You're hungry?" he asked.

She was glad he didn't realize her true discomfort. "Yes, though not enough to keep us from climbing."

He rubbed at his stomach. "My hunger is growing."

He turned his head searching the area. "We best find where that food sack landed so we can feast after the climb."

Duncan and Mercy stood at the foot of the hill and looked up.

"It appears bigger," Mercy said, "more a mountain than a hill."

"That's because it conquered us the last time," he said. "Once conquered, fear sets in, hope dies and most give up." He took hold of her hand, wanting to reassure her. "This time I'll watch my step."

"I trust you," she said with a soft smile. "You are the gallant warrior come to my rescue."

He felt a stab of guilt. While he had wondered over why one of the gentry had been taken prisoner, it stood to reason that more than likely the king had fancied her, or one of the powerful warlords wanted her. It was simply bad luck that she had been chained to him, since it was he the soldiers wanted and planned to kill. She was an innocent in all this, and his guilt soared with that acknowledgment.

They once again started their climb, Duncan more careful, though only because she was with him. If he had been on his own and fallen, he would have cursed the damn hill and returned to climb it with vengeance. He couldn't do that chained to Mercy. He had her safety to consider.

Step by careful step, they climbed and, as before, the

terrain turned rocky and more treacherous. Duncan paused when they reached the spot where he had previously lost his grip. He looked around and was more watchful of the rocks he chose to grab.

His hand latched on to a sturdy rock when he heard the rumble of falling rocks below, and he instantly tightened his grip on the ragged stone and locked his fingers with Mercy's just as she lost her footing.

"Duncan!"

Her frightened scream tore at his heart, but his firm grip stopped her from falling too far and from taking him with her.

"I've got you," he reassured her with a shout. "Find a firm footing."

More rocks went crumbling and he knew that the hill was protesting their presence. It had had enough of their trespassing and wanted them gone. It was a strange thought to some, but not to those who knew the land.

"Stay still," he yelled. "I'm going to pull you up."

She weighed little. It was no struggle at all to pull her up beside him. As soon as he did, her free arm wrapped around the back of his neck, and she tucked her head beneath his chin, resting her face in the curve of his neck.

Her chest heaved, her slim body trembled and she clung to him for dear life.

"Hold on, I'll get us to the top," he said.

"I can do it," she reassured him, though he was well aware that she was trying to reassure herself.

"I know you can, but leave this to me."

"If you insist," she said, her voice quivering.

"I do," he said, and almost kissed her forehead. He had no intentions of wasting his kiss on a reassuring peck. When he kissed her, she would remember it—and no doubt would he.

"Have we far to go?" she asked.

He glanced up at the distance and though not far, it was treacherous. Not wanting to add to her distress he said, "It's a short distance. We'll be there in no time."

"Tell me how I can help."

"Hold tight," he said. "I'll get us the rest of the way up."

Her arm never left his neck. She remained locked firmly against him, and with brute strength he caught hold of rock after jutting rock, her shackled hand not much help, though she retained his rhythm as best she could as they climbed. With only inches from the top he swung her up past him and, with his hand to her bottom, he pushed her to safety and then joined her.

They lay side by side, hands joined, Duncan's breathing labored.

"We made it," she said in a rough whisper, almost as if she didn't quite believe it.

His cough was more a laugh. "We have yet to climb down."

She laughed, too, and turned to nestle in the crook of his arm. "Down has to be easier than up, especially if we take another tumble. At least then we'll be at the bottom and not have to climb again."

"No more climbing today," he said, his arm settling around her and keeping her close. Close and safe. "We reach the bottom and we feast and rest."

"You'll not find me objecting."

He turned so that their bodies faced. "Were you taught to be so agreeable?"

Her eyes sprung wide for a moment and then retreated to a natural flutter. "My circumstance taught me that objection could often prove futile and so I learned how to adapt."

"As you do now shackled to me?"

"What else is there to do?" she asked. "But survive."

He couldn't help but notice how her eyes had turned such a brilliant blue, although it could have been that her long, curled, dark lashes intensified the color. Or was it that every inch of her face seemed to grow lovelier before his eyes? Her lips even appeared more plump than usual and of course more tempting to kiss. Or was it that he had the promise of a kiss on his mind?

"We need to get moving," he said, not trusting himself not to kiss her there and then. Her lips were much too inviting and he was much too hungry to taste them. "The darkening sky threatens another storm."

"We should find shelter then," Mercy said, sitting up.

Duncan followed and got to his feet, taking her along with him.

Mercy brushed the debris from her blouse and skirt as she asked, "How far to your home?"

"Four days if we keep a good pace and do not have to detour further to avoid the soldiers." He was truly anxious to get home. He had much news to share and there was still much to be done, though he had no doubt his brothers would have much to say about the shackles.

They began the climb down, hands joined and their steps confident.

Chapter 9

They found shelter in an abandoned cottage weathered and beaten by time. Though four walls remained intact, the sky was clearly visible through a gaping hole. Still, it provided sufficient protection from a light rain that had started falling.

A pallet whose stuffing leaked through torn patches was bunched up in a corner and Mercy went to its rescue, forgetting Duncan was attached to her. She stopped and turned her head when she heard him stumble to keep up with her.

"I'm sorry, but that worn bedding looks fit enough to save us from another night's rest on the hard ground."

"A tempting thought," he agreed, and led the way.

It startled Mercy to realize that she enjoyed watching him move. There was courage and confidence in his steps that she didn't often see in others. And his thick arms rippled with muscles even in the slightest of movements and hardened like the blade of a mighty sword when a stronger strength was needed. She could easily attest to that, since he had captured and held her in his arms often enough since they first met. His neck also fascinated her, thick and wide, the perfect haven for her to tuck her head.

She counted herself lucky, in an odd way, for being chained to this man. Otherwise she would have never been able to know him so intimately, and she was glad for it. From what she had learned so far, she believed him to be a special man. Or was it that she found herself deeply attracted to him that made him so special in her eyes?

They spread the lumpy bedding on the floor near the corner and away from the hole in the roof. Then they both plopped down on it and smiled at each other.

"It's a fine bed we have for tonight," Duncan said.

She reached for the sack he had dropped to the ground before helping her. "And we have food and a blanket. We are living well."

She placed the folded blanket on the ground in front of them and then began placing the food on top.

"You are accustomed to living well?"

His inquiry startled her, but she had to expect him to be curious about her, since she was about him.

Still, she was cautious. "Why do you ask?"

He reached out and took her hand turning it over to trace a finger around her palm. "Your lovely skin bears no signs of hard labor."

For a moment Mercy's thoughts could center on nothing but the tantalizing play of his finger on the flesh of her palm. It teased her senses to the point of igniting her passion, just a spark here and there, though it would surely flare if he continued. She was relieved yet disappointed when he stopped, though it allowed her to slowly regain clarity and respond. Not that the sparks completely dissipated. They lingered and threatened to ignite if she didn't ignore them. Not an easy task.

"I have been fortunate to have had a privileged life," she admitted, seeing no reason to deny the truth, with evidence proving otherwise.

"You seem too adventurous for being privileged."

Mercy laughed, recalling old memories. "My parents weren't always privy to my actions. I loved climbing trees, using branches to sword fight and riding my beautiful mare presented to me for my birthday one year."

She almost choked on her last few words, the hurt of leaving her beloved mare, Sky, behind rising to torment her. She loved that horse dearly and rode her every day, but there had been no time to get to her. There had only been time to do as her mother said.

"So adventurous, and yet you never learned to swim?"

Mercy returned to spreading out the food. "My mother's doing. She had a deathly fear of water and refused to allow me near it." She didn't bother to explain where her mother's fear came from—that her mother's own father nearly drowned her when she was young. She didn't want to have to explain that her mother's mother was a kept woman and that when the wealthy man's wife finally gave birth, he wanted to make certain no bastard of his stood in the way of his true daughter's inheritance.

Mercy's grandmother had saved her only child and ran, and taught her daughter never to trust a man, just as she, Mercy's mother, had taught her daughter—Mercy, though, had no choice but to trust Duncan; and the more she trusted him, the more she felt she could trust him.

"I'll teach you how to swim."

"If there's time," she said agreeably.

"There'll be time."

He sounded so confident she had to ask, "How do you know that?"

"You admitted that you have no one and no place to go. You will remain with my people where you will be safe and where I will be able to teach you to swim."

Mercy didn't argue. If there was one thing her mother had taught her it was not to challenge when it would do no good. Simply allow the person to think you agree and proceed as you wish when the time comes. As much as she wouldn't mind accepting Duncan's offer, she knew that eventually she would have to take her leave.

"You will like my home. There are good people there and you will find it a good place to settle."

"I did not think you would want me around after being shackled to me for so long," she said teasingly as she tore off a hunk of bread and handed it to him.

He took the bread and grinned. "We will be shackled no more. We will be free of each other, never having to be tied to one another again."

Had his grin faltered and his words lost enthusiasm, or had she merely imagined it? And had she felt her own smile fade and a shiver run through her when she realized that there would be no reason for them to spend every moment together? Was that truly sorrow she felt? Did the thought of not being with him disturb her so much? Whatever was the matter with her?

"It's been a long day," he said. "We should eat and sleep so that we can get an early start in the morning."

She nodded, and though not as hungry as she first thought, she nibbled at the food. Conversation was sparse, but then they both seemed more focused on their meal than anything else. And when finally they finished, the remaining food stored in the sack, they settled on the pallet beneath the lone blanket.

While exhaustion washed over her, Mercy found it difficult to sleep. She blamed her chaotic thoughts for keeping her up, though she wondered more if it was a single thought that crept in, nudged hard and demanded attention.

The kiss.

Why couldn't she stop thinking about Duncan kissing her? Sure, she had never been kissed and was curious, but that didn't mean she had to obsess about it. Her mother had warned her to remain pure, insisting that then they could find a man who would pay dearly to have her as his own. Then Mercy would never have to worry.

Mercy hadn't quite seen it as her mother had. Being a mistress to a wealthy and powerful man didn't guarantee a woman anything. It certainly hadn't proved beneficial for her grandmother, and as for her mother? Her mother's scheming helped do her in, but it also made Mercy realize that her father cared naught for her. How could he when he had ordered her death?

The heartbreaking thought had her cuddling closer to Duncan and when his arms tightened around her, she snuggled her face to his chest. She had no doubt she was safe with this man, or that she felt a certain comfort with him. And she couldn't deny her attraction to him, or her desire to taste his kiss.

She wondered what it would feel like. Would it intoxicate her into wanting more? Or would it disappoint her? No, she didn't believe that would be the way of it. Certainly, his kiss would steal her breath away, not to mention her senses.

What foolishness!

Mercy almost jumped, so startled was she by her mother's clear voice in her head. While her mother insisted she remain pure, she also insisted that she didn't remain ignorant of pleasing a man. A kiss her mother had taught her was meant to lure a man, make him want more and do anything for that kiss.

Mercy recalled asking that if she was to remain virginal to kisses, how would she ever know how to lure a man with one?

"You respond," her mother had snapped sharply. "Tentatively at first as if unsure and then you taste and you don't stop. You let him feel your eagerness. You press against him, touch him, make him feel how your body aches for his, but"—she had stopped and shook a finger at Mercy—"you always, always remain in control. Never lose yourself to the kiss, for then you will surely be lost."

While Mercy had listened to her mother's warning, she couldn't help but wonder how it would truly feel to lose herself in a kiss. And she wondered if she would get lost in Duncan's kiss.

Kiss him and be done with it so it plagues you no more.

Yes, that would be her mother's advice. It was after all the edict she lived by.

Be done with it.

Her mother never tarried over thoughts or decisions, once done that was it and no more time was to be wasted on it. But this time Mercy didn't want to hurry. She found enjoyment in thinking about the kiss and along with it, came an anticipation that tickled her tummy.

She was looking forward to Duncan kissing her and the anticipation only served to heighten her desire. When? Where? How?

She almost laughed, but caught herself. How would be up to him. Would he one day lean close and simply steal the kiss? Or would he take her in his arms and demand she return his kiss? Or perhaps he would do as her mother had advised, slow, tentative kisses leading to a deeper more demanding one.

Her tummy tingled and she couldn't help but sigh, though it turned into a yawn.

"Settle your thoughts, or we'll both not sleep tonight."

Mercy froze and slowly raised her head to look at Duncan, his dark eyes wide open.

"Whether you realize it or not, your body has yet to settle for the night. A twitch, a tuck, a turn. Your restlessness tells me you have much on your mind. What disturbs you?"

She couldn't admit that she'd been thinking about him kissing her. That just wouldn't do, though she could say, *Concerns.*

"What concerns?"

She should have known he'd probe.

Control.

Her mother's reminder echoed in her head and she did as she had been taught. She turned the question on him. "Don't you have concerns?"

His mouth moved closer to hers and her breath caught. Was he about to kiss her?

"What concerns could I possibly have when I have a beautiful woman in my bed, wrapped in my arms?"

Her sigh freed her breath and while disappointment gnawed at her, she had to admit she was glad she still had the kiss to look forward to.

She smiled. "Then I should think only of the handsome Highlander whose strong arms keep me safe and who rests contentedly beside me."

"No better thought to fall asleep on."

She yawned, turning her face away. "I shall sleep

soundly now." And she rested her head to his chest.

He whispered as his hand caressed her arm, "I will keep you safe and I am content sleeping beside you."

She sighed enjoying his strong caress that helped alleviate the muscle ache in her arm. And she couldn't help but say, "That feels so very good."

"You feel good, so soft and touchable."

She yawned again and rubbed her cheek to his chest. "And your chest is hard, but makes a good pillow."

"You are welcome to rest on my chest any time."

"There you go being chivalrous again," she said, her eyes growing weary with sleep.

"For now," he murmured.

"Yes, for now," she agreed as her eyes closed and she drifted to sleep, though she thought she heard him add . . .

No, he didn't say that and she certainly hadn't agreed.

Had she?

Sleep intruded and reasoning dimmed, but still she wondered.

Had he said it?

Had she agreed?

Make no mistake, Mercy, I will make love to you.

Chapter 10

Duncan and Mercy woke early and agreed it was best not to delay, but to get an immediate start. Sustenance could wait a couple of hours, besides both admitted they weren't hungry. An overcast sky followed them and the heavy mist that hugged the hilltops found its way to the low-lying areas, slowing their pace.

Silence was a necessity since they had to concentrate on their every step, which left Duncan quietly grumbling to himself. Though it wasn't the weather that irritated him, it was that he couldn't stop thinking about making love to Mercy. Forget the kiss, not that he didn't want to kiss her, he simply wanted more. He wanted her naked in his arms, but not chained to him, and he wanted to make love to her.

He shook his head. He'd coupled with enough women, but made love? Now there was the question. Was he feeling more toward this woman than he realized? He didn't know and he didn't know if he wanted to know. All he knew at the moment was that in a strange sense he felt as if she belonged to him and an even crazier thought, he belonged to her.

He needed to be free of her, if he was to make sense of any of this. So he needed to concentrate on getting them home. Then he could put some distance between them and see what happened. Why then did he get a punch to his gut every time he thought of being separated from her?

This whole ordeal was making him crazy. It was time to get back home and attend to his mission. He had no time to fall in love.

Fall in love?

He couldn't possibly be falling in love. Could he?

He shook his head. He had to get home and be ready to do whatever was necessary for their mission. He and his friends had to see about getting the rightful king on the throne. They had been pledged to the task since they were young. It was their task in life. They had trained for it and he was proud to be part of it. Once it was done, then he could think about love, marriage and family. But now was not the time?

But could he make love to her and let her go?

Damn, he didn't need this now. He needed to concentrate on the matters at hand and to make certain he did that, he couldn't kiss her. He knew as surely as the sun rose each day, if he kissed Mercy he'd want more. And it wasn't only coupling he was thinking about.

"Duncan."

Mercy whispered his name as she moved closer to him and he saw the look of concern in her wide eyes.

"I hear something."

Duncan stopped, took her hand, and after assessing their surroundings as best as he could through the mist, walked to a small cropping of trees and took shelter among them.

"What did you hear?" He kept his voice to a murmur.

"Voices." Her voice quivered with fear.

"Are you sure?"

She shook her head.

He grumbled beneath his breath annoyed that he hadn't been paying attention. That was why he couldn't give a woman thought right now. It was imperative he remained alert, not only to this situation, but to his mission. Otherwise they could very well die, or the mission he had trained so very hard for could fail.

He kept his voice low. "We'll listen for a few minutes and see if we hear anything."

She nodded and he felt her fingers latch more tightly to his.

They waited, the mist making it more difficult to see anything. They had to rely on their hearing and stillness spoke loudly. Not a bird cried out, nor did an animal scurry. For some reason the forest was on alert.

Duncan placed a finger to his lips and Mercy nodded.

They heard it then, footfalls and none too light, which meant possibly more than one person.

"I heard something, I tell you."

"Shut up." Someone scolded harshly.

Silence immediately followed.

Duncan wondered how many soldiers were out there. A pair or more? Whatever waited for them, defending themselves would prove difficult being shackled together.

The footfalls grew closer and then stopped. Duncan again pressed his finger to his lips and Mercy nodded. He was glad she understood it was not only silence he sought from her but no movement as well. The smallest rustle and the soldiers would be on them.

They waited, for how long neither knew, though it seemed an endless amount of time, and finally, hearing nothing, Duncan signaled Mercy to follow him. Her brow furrowed and her eyes widened as if questioning his decision.

He squeezed her hand to reassure her and signaled for them to move again. This time she didn't hesitate, she followed. They both treaded cautiously, making as little sound as possible, still wary of what waited for them in the mist.

They had taken only a few steps when they collided with the two soldiers.

Duncan was quick to react, his large fist met the one man's face and he stumbled and fell. He turned to lay low the other soldier and saw that Mercy had already landed a good blow to the soldier's face. Blood poured down his nose and he looked dazed. She took advantage of his stunned posture and landed a kick to his leg that sent him sprawling.

Duncan turned in time to land several blows to the returning man and as he stumbled to regain his footing, Mercy stepped forward and with her free hand claimed the fellow's sword, retrieving it from the scabbard. She was quick to slip it into Duncan's hand and kept her chained arm close to his, giving his sword hand free rein.

The other soldier recovered, though blood continued to pour from his nose, and with several foul oaths spewing from his lips, he charged Duncan. He was no match for Duncan's skilled hand, and with one swing he ended the man's life.

He had no time to worry over Mercy, who was trying frantically to keep pace with the rhythm of his movements, though it wasn't easy for her. It actually appeared as though she flew through the air when he had given a good thrust.

The last soldier didn't hesitate to attack. He gave a wild cry and charged forward. Duncan remained where he was, feet braced firmly on the ground, his hand ready to swing and he saw that Mercy kept her eyes on his hand, prepared to follow.

Duncan waited until the man was close enough, the fool thinking he had an advantage with them shackled together. It was the last mistake he would ever make. Duncan killed him in one swift blow.

He didn't waste a moment. "We take their swords and whatever else is on them that we can use."

Mercy nodded and when they were done, Duncan took only one sword and two dirks, slipping one into his boot and the other at his waist. He also sheathed the sword in the scabbard he had fastened around his waist.

"We go," he said and clasped her hand before marching forward into the mist.

They traveled for hours before Mercy voiced her fatigue and hunger.

"We'll stop, but not for long," Duncan said, scouting the area in a glance and choosing a secluded spot behind two large boulders.

Mercy sighed with relief as she lowered herself to the ground and leaned back against the rock.

Duncan took the food from the sack and handed her a hunk of cheese and an apple. If he allowed himself to linger on her lovely face he would feel even guiltier that he was pushing her so hard. Weariness was evident in her slow movements and a smile that barely made it to her mouth, but he had no choice. He had to keep them going. He had to get them to his land where help would be at hand.

"You fear more soldiers are about?" she asked.

"I'm hoping that only two soldiers were sent to cover this area, since the terrain is more difficult. They would assume we would avoid it."

"They believe I slow you down."

"Being chained would slow down a pair, but for a

pair who works together, it would not be a hindrance," he said and smiled. "We work well together."

"We do, don't we?" she said and though she attempted a smile, a shudder grabbed her first and ran through her. "You have killed men before, haven't you?"

Duncan cursed his own stupidity. He had been so obsessed with getting them out of there and as far away as possible that he had never considered the effect of Mercy seeing two men killed before her eyes.

He wanted to reach out and take her in his arms, but somehow he sensed that wasn't what she needed. "Yes, I have, but you haven't, have you?"

She shook her head. "No, I have never seen a man killed."

"Yet you entered the battle like a brave, seasoned warrior, without fear or delay."

"I was fearful," she admitted, "though it was of dying."

"The best weapon when in battle . . . survival."

She turned her lovely sapphire eyes on him and he was glad to see that their brilliant color hadn't dimmed.

"I want to survive, Duncan," she said adamantly. "I know not what the future holds for me, but I do know I want to live."

He eased her into his embrace, though she went willing. He cuddled her close in the crook of his arm and she rested her head to his chest as she so often did.

"You'll survive, Mercy. I promise that you will survive."

Her head shot up and her eyes turned wide with fear. "You must survive too. Promise me that you will survive."

His heart swelled with how much she cared for what happened to him and a wide smile surfaced of its own accord. "We'll survive together."

"Promise me."

It was such a ferocious demand that he answered quickly. "I promise."

"And you best keep it, Duncan MacAlpin."

"Is that an order?" he asked teasingly.

"Aye, it is."

"And who are you to be giving me orders?"

Her eyes softened and her voice turned gentle. "Someone who cares about you."

Her tender words first stabbed at his heart and then punched his gut and he wasn't even in battle, or was he? If he was, it sure wasn't familiar tactics that were being used. And how the bloody hell did he battle unfamiliar foe?

Uncomfortable in foreign territory, he figured the best thing was to move to more familiar terrain.

"If we pick up the pace we could reach the outskirts of my land in possibly two days."

She moved away from him. "I will do my best."

"Finish eating, so we can get moving," he said.

She handed the uneaten apple back to him.

"Eat it, you'll need your strength," he urged, feeling guilty that his own misgivings caused him to hurry her.

"I'm not hungry."

He grew annoyed, though it was at himself. "You're barely a wisp of a thing. You need to eat."

Her chin went up. "I may not be stout like some woman, but I'm strong enough."

He immediately regretted his words. He had hurt her and that hadn't been his intention. "I worry that I push you too hard."

He was surprised that she smiled.

"You push your warriors, don't you?"

He nodded.

"Well, since you have claimed me a warrior woman, then I expect nothing less from you." She rested a hand to his chest. "And you should expect nothing less from me."

She was a courageous one and his respect for her grew.

"Then let's get moving and get home," he said.

She bounced up and tugged on the chain. "Come on then and see if you can keep up with me."

"There you go challenging me again."

"Are you up to it?" she teased with a smile and a cock of her hip.

He laughed and tugged her to him, his hands resting at her waist. "One day I'm going to show you just how much I'm up to it."

"Promises, promises," she said in a singsong voice.

Her breath was sweet, her lips moist like plump fruit, her cheeks flushed pink and he told himself not to do it. The warning rang in his head over and over.

Don't kiss her. Don't kiss her. Don't kiss her.

He told himself to step away from her, but he could only go as far as the chain would allow. That wasn't far enough. She was close, much too close to ignore. *Turn your head away. Don't look.*

But he didn't listen, his glance strayed back to her lips. They waited for him, slightly open. His heart raced as her tongue peeked out to wet them, the tiny tip slowly moving around, covering every inch until they sparkled like the morning dew on a freshly bloomed rose.

Don't kiss her. Don't kiss her. Don't kiss her.

The warning rang like thunder in his head and finally realizing that a storm brewed if he didn't take heed, he turned and reached down for the sack of food. Turning back to look at her once again was a mistake, for he saw something in her eyes, something he couldn't deny. He saw that she wanted him to kiss her.

He dropped the sack, reached out, yanked her up against him and brought his lips down on hers.

Chapter 11

Mercy found herself in Duncan's arms and his lips on hers before she realized what was happening. Mercy forgot everything. Time stood still. Nothing existed except the kiss. His lips proved as powerful as the rest of him. They took command, melting her senses. And though the intrusion of his tongue at first startled her, it took only a fleeting moment for her own to respond. It was as if his tongue had invited hers to dance and she couldn't resist.

She didn't know when she slipped her arms around his neck, or when her body gravitated up against his, or when she realized she never wanted this heavenly moment to end.

His hand roamed down her back and over her backside to cup her buttocks and press her more intimately against him. And that's when she felt the first tingle of heat between her legs and as their kiss deepened, the sensation turned into a steady, aching throb.

She was lost, utterly lost in the magic of his kiss and . . .

Fool!

Her mother's angry voice was like a splash of cold water in the face that cooled her ardor immediately. And she could think of nothing more than her mother admonishing her not to get lost in a kiss. And under the circumstances this wasn't the time or place to allow herself the pleasure.

She eased the kiss to an end and reluctantly stepped away, though Duncan planted his hands on her waist and refused to let go.

They stood silent, staring at each other, and Mercy wondered if her unrequited passion showed so vividly in her eyes as Duncan's did in his. And she clearly knew, or perhaps clearly felt, that if something wasn't done they would soon be locked in another kiss that would end far differently than this one.

She mustered up the courage to say, "Your kiss has been claimed."

He grinned and though he tried to urge her to him, she refused to budge, digging her boots firmly in the ground to keep a safe distance between them.

"You cannot tell me you didn't like it," he said confidently.

"I certainly will not deny that I liked it," she said, "even more so than the first kiss."

His grin faded and his dark eyes narrowed. "Who is it you compare me to?"

She smiled. "When you first kissed me was the first

time I had ever been kissed. While I cannot deny I enjoyed that kiss as well, this kiss was more . . ." She chewed on her bottom lip for a moment, trying to find just the right words. One came to mind and her smile turned generous. "Memorable."

Duncan appeared confused, shaking his head. "I was the first to ever kiss you?"

She nodded.

"No man's lips but mine have touched yours?"

"No man but you."

He looked at her strangely for a moment and then reached out to brush her lips with his fingertips. "They belong to me now."

Belong.

Mercy had not wanted to *belong* to anyone. Her mother had belonged, and while belonging could have benefits, in the end it proved worthless.

Mercy again took a step away from him. "Neither my lips, nor I, belong to anyone."

He seemed surprised by her response, and she assumed he would argue the point. He didn't, though she wasn't foolish enough to believe that he thought differently from his claim. By not arguing he was simply choosing not to debate the matter with her. And she as well would not waste precious time on it.

She belonged to no one and that was that.

"I am pleased you thought my kiss memorable," he said. "I will strive to make all kisses that follow even more memorable."

"There'll be no more kisses," she said candidly, "except of course for the one I promised you once we are freed."

"Afraid to kiss me again?" he challenged.

Truth be told she was, but that was not a truth she intended to share with him.

"We have no time for kisses. We must concentrate on staying alive."

His smile faded and he stepped forward, taking her hand. "You're right about that. We do need to focus more clearly on our situation, but"—he paused and his smile returned—"there's always time for kisses."

To prove it, he gave a quick kiss to her lips.

She silently cursed her body for instantly responding to his playful kiss. And she grew annoyed with him, for he kissed her for one reason and one reason only, to prove that he could. He had no intention of paying heed to her declaration that there would be no kissing. He was letting her know he would kiss her whenever he pleased.

The worst part was that she had no doubt she would eagerly respond.

Don't let him control.

All well and good for her mother's warning, but how did she stop him when she so enjoyed his kisses?

Duncan made sure to keep a keen ear and eye on his surroundings as they continued on their journey. Neither was talkative and he had expected that, the kiss having had a profound effect on them both.

The idea that his lips had been the only ones to have kissed Mercy left him feeling extremely possessive of her. It was as if he had branded her his and branding was for marriages, not kisses. So why did he feel like this? It irritated him, and yet he couldn't shake the thought. Not to mention that rage overwhelmed him, if he even gave brief thought to another man kissing her.

No one had that right, but him. He, and only he, could kiss Mercy. And kiss her he wanted to. Their kiss came as natural as the dawning of the day and continued to rise with as much fervor and heat as the sun did. And like the sun that joined completely with the sky did it finally settle and slowly descend, and that was how he felt with Mercy.

How then could he stop himself from kissing her again, or could she stop from responding? He was no fool. He knew that she wanted to kiss him again as much as he did her, and they would. They'd both be foolish to think it wouldn't happen again, but if Mercy felt better dictating otherwise, he'd let her.

She'd come to her senses sooner or later. Future kisses would see to that and then? He grinned with thoughts of the future.

By the time they found a stream they were both so parched that they fell to their knees and hungrily drank.

Mercy stopped drinking before Duncan and was startled by her reflection in the water. Her face was smudged with dirt, her long black hair wasn't only an unsightly mess, but its brilliant luster was gone, and exhaustion stamped its heavy mark around her eyes. Her mother would be mortified by her disheveled appearance and frankly, so was she.

That she had a reasonable excuse for looking so unkempt was no excuse at all to her. And she felt a sudden need to tidy herself up as best she could. She leaned over the water's edge and with a scoop of her hand splashed a generous amount in her face. She didn't care that it trickled down her neck and over her blouse, she simply wanted to rid herself of the grime.

She scrubbed her face and neck with her hand and gently patted around her eyes. She wished she could have taken her clothes off and dunked herself in the refreshing water. And while she didn't doubt that Duncan would eagerly agree and join her, it wasn't a wise idea.

"You're beautiful."

Startled by Duncan's firm declaration, Mercy turned to face him. And the truth and caring in his dark eyes had her saying, "You truly mean that, don't you?"

His laugh was gentle, just a slight ripple though it came deep from his chest, and for some reason it sent a tingle through her.

"I wouldn't say it if I didn't mean it. You are a beautiful woman." He smiled and ran a finger down her wet cheek. "Grime and all."

Mercy sat back on her haunches with a slump. "I am rumpled."

He laughed. And when she sent him a scowl, his laughter instantly ceased.

His hand slowly reached out and cupped her chin. "You look like a woman who has been at play with her wee bairns, or busy in the field working alongside her husband, or tending the cook fire so that her family can eat a hardy meal. Or running to survive so that someday she can have bairns and a loving husband, and that, my wee lassie, is true beauty."

"Thank you, you are generous," she said. Her mother may have filled her head with becoming a kept woman, but it was always Mercy's dream to find a man who would love her as much as she loved him and that they could share a life together. Duncan's words had reminded her of that dream, and she wished with all her might that miraculously her dream would come true.

"I am truthful and that makes the difference."

"Chivalry and honesty, you will sweep me off my feet if I'm not careful," she said with a smiling laugh.

"Another challenge, I am sure to win," he declared confidently.

A heavy rustle of leaves sounded, as if someone approached and they both swerved around, Duncan's hand quickly moving to the hilt of his sword.

Relief flooded Mercy when she caught sight of two squirrels tumbling playfully along the ground, then scurrying up a tree one in pursuit of the other.

"I will be grateful for a reprieve from this constant worry," she said, though she knew it would be short-lived.

Soldiers would continue to search for her until the king's edict was carried out . . . until she was dead.

"You will have it once we reach my home. A good meal, a bath, fresh clothes—"

"Then why are we lingering?" she asked with a wide smile. "Let's get moving."

He took hold of her hand but made no move to leave.

She waited, knowing he had something important to say to her.

"Soon we will be in an area that provides little shelter."

"Then it will be the same for the soldiers."

"Aye, it will and more of a chance we'll face battle," he said.

"I'll be ready." She nodded, though fear crept slowly along her spine.

"Then we forge ahead," he said and kept hold of her hand as they once again resumed their journey.

Night seemed to fall more quickly, but then they had walked longer than usual. And after a quick and light meal, since food dwindled, they settled to sleep. However, as exhausted as Duncan was, sleep eluded him. Thoughts stampeded through his mind like a herd of cattle, not sure where they were headed, knowing only they needed to keep going. Like a herd that would eventually be sorted, so would his musing, though not so easily. Some thoughts had easy solutions, others more difficult, and one of them was Mercy.

He didn't know how in less than a week a single woman could so change his life. He had always been focused on his mission. All of them had—he, Trey, Bryce, and Reeve had lived and breathed it since they were young. Nothing would prevent them from seeing it through, nothing would stand in their way, particularly a woman . . . or so they had agreed.

So how had he allowed this wisp of a woman asleep in his arms to sneak so close to his heart? His mind warned him that once free of her he had to let her go, forget her and focus on what was important, but his heart responded differently. It twisted and wrenched in pain whenever he thought about being separated from her.

He actually feared he was falling in love with Mercy and he reminded himself that now was not the time. But no matter how many times he warned himself against such thoughts, they crept right back and insinuated themselves even deeper in his mind and heart.

Worst of all he feared what would happen if he made love to her. He feared he would never want to stop. He couldn't even say for sure what it was that attracted him. She was a beauty, a lovely body, a good mind, strong and brave for sure, and yet those attributes weren't what made her so damn appealing. He believed it might have been when she had jumped off the cliff with him, knowing she couldn't swim. Not for one moment had she doubted that he could save her, not for one moment had she hesitated in believing in him. And he had never known such undiluted trust from any woman he had ever been with, and more so, that trust had remained strong and fixed in those wild blue eyes of hers. He saw it there every time he looked at her, even in the worst of circumstances, it had been there. She believed him, come pain or gain, she believed in him and the sense of pleasure it gave him was indescribable.

Did love spark to life that way?

Love.

It kept creeping into his thoughts until he had no choice but to consider it, until he fully accepted the possibility that he could be falling in love with Mercy.

He didn't need another complication in his life, not now, but then he knew love didn't wait for the perfect time or place. But he also knew love could complicate as it had for Trey. He remembered his friend's suffering over the pain of losing the woman he loved. He and the others had suffered along with him. The worst part being that Trey hadn't been able to protect her, she had been ripped away from him. Never again would he hold her hand, kiss her, touch her, love her.

The thought of never seeing Mercy again so overwhelmed Duncan that he tightened his arms around her, as if by holding her close she would forever remain by his side. But Trey had done the same with the woman he loved, and still he had lost her.

Duncan wondered then if love was worth it. If loving

someone left you with such pain, such heartache, was there any point in loving at all? He found no answers to his questions.

So what wisdom then had he gained from his musings?

That he had yet given love a chance. Love would come in its own good time, in its own way, and nothing would stop it. If he battled it, he would surely taste defeat and possibly in more ways than one.

Besides, if love was introducing itself, then he should enjoy the introduction and he looked forward to getting to know it better. Time was the only sensible weapon when it came to love, so therefore, he and Mercy would need more time together.

He almost laughed, thinking that he should simply keep her chained to him, but that would solve nothing. They needed to be free to make sense of what was going on between them. If it was love, there would be no denying it, thus the outcome would see to itself.

Once again he saw that his decision to have Mercy make her home with his people had been a wise one. He yawned. Reaching good solutions always did that to him, made him sleep better.

Now he could get a good night's sleep and in a matter of three, possibly two days, they should be home and safe. The chains would come off and they would be free.

And then he would make love to her.

Chapter 12

By late morning Mercy was feeling the fast pace they had kept since dawn. Her calves hurt and her feet ached and her back caught in pain now and again, no doubt from sleeping on the cold, hard ground. And if that wasn't enough, her stomach growled in want of food, the morning meal having been woefully inadequate.

Still, Mercy forged ahead, hoping that all she endured would be worth it, that somehow she would find a home and a peaceful life. Perhaps the seer's prediction was true and the rightful king would reclaim the throne and bring peace to Scotland. She hoped and prayed it was so, for his arrival would mean her survival.

She wondered what Duncan thought and asked as they continued walking. "Do you believe the rightful king of Scotland will claim the throne?"

"Do you believe the wrong king sits on the throne?"

"I cannot say for sure, only what I have heard," she answered.

"Which is?"

"That Kenneth the third who sits on the throne is no descendant of Cinaed, the first King of the Scots. And to be rightful king, ruler of the Scots, he must be of his bloodline."

"So it is told. It is also told that Kenneth took the name of the true kings of Scotland before him, but has not an ounce of Cinaed's blood in him."

"Then the seer's prediction could very well be true," she said with a shake of her head. "Though I must admit the prediction makes no sense to me."

"It need not," Duncan said. "Only he who would be king needs to understand it."

"But the prediction says that when he meets death on his own, that is when he reclaims the throne. If he meets death, how can he ever sit on the throne?"

"The one who will be king will know and that is all that matters." He smiled. "You seem to know the prediction well."

Mercy nodded, not wanting to tell him how her mother had repeated it often enough while trying to determine how to find this king and, Mercy assumed, offer her only daughter to him.

"Recite it for me," he said.

"Do you not know it?"

"Not particularly well."

Mercy cleared her throat and in rhythmic tone began, "When summer turns to winter and the snow descends, the reign of the false king begins to end, four warriors ride together and then divide, among them the true king hides, when he meets death on his own, that is when he reclaims the throne."

"And the Scottish people celebrate," Duncan cheered.

"You favor the true king?"

"A true king serves his people. The present king serves no one but himself."

"What do you think will happen to King Kenneth?" she asked.

"That will be a decision left to the true king," Duncan said, taking her hand as they maneuvered around a rocky path. "However, those who have suffered under his reign might demand his death."

"Hasn't there been enough death?"

"Blood is always spilt in the battle for freedom."

Mercy knew the truth of his words. Whether it was a country's battle or an individual's, freedom came with a high price. She fought for her freedom now, more so since she had finally tasted it. No longer did her mother dictate to her, or plan her future without thought to her daughter's hopes or dreams. And though her mother's death saddened her, she also felt a preponderance of guilt for the relief it brought her. That left only one person with the power to decide her future and he already had.

Once she survived the king's edict, then she would truly be free.

Duncan wrapped his arm quickly around her waist before he brought them to an abrupt halt.

She turned wide eyes on Duncan and as soon as she saw how his glance carefully scanned their surroundings and how his head turned slowly, as if searching for a sound, she knew enough to remain silent.

With his arm secure at her waist he walked them both to an outcropping of large boulders nearly encircled by trees, then slipped behind the biggest one.

"Did you feel the ground rumble?" he asked with barely a whisper.

She shook her head. She had been too lost in her thoughts to notice anything and knew that would not happen again. She would not let it.

"I believe riders approach."

Mercy felt her skin crawl with fear. If it were a troop of riders, they would have no chance against them. Their only option would be to hide. But if the troop remained in the area, it would only be a matter of time before they were caught. And they were so close to Duncan's home, so close to safety.

She squeezed his hand without realizing it, and when he returned the squeeze it not only comforted her, it gave her resolve. They had faced and survived difficulty together and now was not the time to surrender to her fear.

She was not alone. Duncan was with her and together they could do anything.

Her body froze when she heard it, a distant rumbling that sounded like thunder, but wasn't. It was a troop of soldiers headed their way. If they remained where they were, they should not be noticed. But then there were scouts to worry about. Could one have already spotted them?

They would need to be more vigilant and take roads less traveled, delaying them once again. Then there was the vast moorlike area they had to cover. Could the troops be going there in hopes of setting a trap for them?

Mercy let her mind conceive what it would. Then she would discuss the possibilities with Duncan and see what could be done.

She squeezed his hand again and this time he looked over at her. His dark eyes so intense suddenly softened and he leaned over and brushed his lips across hers, teasing a response from her, then returned his attention to the sound that reverberated through the ground beneath them.

Mercy reveled in the light kiss. She would not have wanted to meet death without having shared a kiss with Duncan one more time. Now she was ready; with Duncan at her side she was ready for anything.

She maintained her silence and her courage as the riders' approach grew louder. Just before it seemed they were upon them Duncan turned and flattened himself against the boulder just as Mercy had done.

She knew Duncan could not take the chance and be seen, though it was difficult not to have a peek and see how many there were. It took several minutes for them to pass, which led Mercy to believe it was a good size contingent. The king was certainly determined to see them dead.

The dreadful thought caused her to shudder and as it trickled from her body to Duncan's, he stepped in front of her. He kept hold of her hand, pressed his body to hers and rested his mouth next to her ear.

"I will keep us safe and do you know why?' he murmured.

His warm breath tickled her skin and if his mouth hadn't rested so near she would not have heard him, that's how low his murmur. She shook her head.

"Nothing—" He paused and faintly kissed the tip of her ear. "Nothing, not even the king's men, is going to stop me from making love to you."

She didn't have to worry about remaining silent, she was stunned speechless and glad for it, since she didn't know how to respond. Instinct, however, did and when his lips moved past hers, she captured them with her own and kissed him.

Their lips barely had time to enjoy each other when they heard.

"Turn around nice and slow, unless you want to die before her."

Duncan moved his lips off hers and mouthed, *How many*?

She had to raise herself on the tips of her toes to glance over his shoulder. And when her feet were once again planted fully on the ground she mouthed, *One*. He moved slowly away from her, and as he did, his hand carefully slipped over the handle of the dirk tucked at his waist. The problem was that it was his hand that was shackled to hers. What did he expect her to do?

She studied his eyes and it took only a few moments for

her to get the gist of what he wanted her to do. With the
breadth and width of him concealing her from the soldier,
she had little worry of being seen, and acknowledged
her assent with a smile.

He returned her smile and slowly moved away.

The soldier grinned victoriously, though it didn't last.
Duncan's slow movements changed in a second as he
rushed down on one knee and in one fluid motion thrust
the dirk forward into the soldier's stomach, Mercy in
rhythm with his every move.

One more thrust to his chest finished him and he
fell to the ground dead. Mercy watched his blood pool
beneath him until the ground appeared saturated with it.
She placed her hand to her stomach and couldn't help but
imagine how differently this scene could have played.

Suddenly her view was blocked by Duncan's chest
and without thinking she pressed her face right in the
middle where his shirt separated. His warm, damp flesh,
the quick beat of his heart, his familiar, rich scent and
his arm wrapped tightly around her waist brought such
a sense of safety and relief to her that she feared she
just might weep.

"I'm sorry," he whispered. "You should not have to
see this as well as be part of it."

"But I do," she said and raised her head to meet his dark
eyes. For a moment she stared speechless into those dark
absorbing depths that so keenly expressed his profound
concern. And her heart swelled with the magnitude of
his compassion, or was it more than that? There was

something . . . something in his eyes she couldn't quite understand, though felt the need to.

"Why?" he asked with a shake of his head.

She realized then that they both had stood speechless, staring at one another until finally Duncan had snapped out of whatever had hold of them and had spoken.

"It teaches me how to survive," she said with a bravado that wasn't quite as courageous as it sounded.

"I told you that you will survive, I will make sure of it," he said sternly, as if annoyed she doubted him.

She placed her hand to his chest and spoke softly. "And I will make certain you survive. Remember we work well together."

He smiled and chuckled, jingling the chain. "I couldn't do it without you."

"That you couldn't," she agreed with her own smile.

Duncan walked her away from the lifeless body, but not from the protection of the boulders. "We need to be extra vigilant."

"How is it that only one soldier found us?"

"He's probably a scout that covers their rear and somehow caught wind of us," he explained. "Once he doesn't return they will send others to search for him."

"Which means the area will be swarming with soldiers soon enough."

"A good reason for us to take cover and travel no further today," he said.

"I know it might be more difficult, but perhaps we should consider traveling at night."

"Traveling the woods and land at night can be treacherous."

"It appears traveling during the day is just, if not more, deadly," she said and could tell by the squint of his brow that he was considering the suggestion.

"It would take us more time."

"Want to be rid of me so soon?" she teased.

He leaned down, their noses almost touching. "I want this chain off and then . . ."

There was no misunderstanding the fiery passion in his eyes and suddenly she felt that for the moment it was better they were shackled together.

"We better go," she said.

He gave her a quick kiss. "You're right. We need to get out of this area and find a place to rest until dusk."

Carefully, they made their way out of their hiding spot and when relatively certain no one lurked about, they darted across the path they had traveled and disappeared into the woods hoping to take a wide berth around the contingent of soldiers that continued on the road not far ahead.

Travel soon grew burdensome as they attempted to forge a path through the dense woods. How they would be able to accomplish the same feat at night was a question that troubled Mercy. But then her accomplishments had been many since being shackled to Duncan and time and again she was grateful for his presence.

She nearly tripped on a fallen branch, though caught herself quick enough. She silently admonished herself for not concentrating on her steps. She had to be ever watchful of each and every step she took. And so she turned her attention to what was important and silenced the endless chatter in her head.

Mercy wanted to shout out her joy when Duncan finally stopped a few hours later. They had not taken a minute's rest and lord, could she use a minute, or a few, maybe an hour or two.

"You're worn out," he said glancing down at her.

She wanted to be courageous and deny the truth, but she simply couldn't. She was bone-weary from all that had taken place today and she needed a small reprieve, to refresh and grow strong once again.

"Aye, that I am," she admitted.

He smiled. "I'm glad you admitted it, for I feel the same myself."

"Good," she said, though quickly added, "not that it's good you're worn out, but that I feel less guilty knowing you require rest as well."

"Then rest we shall have," he said and before he released her chin, he kissed her softly and then took her hand as he headed for a thicket of bushes.

She was becoming all too accustomed to his kisses, even looking forward to them. She considered that perhaps the lovely and often intense feelings she experienced with him were the prelude to falling in love. If that was so she was in trouble.

She would dearly love to remain with his clan, build a life there and even continue to explore her mounting attraction and desire for Duncan. Unfortunately, that was a dream that would not see fruition. She simply could not allow it to, no matter how enticing it seemed. In doing so she would endanger many lives, just as she had Duncan's.

She could not allow herself the luxury of believing she could have a normal life. It just would not happen, not now, perhaps not ever, unless of course the seer's prediction proved true.

Sorrow stabbed at her heart. Her father had not been a loving man. He could even be harsh at times, though it had been worse when he simply ignored her as if she didn't exist. She had wanted for nothing, except of course his love, or a minor demonstration of it. Time had taught her that she was more of a pawn for her mother and father to use in their games for power and influence. It explained why she was treated well, though not cherished, why she was taught various languages, why she was schooled in the manners of the high-born. Her mother wished to match her with the king who would claim the throne. Her father planned to sell her to the highest bidder, and she would be as her mother, a kept woman.

"We may suffer a few scratches," Duncan said after wrestling with the thick bushes. "But there's a small clearing in the center that should offer us sufficient protection."

Mercy chided herself for getting lost in her musings. She simply had to pay more attention, but then wasn't she? She was assessing her situation and planning for appropriate action.

"We'll need to remain silent, so as not to be detected," he said.

"I'm well aware of that," she assured him.

He leaned his face close to hers. "I know how to keep our lips silent, though occupied."

She smiled. "We simply need to keep them sealed."

"Locked," he corrected with a grin. "Locked together." He kissed her then, and gallantly used his arm as a shield to draw back the bushes so she could squeeze by without a scratch, then he followed.

Mercy immediately surveyed his scratched arm and, with the end of her skirt, dabbed at the blood that oozed slowly from the narrow abrasions.

He told her it was nothing, but to her it was. "You shielded me and suffered for it."

He laughed. "Minor scratches."

"Chivalrous wounds," she corrected.

He kissed her then, his mouth swooping down to claim hers in a heart-pounding kiss that left her legs weak.

Mercy knew then and there that she truly had no choice, and the more Duncan kissed her, the more she knew she couldn't remain with him. His kisses stirred more than her passion, they touched her heart and soul. She could easily fall in love with him, if she hadn't already.

And loving him would mean his death.

Her father would never stop hunting her and she would not see Duncan, or his people, suffer because of her.

He would protest, of course, and so she could not tell him that she would eventually leave. One day she would simply disappear.

And he must never know that she would have preferred to remain with him. Certainly never know how easily she could have fallen in love with him. Most of all, he could never learn her father's identity.

That her father was Kenneth III, King of the Scots.

Chapter 13

Duncan studied the open field with the eye of a warrior planning an attack and though night's darkness
laid claim to it, memory had him seeing it as if the sun
was high in the sky. It was a wide expanse of green land
peppered with rocks. It could prove a troublesome terrain
during the day and a treacherous one at night. He had
crossed it numerous times, each time with a smile and
a hardy step, for beyond it lay his home.

A soft yawn diverted his attention and he glanced down
to see that Mercy had rested her head against his arm.

Fatigue had claimed his limbs hours ago; he could not
imagine how she felt. He had not realized until recently
that it took her two strides to keep up with his one, and
yet she had and without complaint.

The last two days had been exhausting, having to find
safe sleeping shelter during the day and travel at night.
And even though they had eaten sparingly of their meager
food, they hadn't been able to make it last. With dawn's
light but two hours away, it would be a full day since they
had eaten and the third day of their nightly travels.

If they could make it across this field and into the woods, they would not be far from his land, and if luck was with them they could be at his village in a day, two at the most.

Another soft yawn from Mercy had him asking, "Can you do this?"

Her head shot up. "Let's see if you can keep up with me."

The night was too dark for him to see her bewitching blue eyes, but he knew they shimmered with determination. And that sultry voice of hers quivered with annoyance that he should even doubt her.

"It is good that the moon is but a sliver tonight, providing us with a cloak of darkness. However, it also burdens our steps, since the terrain surprises with rocks that hide amongst the grass."

"We will make it before sunrise?" Mercy asked.

"We should have time to spare, allowing us to seek the shelter of the thick woods that lie beyond."

"We will seek shelter there for the day?" she asked, a yawn rushing out afterwards.

"I know you must be exhausted, but if we can keep going for a few more hours it would bring us that much closer to my home, which we can reach within a day's time, two if we slow our pace."

"Truly?" she asked with enthusiasm, though she didn't allow him to answer. "We could soon sleep in a bed. I could bathe. Have clean clothes."

He didn't interrupt her and he didn't remind her that

they could also be free, their shackles gone. Soon they could sleep alone for the first time in nearly two weeks and for some reason he didn't care for the thought. He wondered if she felt the same.

"What are we waiting for?" she asked standing. "Let's be on our way home."

He liked the sound of that. "On our way *home*." She was already thinking of his home as hers and he felt a sense of relief. Though his mission had to remain first in his mind, there was no reason he couldn't pursue her and see where it took them. Though he had no doubt she would occupy his bed before long, and once there? He doubted he'd ever let her leave it.

He stood and clasped hold of her hand, more determined than ever to keep hold of it. And with that thought in mind he led them out of the woods and into the field.

They spoke not a word, both understanding that their voices would easily resonate over the empty expanse. And their hands remained firmly locked together, so that they could help balance each other's steps.

It was a dance of sorts, he even lifting her in graceful form before she took a tumble, her foot catching now and again on rocks strewn in her path. The walk was going more smoothly than Duncan expected, though he was not foolish enough to be overly confident.

He kept their pace steady, not rushed or unhurried and he kept his ears alert. He was familiar with the sounds and creatures of the night. He and his brothers had often bedded beneath the stars and he would lay awake thinking, dreaming and hoping for a victorious outcome to the mission they had not only trained so hard for, but had dedicated themselves to.

So as soon as the unfamiliar sound reached his ears, he slowed his steps, Mercy following his, until he came to a complete halt.

He pressed a finger to her lips, cautioning silence and then tapped her ear so that she would know to listen.

The sound came again, though this time it was familiar. It was the snorting of horses.

He felt Mercy tense beside him and her fingers wrap tighter around his. He tugged her hand, signaling for her to follow and she did spreading out in the grass alongside him.

He thought a moment and didn't like his own conclusions. No doubt soldiers either waited for them in the woods or were camped there for the night. And there was no telling how many. The snorting could have come from a couple to several horses.

With his lips pressed against Mercy's ear, he murmured, "We're going back."

She nodded and they slowly stood, though remained crouched as they turned and began to make their way back to where they had started.

He wanted to run, gain speed and not stop until they returned to the safety of the forest, but that would have been a foolish move. Surely, the soldiers would hear their rushing footfalls and though dark, one or two brave ones might attempt to hunt them down.

A shout froze them a few feet from the woods.

"Nate?"

Duncan grabbed the chain so it wouldn't make a sound and rolled over on Mercy, shielding her just as a soldier and his horse walked out of the woods.

"Quit shouting, you fool," a strong voice answered.

Nate paid no heed. "Someone was to relieve me hours ago."

"Stay put until he arrives. I don't intend to miss catching the pair if they try to cross."

"When's he coming?" Nate shouted.

"He's on his way. Now shut up."

Duncan realized he had little time to get them out of there and on a different trail that would take them far from the soldiers, though further from his home. He needed to distract the soldier so that he and Mercy could sneak past them and be on their way.

With his free hand he carefully felt the ground around him until he connected with a large stone. He gave Mercy a nudge, letting her know to be ready and she squeezed his hand in response.

He heaved the stone as far as he could opposite of where they lay.

"Hold, by order of the king!" Nate shouted and hurried in the direction of the sound.

Duncan and Mercy scrambled to their feet and ran for the woods and didn't stop once in its safety. They both knew distance was needed, so they hurried their pace as best they could.

The thick darkness of night proved a hindrance, causing them to alter their pace considerably, but it didn't stop them.

Finally, after what seemed like hours, Duncan drew to a halt. "We need a brief rest."

"Do you know where we are?" she asked breathless.

"I have a general idea."

"The soldiers seem to know our every move," she said.

"They assume we head to safe land," Duncan explained. "Land they are not welcome on and will not tread upon without approval from the king. And with the way things are at the moment, I don't believe the king wants to war with a ruling chieftain from the north."

"What do we do?"

"What I should have done from the beginning," he said. "Take the long way home."

"How long?"

"A week or more," he answered.

He thought perhaps she would protest, though he wasn't surprised when she didn't. Survival was their main concern. She understood that and had done what was necessary, so there was no reason she would brook objection now.

"We best get moving," she said. "We can find a place to rest some time after dawn, hopefully after we find something to eat."

"I agree wholeheartedly."

They continued, though kept a slower pace, their limbs

protesting from the long day's hike. Neither spoke, they simply kept trudging along.

"Do you think the soldiers will find our trail?" she asked.

"They seemed convinced that we would cross that field, a logical expectation, so I assume they will remain there for a day or so."

"Will other soldiers follow the trail we're on?"

"It's doubtful," Duncan said.

"Why?"

"It leads to pagan territory. The king's rules hold no importance there. It is where the Picts live."

"I thought the Picts were no more."

"While most Scots and Picts blended when Cinaed brought them together, there were a few who preferred to keep to their ways. Not many tread on their land, most out of fear, though more from ignorance."

"You don't fear them."

"There's nothing to fear," he assured her.

"When will we reach their land?" she asked.

"A day at the most."

They continued walking, at times their pace hurried and other times slowed. By the time dawn broke on the horizon they had put a good distance between themselves and the soldiers.

They stood on a small hill and greeted the sun, their hands clasped and their limbs aching.

She swayed against him and he wrapped his arm around her. Her head went to rest on his chest.

"We'll find shelter and rest. We both need it."

"That would be best," she said.

"You're tired," he said, feeling guilty that he had pushed her so hard yet again. He slipped his finger beneath her chin, wanting to gaze into her lovely eyes as he offered what encouragement he could.

His eyes sprung wide when he saw the blood caked above and around her eye.

"Why didn't you tell me you were injured?" he said and scooped her up into his arms.

"You would have stopped." She yawned. "And that would have been foolish."

"You should have told me," he scolded and looked around, not sure what he should do first.

"Water to cleanse the wound, food to give me strength and rest so I can heal," she said as if providing him with an answer.

"There's a stream not too far," he said and began walking.

"How far?"

"Thirty or so minutes."

"Put me down. I will walk," she said.

"No!"

"Don't be foolish," she warned gently and rested her hand to his cheek. "If you tire from carrying me, how then will you be able to tend me?"

"Damn," he mumbled. "Why must you make sense?"

"One of us must," she said with a smile.

He eased her gently out of his arms, keeping his hands

at her waist until he was certain that she had the strength to stand.

"I'm fine," she assured him.

While he wanted to believe her, it was difficult. The blood was caked thickly above and around her eye and he feared if he disturbed the wound it would begin bleeding again.

"You should have told me," he said again.

She rested her hand on his arm. "Wouldn't you have done the same?"

He had to smile. "You know me too well."

"That isn't hard to do," she said and tugged his hand for him to walk along with her.

He wanted badly to scoop her up and carry her, but she was right. They were both already exhausted and he would need what strength remained to not only see to her wound but to find a way to feed them and arrange a good shelter.

Silence followed them and by the time they reached the stream, fatigue was near to claiming them both.

They sunk down together in front of the stream and both leaned over, eagerly scooping up handfuls of water.

Duncan was busy quenching his thirst when suddenly his hand was yanked away. He turned, thinking to tease Mercy about her eager thirst and saw that she was falling facefirst into the stream.

His hands shot out and grabbed her though not before her face and shoulders disappeared beneath the chilled water.

Chapter 14

Mercy licked her lips. She could almost taste the fresh cooked fish. She certainly could smell it. The delicious aroma tempted her nostrils and made her stomach roll with the want of it.

As her eyes slowly drifted open and she recalled where she was, she knew it was nothing more than a dream, and yet the luscious scent persisted. She almost didn't want to fully wake and lose the lovely mirage.

"Wake up, sleeping princess. It's time to eat."

Mercy's eyes popped open. "I'm not dreaming?"

Duncan smiled. "No. You're not dreaming."

She struggled to sit up. Duncan's hand was quick to assist her, going around her and helping her up. She realized she lay on a bed of pines and that the lone blanket they possessed was tucked around her. She was sheltered under the branches of a towering pine and a fresh cleaned trout was cooking on a spit over a campfire.

Her hand went to her head, recalling her wound and Duncan grabbed hold of her wrist.

"Your wound wasn't that bad. I cleaned it. I have no doubt it will heal nicely."

She shook her head. "How did you manage with—"

"You passed out?" he finished.

Mercy's hand flew to her chest. "I passed out?"

"You don't remember?"

"I recall looking at my reflection in the stream, not at all pleased with what I was seeing, when suddenly the water appeared to move closer to my face and then . . ."

"Nothing?"

"Until now," she said. "I surely must have been a burden to you."

"You're never a burden," he assured her, his tone so reassuring that a sense of safety settled around her.

"But how—" She shook her head again as she looked around. "How did you manage?"

"As you advised earlier, I addressed one issue at a time," he said. "I saw to your wound first, which thankfully wasn't that bad. Then I carried you over my shoulder while I hunted down firewood and what I would need to make a sturdy fishing pole and then found a spot under this tree to bed down."

"Oh my," she said, suddenly realizing it was hours past dawn. "Have I slept a whole day away?"

"That you have," he said breaking off a bit of fish in his hand and blowing on it to cool as he handed it to her.

Mercy cupped her hand and gratefully accepted it, popping small pieces into her mouth. It was the most delicious fish she had ever tasted and she wanted more, much more.

"I slept myself, just getting up at the break of dawn, and then I caught two fine fish."

Mercy gasped. "You mean this fish is all mine?"

"It is," Duncan said. "I already ate mine."

"You are my hero," she said with a wide smile.

"And it only took a fish," he teased and dropped a good portion of meat into her hand.

"What of the soldiers? Won't they see the smoke, smell the fish?"

"I believe we're far enough away. And that they are still busy waiting for us to cross that field."

"We fared well against them," she said with a nod and popped more meat into her mouth. "You cook a delicious fish."

"It helps that you're starving or you might think differently."

Mercy laughed and held out her hand. "Starving or not, it's the tastiest fish I've ever eaten."

Duncan slapped his hand to his chest. "You've won my heart, lass, you have."

A tingle raced through her at the thought that she could even have a chance at winning his heart.

Foolish.

She wished her mother would stop creeping into her mind. She had heard it enough through the years and didn't want to hear another word or warning. She wanted simply to spend what time she had left with Duncan and learn for herself, judge for herself and experience for herself.

"More?" she asked, her cupped hand held out to him, and her request not only for the fish.

"All yours," he said plucking another fat helping of meat off the fish and into her hand.

"All mine," she whispered, her gaze on Duncan and not the fish.

"Do you feel rested enough to travel?" he asked.

"More than enough," she answered with a nod. "And I suppose we should be on our way."

"The further we travel into Pict territory, the less likely the soldiers will follow."

"How long before we enter their land?"

"Half day's journey," he said.

She finished eating, thinking that no doubt the Picts would have sufficient tools to free them of the chain. Once again she wondered, what then? But there was no time and certainly no sense to dwell, only time to act.

When the last of the fish was eaten, Mercy went to the stream, Duncan following without protest, and refreshed herself. This time her reflection didn't shock her. Duncan had cleaned not only her wound but the grime from her face. She turned to where he knelt beside her.

"Thanks to you I didn't frighten myself when I looked upon my reflection."

He grabbed hold of her chin. "Your reflection could never frighten. You're too beautiful."

And with that he kissed her. She hadn't expected it,

though she certainly welcomed it. He took his time and was ever so gentle that she simply melted against him and allowed him to steal her senses.

She cared for nothing at that moment except the kiss and the way his arm slipped around her, ran up her back and down again while all the time he continued to kiss her. She was lost and didn't care. She wanted only to enjoy this moment with him, this kiss, and so she did. Every weave and tangle of their tongues sent tingles down to her toes and his lips were so very firm and confident, tempting her, urging her to respond that she did so without thought or reason.

They could barely breathe when he finally and reluctantly ended it, resting his forehead against hers.

"One day," he said breathless. "One day."

He didn't have to say more, she knew what he meant, felt what he meant and agreed. One day they would satisfy the passion that continued to grow between them. It was inevitable.

"We better go," he said and turned to douse the campfire with dirt. "We may come upon a croft or perhaps a field yet harvested as we travel and get to enjoy another hardy meal."

"Nothing will ever taste as delicious as the fish you cooked for me," she said as they bent down, gathered and folded the blanket into the sack.

"I will always be there for you. I will keep you well fed and see you safe, of that you have my word."

He sounded as if he recited a vow and the thought

warmed her heart. It was so very nice to know someone cared enough to watch over her. Her mother and father may have professed to do the same, but it was for selfish reasons. Duncan did it for . . .

She would have halted her steps, the thought jolted her so, but Duncan would surely question her abrupt halt and she would not know what to say.

Her thoughts far surpassed the gait she kept alongside him. Why did he do it? Why speak as if he took a vow? Why pledge anything to her? He owed her nothing. They worked together to survive. That was the way of it, pure and simple. And yet . . .

She recalled with clarity the moment that she and Duncan had been chained together. How could she forget it? Here had been this large Highlander warrior that towered over her and whose width even thwarted her shadow as the shackles were locked. And he had been scowling. She thought he had looked ready to devour her.

They had no time to speak, nor had Duncan looked as if he had wished to say a word to her. They had been forced to walk at a grueling pace and it had been through his actions that she had gotten to know his nature.

The first time she had tripped, his large hands had been quick to grab her and more gently than she had expected. He then had told her to be careful here and watch her step there. She had soon found herself taking hold of his hand if she felt herself unsteady. And when she had, he had wrapped his fingers around hers.

In a short time she had learned he was an honorable

man whom she could trust and she supposed that had been why she had so easily stepped off the side of the cliff with him.

"Your thoughts are deep this morning."

Mercy glanced over at him. Her heart fluttered and for a moment she felt that she couldn't catch her breath. She didn't know what it was she saw in Duncan this time that she had never seen before, but there was something there and it touched her heart in a way she had never known.

She shook her head. "*Too* heavy."

"Share what burdens you."

"Haven't I burdened you enough?" she asked with a tinkle of laughter.

"You are no burden and what burden there is"—he raised their clasped hands, the chain rattling—"we share."

A sudden thought had her asking. "What did you think when the soldiers chained us together."

"How lucky I was to be shackled to a beautiful woman."

"You did no such thing," she accused, her eyes and smile wide.

"I give you my word."

"But you must have had doubts—"

"Doubts about what?" he asked.

"How our differences would hinder us?"

"What differences?" he asked.

She poked his chest playfully. "You big. Me small."

He laughed. "What you lack in height, you make up for with your tenacious nature."

He was praising her courage again and she appreciated it, especially with it coming from a Highlander warrior.

They talked on and off throughout the morning and grew silent as they traversed a steep hill and just after entering the woods beyond, Mercy sensed a change. She couldn't say what it was but somehow she sensed this land was different. There was a reverence to it, as if it demanded respect, and she didn't mind at all paying homage to it.

"We're on Pict land now?" she asked softly.

"Once we came over that rise we were, but they saw us approach long before that," Duncan said.

"Then we are welcome?" she asked.

"Anyone who means no harm is welcome."

"They will greet us?"

Duncan shook his head. "No. They will watch us."

They walked for a couple more hours before coming upon a croft. Duncan didn't pull back as he had done on other occasions. He simply approached with a smile and a wave to the man on the roof repairing the thatching.

He was a slim man, though solid with light hair and smooth skin and a pleasant smile.

"Good afternoon to you," Duncan said.

"It is a good afternoon. The sun high, the day warm," the man said. "If it is food and rest you look for, you are welcome."

"Thank you for your generosity. I am Duncan and this is Mercy. And we could use nourishment."

"I am Able," the man said, climbing down the ladder resting against the front of the cottage.

A robust woman emerged from behind the house, a basket brimming with freshly picked greens on her arm. Her full cheeks were flushed, and her light hair a mass of curls escaping a single ribbon and bouncing around her unmarred face. A lovely embroidered green blouse was tucked in the waist of her dark blue skirt and a pale yellow apron covered a good portion of that.

"This is my wife, Eleanor," Able said.

"Welcome to our home," she said.

Any doubt that these people were other than who they presented themselves to be faded quickly from Mercy's mind when Eleanor smiled. It was sincere, warm and welcoming. They were safe. These people meant them no harm, though she couldn't help but notice the strange markings that wrapped around Able's upper arm and there was one around Eleanor's wrist.

Mercy knew little about the Picts and the little she did was from those who believed them their enemy. The talk she had heard certainly didn't match what she was seeing for herself.

"So is that a new way the Scots have of holding on to their wives?" Eleanor asked, her dark eyes twinkling as she pointed to the shackles.

Duncan gave a nod to Mercy. "She fears I will stray."

Mercy grinned and raised her arm. "Aye, and so I solved the problem."

The couple laughed.

"Come and eat," Eleanor invited.

It was a hardy stew she gave them with fresh baked bread along with cider and ale, and friendly conversation. When it was done Able approached the matter of their shackles.

"Was it the king's men who did that to you?"

"Aye, it was," Duncan said.

"I hope the true king does return and set things right," Eleanor said. "He would know how to bring peace to this land since the blood of the Picts and Scots run through his veins."

Able nodded. "He would understand and respect our ways."

"This king who is to return is not merely a myth?" Mercy asked.

"Some believe it is," Eleanor said, "but those who know understand otherwise. The time will come for him to rise and claim the power that is his. Now about this chain." She looked to her husband.

Able turned to Duncan and shook his head. "I have no tool capable of removing them. You're going to need a smithy to get them off."

"Is there one nearby?" Duncan asked.

"Are you headed to MacAlpin land?"

"We are," Duncan confirmed.

"There would be the closest smithy, otherwise you

would travel further away from your destination to reach one."

"Bliss could help you with those wrist sores," Eleanor said.

"She's a healer?" Mercy asked.

Able smiled. "She's many things, and she has a good healing touch."

"Her cottage is a bit off course for you," Eleanor explained. "But it may be worth it."

Mercy and Duncan thanked the couple and left with their sack full and directions to Bliss's cottage.

When they were a distance away from the croft Mercy turned to Duncan. "There is no reason to add further delay to reaching your home. We need not visit this healer."

Duncan stopped walking, forcing Mercy to do the same. His fingers went to the wound at her head and she winced when he probed the area.

"It looks as if it's turned an angry red, so there is no question to it," Duncan said. "We go to the healer."

"Able never claimed her to be a healer. He said she had a healing touch."

"It matters not how she heals you," Duncan said and brushed his lips across hers. "As long as she heals you."

Chapter 15

Rain clouds thwarted the setting sun as Duncan and Mercy approached Bliss's cottage. Duncan stopped a few feet from it and glanced around. It was exceptionally quiet, but then that was more likely due to the land. This area had always been more serene than anyplace he had ever been. Though the cottage was a bit larger than the usual, it had familiar characteristics. And somehow he knew it welcomed.

He had no doubt they were being watched and had been since entering Pict territory. In a way it lent comfort, for the king's soldiers would be quickly noticed and not last long here.

"Something troubles you?" Mercy asked.

He smiled and with the urge stronger than ever to kiss her, he did and then said, "The only thing that troubles me is that I want to kiss you all the time. Your sweet, warm taste is addictive." He kissed her again, needing to confirm it for himself. "I will never tire of the taste of you."

"Then savor all you want," she invited.

He wrapped his arm around her and drew her up against him, their bodies coming together in a perfect fit. "Be careful what you offer."

"I offer it freely," she said with bitter sadness that disturbed him.

He wanted to tell her that his offers came with conditions and promises, but now was not the time. There was much that had to be done, the chain coming off being one; and then it would be time to talk, and much needed to be said.

"Welcome."

Duncan and Mercy turned at the sound of the melodic voice that called to them and both their eyes spread wide. The woman standing a few feet from the cottage was stunning. Her beauty actually captured their breath and left them speechless.

While her garments were those of a peasant woman, plain brown wool skirt and soft yellow blouse, her features were those of royalty. Her long blond hair varied in shades of shimmering gold and cascaded softly around her face and down over her shoulders, ending just past her breasts. She stood a good seven inches over five feet and was of slender build, but it was her face that caught and kept the attention.

Surely, she was of heavenly descent for only angels could be that beautiful.

"Come," she waved to them. "The rain will start any moment now and bring with it an autumn chill."

As if the sky heard, fat raindrops suddenly began to fall and Duncan, taking firm hold of Mercy's hand, ran with her to the cottage.

The woman closed the heavy door behind them and motioned them to the large fireplace. "Go warm yourself while I get you hot cider."

Duncan and Mercy eagerly accepted her hospitality and sat on the floor in front of the roaring flames and let the heat soak through them.

"You are Bliss?" Duncan asked as she handed him a tankard of cider.

"I am and you must be Duncan," she said and then turned, handing Mercy a tankard. "And you must be Mercy."

Duncan furrowed his brow, wondering how she could possibly know who they were. She quickly satisfied his curiosity.

"News travels fast in these parts, especially when it concerns the king's soldiers chasing after a man and woman shackled together. Though none were sure you would come our way."

"We had no choice," Duncan explained.

"The king must want you both badly to send so many of his men after you," Bliss said.

Duncan allowed her her conclusions. He didn't want to draw any special attention to himself. It might jeopardize his mission.

"You both must be exhausted, that chain is a heavy burden."

"No!" Duncan and Mercy sang out and stared at each other, startled by their harmonious reply.

"The chains are no burden," Duncan said, though his eyes were on Mercy. He had reiterated it often enough, but he wanted her to know again and again that she was not nor ever would be a burden to him, chains or no chains.

"Aye, Duncan is right," Mercy said. "The chains are no burden at all."

He smiled, pleased that she was letting him know that she felt the same.

The flames suddenly spit and roared, casting light upon them and making Mercy's head wound appear far more damaging than it was and causing Duncan alarm. But before he could voice his concern, Bliss spoke.

"I have salve that will help heal your wounds," she offered and set about fetching it before either of them could thank her.

"You live here alone?" Mercy asked.

"So to speak," Bliss said.

Duncan wondered what she meant, since she offered no further details, but he didn't ask. There was a sense of safety in her cottage, and he instinctively knew there was no need to worry while here.

While Bliss applied the salve to Mercy's head wound and then her wrist, she talked with them. Duncan noticed that her answers to questions that concerned her were vague, though she was quite informative about the land and her people.

He decided to respect her privacy and did not venture

any further than she wished. When she was done with Mercy she started on his wrists, rubbing the soothing salve over his wound. He had thought the cream would sting and her touch would hurt, being the skin was raw, but surprisingly, the salve was cool and her touch light.

Able had said she had a healing touch and he certainly agreed. Remarkably, his wrists were already feeling better.

When Bliss was done, she stood. "I have fresh clean clothes you both are welcome to if you'd like."

Mercy's face lit with joy and then faded.

As if Bliss knew Mercy's mind, she said, "You can bathe first if you'd like."

Mercy pointed to the chains. "It would be difficult, though I would dearly love to bathe and have fresh garments."

"You can have both," Bliss said. "There is a spot where I bathe. It is secluded and the water warm. And we'll work around the chains with some needle and thread."

Mercy looked to Duncan. "What say you?"

He found himself speechless. While he wanted to bathe and have fresh clothes also, it would mean being naked with Mercy once again. And he just didn't know if this time he could keep his hands off her.

So far he'd been a chivalrous man, but that was before he'd kissed her again and again and damn if his hands weren't aching to touch her intimately.

"A bath it is."

Had he truly said that? What was he thinking?

Long, lazy kisses, soft, exploring touches and endless hours of love making.

Damn he was in trouble.

"I'll take you there," Bliss said, "and return for you in an hour."

"Perhaps two hours?" Mercy asked. "If the water is warm, as you say, I would love to linger."

Yes. Yes. Let's linger. No, you fool! No lingering.

Duncan warred with himself. How would he ever last two hours without touching her or making love to her?

Bliss nodded. "Two hours gives me time to cook a substantial supper."

"You are very generous," Mercy said, "tending us, offering us fresh clothing, and feeding us. I hope someday I can repay your generosity."

"You will," Bliss said. "Now let me get the things you'll need while you finish your cider."

Mercy leaned close to Duncan once Bliss walked away and whispered, "She speaks as if it will be so, as if she knows."

"She has good instinct," he said, having noticed the same, though wondered if it was more than mere instinct she possessed.

"Did you notice that her touch soothed and caused no pain?"

"I did," he admitted, wondering over it himself.

"And this place is like none I've ever known."

"You don't wish to stay?"

"No, I don't wish to leave," Mercy said, smiling. "The

only other place I feel so safe and comforted is in your arms."

He slipped an arm around her and grinned. "Now you're doubly safe and comforted."

Her soft laughter rippled over him and grabbed at his heart and made the thought of bathing naked while chained to her all the more appealing.

"Ready?" Bliss asked.

Duncan stood, taking Mercy along with him as *he* had grown accustomed to doing. And she had taken his hand, moving along with him as *she* had grown accustomed to doing. They worked as one, without thought or complaint and it felt right.

The rain had changed to a fine mist as Bliss, carrying a torch, lead the way.

There was a chill in the night air and Duncan worried that the water would be too cold for them to bathe. Bliss addressed his unspoken concern as if she had clearly heard his thoughts.

"The spot I take you to is in a cave, the water warm year round and not more than five feet deep."

Duncan nearly groaned aloud. Bliss described the perfect secluded setting for seduction.

And secluded it was. Brush and trees guarded the cave entrance. If one didn't know the cave was there, it would never be found. Once inside, Duncan was amazed by the warmth and quiet beauty of the concealed place. Flat rocks encircled the water.

Bliss put down the basket she'd been carrying. "All

you need is in here. Enjoy." And with that she turned and was gone.

They stood staring after her, even though she was gone from sight. Silence hung heavy, neither of them exchanging a single word.

Mercy finally spoke, her sultry voice a soft echo in the cave. "It looks so inviting."

"Then we shouldn't waste a minute," Duncan said and meant it. He wanted every second he could get alone with her.

Mercy nodded. "We should see what's in the basket."

Duncan agreed, bending down along with her as she removed the cloth covering the good-sized basket and removed the items to lie upon the flat rock.

Towels, sweet-scented soap, fresh garments, as promised, and a knife to cut off parts of their clothing the chain wouldn't allow them to relinquish. And a small jug of wine and hunk of dark bread, which they both looked at and smiled.

"Bliss is blessed with a magical mind," Duncan said.

Mercy broke off a sizable chunk of bread. "For which I am forever grateful."

Duncan joined her.

They lingered over the food and drink and Duncan wondered if it was due to hunger or apprehension over bathing naked together. It wasn't as though they had not been naked in front of each other before, yet this time seemed different. And he knew why.

He wanted her and not simply for the sake of satisfying his lust. No, it was more than satisfying a need. It was satisfying that wrench in his gut, or that stab to his heart. He wanted to make her his. Put his mark on her. Claim his territory.

However it was, he wanted her to belong to him and him alone.

Did he love her?

He almost laughed aloud.

What else would make him feel so strange and yet make it all seem so right?

"Have you second thoughts about this?" Mercy asked.

"No," he said, resting his hands at her waist and squeezing lightly. "Not at all. I look forward to it."

He saw the flash of apprehension in her brief smile. And wanting to ease her concern he scooped up the knife and held the handle out to her.

"Divest me first of these filthy garments, and then I shall do the same for you."

Her worries seemed to melt if only a little, but it was a start.

"Wait," he said and tugged his boots off, tossing them aside. Then he tugged at his plaid until it fell to settle around his feet. "I'm ready."

He had to smile, for her hand did not tremble, nor

did she hesitate. Courage did not fail her as she sliced at his shirt until it finally joined his plaid. He shoved both aside with his bare foot. Then he reached out to take the knife from her.

"Your turn."

She nodded slowly and bracing her hand to his shoulder, she rid herself of her boots.

He liked that she didn't hesitate to lean on him. It told him that she was comfortable in relying on him and he liked that.

She dropped her skirt to the ground and announced, "I'm ready."

He made quick work of slicing off her blouse. It dropped to her feet in seconds, her glance following its descent. When she didn't raise her head he lifted her chin with one finger.

"You have nothing to fear from me," he said.

"I know," she whispered.

"Then what's wrong?"

She placed her hand to his chest.

Her innocent and gentle touch had him struggling to keep control of his passion. This was not going to be easy. He could feel desire pulsating through him like hot fire and any moment now his member would flame to life and let himself be known.

She hesitated, and he could see she struggled to speak.

He encouraged her. "You can tell me, Mercy. You can tell me anything."

"But what of the consequences?"

He ran the pad of his thumb over her soft, rosy lips. "There are no consequences for us, only solutions."

"Oh, if that were only true," she said with a sigh.

"Tell me what worries you and I will provide the solution."

"You are so sure," she said.

"I am," he boasted and gave her waist a loving squeeze.

She thought a moment and nodded, her decision made. "It is simple, but then again not so simple."

"Tell me," he urged and she did.

"I want you."

Chapter 16

~~~

If Mercy had hesitated even for the briefest of moments, she would have never had the courage to speak her mind. Even now she wondered if she had done the right thing, though her body was certainly tingling with glee. That didn't mean it was the wisest of choices. Whatever was she doing?

Falling in love.

Mercy snapped her head around, the voice so clear that she thought someone stood behind her. But no one was there, though the words lingered in her mind. Was she truly falling in love with Duncan? Was she afraid to admit it?

She shook her head, not certain if she was shaking away the thought or denying it.

"No changing your mind," he warned laughingly and slipped his arm around her slim waist.

She didn't want to change her mind. She wanted this time with him. She wanted to make memories with him, no matter the consequences.

"No, I will not change my mind," she said. "I don't want to."

"You know just the right words to stir a man."

She chuckled. "By sheer luck."

"No," he whispered close to her lips. "By sheer desire."

His warm breath faint with the scent of wine fanned her cheeks and sent tingles through her. And shivers rippled over her body, running down to the tips of her toes.

Duncan took firm hold of her chin. "You and I are meant to be."

"You are so sure?"

"Aye, with clear certainty," he claimed with a sharp nod.

She wished to ask what he meant. Were they to be lovers, friends, or more? But she didn't have the courage. She was much too afraid of the answer.

"We shouldn't waste what time we have talking," he said and took hold of her hand.

She quickly scooped up the soap before keeping step with him. And before her foot touched the water, he swung her up high into his arms, kissing her quickly and cradling her, then walked them into the comforting warm water.

Her arm went around his neck and her head to his chest as he slowly surrendered their aching bodies to the water's heat.

"I think I've died and gone to heaven," she said.

"Not yet you haven't, but fear not, I will take you there."

Mercy chuckled. She loved his humor. Oddly, it calmed her. And whether this decision of hers was right or wrong, she had made it, and she would have no regrets.

"I wish to wash," she said, wanting to be sweet scented for him.

"We do think alike."

He set her on her feet, the water rushing to tease the tips of her rosy nipples, while his chest lay fully exposed. Hard muscles rippled over hard muscles and her eyes drank in the enticing sight until . . .

He was suddenly gone, dunking himself until he disappeared beneath the surface, leaving behind him a rash of small waves that descended on Mercy. Then unexpectedly he rose up out of the water, grabbed her around the waist and plunged them beneath the surface.

Mercy wasn't ready, wasn't sure what to do and when they rose out of the water, a moment later, her arm wrapped tight around his neck, she was coughing and spurting.

He wiped the rivulets of water from her face. "Easy," he cautioned. "Breathe easy." He demonstrated taking slow breaths himself and when she finally maintained the rhythm on her own, he apologized. "I forgot you are not accustomed to the water."

"Teach me," she insisted.

"Now?"

She nodded. "I never want to be caught in such a position again. The next time it is necessary for me to jump or dunk in a river or stream, I want to do so with confidence."

He hesitated and she knew why and commiserated. She, like he, had expected this time to be one of intimacy. But the unexpected dunk beneath the water had frightened her, chilled her to the core with the memory of jumping off the cliff. And while he had been there to keep her from drowning, the truth was that she couldn't count on him always being there. Even though he claimed he would always be there for her, there might come a time when she was on her own.

He suddenly seemed to understand. "You do need to learn to swim."

"I do," she agreed hastily.

"It may take more than one lesson."

"I learn quickly."

He grinned. "That is good to know."

She chuckled. "Of course that depends on what kind of teacher you are."

His laughter was more a seductive growl. "I'm an excellent teacher . . . in all things."

She brought her lips close to his. "Then I look forward to learning from you."

He stole a kiss and while she knew he intended it to be a quick one, it wasn't. Once their lips touched, their hunger took command and nothing mattered, nothing at all, expect satisfying their voracious appetite for each other.

They feasted, enjoying every succulent taste, drinking in the nectar of their passion while never quite appeasing it.

His hands drifted to her bare bottom and hoisted her up against him. That he wanted her was undeniable, she could feel his strength, his thickness, his hungry need, and her own.

She tingled between her legs so badly that she wanted nothing more than to feel him hard and bulging inside her, to satisfy her aching need. It would be easy and done with and that sudden realization quickly cooled her ardor.

She did not want her first time with him to be a quick spurt of lovemaking. There was more between them that needed to be explored and felt, and understood. She reluctantly ended the kiss nibbling along his lip before she was finally able to pull away.

"I—I—" She stuttered unable to voice what she was feeling, since she barely understood it herself.

She wasn't surprised that he already knew. He seemed to have the uncanny ability to understand her before she understood herself.

He nuzzled her neck with his mouth and then his lips drifted to her ear. "Our first time making love will be special. It will not be planned, or done in haste. It will come naturally, as it should, and we will remember and cherish it always."

She laid her hand to his moist, heated cheek. "You are a good man."

"What happened to chivalrous?"

She smiled. "You are that too."

"And I am a teacher," he said, "and you my pupil. Now you will learn to swim."

He turned her over on her stomach, his free hand around her waist and his chained one extended so that she could have use of hers.

"This will be difficult due to the shackles," he said.

"I believe if I acquaint myself with the fundamentals, then I will be able to learn fast."

It was more difficult with the shackles than either of them imagined and several times Duncan had to keep her from sinking. Finally, Mercy stood and slapped the water hard sending it splashing over the two of them.

"I've had enough," she cried. "I'll never learn to swim.

"Aye, you will," Duncan said sternly. "You're a warrior woman and warrior women never give up. And besides, if I can manage to continuously stare at your beautiful round, bobbing derrière and keep control of my ardor, then you can learn how to swim."

She opened her mouth and he pressed his finger over her lips. "Don't dare tell me how gallant I am, for I have the most ungallant thoughts right now."

Mercy wished to know his ungallant thoughts, every last one of them, but knew it unwise. It would be far better if they simply did what they came here to do, be done with it and wait for Bliss to return.

"Perhaps we should wash," she suggested.

"A good idea," he said. "We only need to find the soap.

"I dropped it," Mercy said realizing for the first time that she had done just that. "It must have sunk, we'll never find it."

"Actually, it's floating a short distance behind you."

Mercy turned to see the bar bobbing in the water. "I've never seen such a thing."

"Bliss's soap must be magical; lucky for us, since it will take magic to get this ton of grime off us," Duncan teased.

He retrieved the soap and offered it first to her.

She was quick to lather her hair, and return it to him, and they scrubbed the grime laden strands in relative silence. They dunk, rinsed and scrubbed their bodies, asking only that each of them scrub the other's back and did so quickly and thoroughly.

When they finished, they bobbed in the water, at the safest distance the chain allowed, enjoying its soothing balm.

While they didn't touch, didn't even hold hands, Mercy felt it an intimate moment. It was as if awkwardness disappeared, vulnerability vanished and pure trust took hold. She knew this man placed her importance before his and there wasn't anything he wouldn't do for her. Hadn't he proved that by attempting to teach her how to swim instead of making love to her?

He could have easily cajoled her into making love, but he hadn't and she loved him all the more for it.

Love.

That word haunted her, simply refused to leave her alone and while she would love to love and be loved, if she dared do so it could have dangerous repercussions.

Her life was in such turmoil. If only none of this had ever happened.

Her heart suffered a sudden stab and she realized that if her life had continued on uninterrupted she would have never gotten to know Duncan. And that would have been the greatest loss in her life.

Oddly enough, her mother's choice had provided her with a good man. Perhaps not one her mother would have chosen, and more than likely would have objected to, but a man Mercy found utterly appealing, full of humor and gallant beyond words and one she was easily losing her heart to.

Without realizing it, she released a heavy sigh and Duncan came immediately to her side, slipping his arm around her, an act so simple and yet so meaningful to her. His arm lent support, comfort and protection, and though she had never admitted it, it was also a loving gesture.

"Why the sigh?" he asked.

"Memories and thoughts," she said.

"That trouble or sadden?"

"A bit of both."

"Then it is new memories we must make," he said with a grin and a wink.

She laughed and felt her heart grow light. "I like that thought."

"See, a new memory already."

Her face sparkled with happiness as she said, "This time, this moment here with you will be a memory I will always cherish."

His grin turned wicked. "This cherished memory will pale in comparison to what I have planned for you."

A tingle of pleasure shot through her and she wondered that if his words could so easily entice, how would it feel when he made love to her?

She shivered at the tempting thought.

"You grow cold, time to get dried and"—his dark eyes twinkled with mischief—"unfortunately clothe ourselves."

She agreed, though silently, that it was unfortunate and reluctantly walked with him out of the warm water. With her thoughts where they shouldn't be, she didn't pay attention, and as soon as her wet foot connected with a smooth, though wet and slippery stone, she found her feet going out from under her, her hand grabbing for Duncan, and he grabbing her forcefully around the waist, twisting them and taking the full brunt of the fall.

She came down hard on top of him, her breath rushing out of her and her senses shocked. It took a shake of her head and a deep breath to regain her wits and hear the groan.

"Duncan!" she cried and looked down to see him grimacing and groaning. "Where are you hurt?"

"Why? Will you kiss it and make it all better?"

"You tease so you must be all right," she said with a smile.

"Anytime that you're lying on top of me, I'm more than all right."

She laughed. "You are wicked."

"As wicked as you want me to be," he whispered in her ear and then stole a quick kiss.

A rush of tingles ran through her and she couldn't stop her body from shivering.

"Hmmm, now I'm wondering if perhaps it isn't the cold that disturbs you, but rather the *heat*." His teasing eyes suddenly sparked with desire.

"It is," she admitted freely. "You know that I want you. I have not denied that."

"Which makes our present position even more difficult."

She felt him then, rise against her naked flesh and damn if the size of him snuggling its way between her legs didn't feel good and didn't make her want to surrender.

He faintly brushed his lips over hers then said, "As much as I would love to dive deep inside you and pleasure you beyond reason, there simply isn't time."

As if on cue, Bliss called out, "Are you done?"

They scrambled off each other.

"A moment, please," Mercy called out. "We're almost finished."

They both dressed with haste, and while Mercy had longed for clean garments, the sweet-smelling clothes were lost to her as her mind remained occupied with thoughts of Duncan. And continued to do so even after Bliss entered and began stitching the garments closed around the chains.

Food, clothes, shelter, nothing seemed to matter to her at the moment except Duncan. Her body refused to relinquish the thought of making love with him. The tingles in her body would not subside and she worried that they never would, at least not until her body was satisfied, not until Duncan and she made love.

And that day was coming soon . . . very soon.

Chapter 17

Duncan and Mercy set out early the next morning with a sack full of food, fresh clean clothes on their backs and confident that the remainder of their journey would be relatively safe.

Bliss had made it known that the king's soldiers were not welcome on Pict land and mostly avoided it. Those who dared venture into Pict territory rarely made it out. She, therefore, advised that they had little to worry about, that is, until their feet left Pict soil.

Duncan was well aware that before reaching home there was a small area of land where the King's men could very well be lying in wait. He and his brothers had already scuffled with the king's men there and a scuffle it was, since the four of them sent the small contingent home licking their wounds.

However, the king knew that time drew near for the true king to surface and claim the throne. He wasn't taking any chances. He had his soldiers out in full force scouring the land for the man who could possibly take the throne from him.

"Your brow draws together," Mercy said. "Something concerns you."

Duncan shared his unease. "Once off Pict land there's a possibility we may run into the king's men."

"Then we'll need to be alert and cautious."

"The terrain can be troublesome if unfamiliar with it," he said.

"Then we have an advantage, since I assume you are familiar with the land."

Duncan nodded.

"Then it's less of a concern than you think," she encouraged. "And besides, your warriors could be lying in wait as well."

"We do have sentinels in the area."

"Then we have no worries," she assured him.

He smiled and locked his fingers with hers. "At the moment not a one, we are free to enjoy the next few days."

"That will be nice," she said.

He agreed, though silently. Their time together had been one of survival and while it remained that way, for the moment they didn't need to worry about it. No thought of soldiers sneaking up on them. They would be undisturbed, uninterrupted and the thought brought a grin to his face.

"Now you're happy," she said with a smile of her own.

"I am, since presently we have no cares."

They both grew silent, each lost in their own thoughts

and concerns, though their hands remained firmly entwined. And he intended to see that they remained that way. Perhaps that was why he always reached out and took her hand. Even though the shackles kept them together, it was that moment when her fingers wrapped around his and held tight that their shackles were of their own doing.

He would never stop taking hold of her hand and he hoped she felt the same. He thought she did, since she didn't wait for him to only claim her hand, she claimed his and often. Her hand felt good in his and though it was petite and could appear lost in his massive one, it didn't. It was a perfect fit.

That perfect fit seemed to apply to every part of them. Whether sleeping side by side, naked together or snuggling in the smallest of shelters, their fit had been flawless.

A crack of distant thunder interrupted his musings and he saw that dark clouds lay in the distance.

"A storm brews," he said.

"We have time yet," she observed. "If we hasten our steps we could cover more distance before we're forced to seek shelter."

Duncan nodded in agreement and they picked up their pace, hurrying along.

The thunder grew, though no rain fell and it wasn't until dark clouds thickened heavily in the sky that Duncan and Mercy finally surrendered and took shelter in a small abandoned cottage Bliss had told them about.

After leaving their bundle inside they hurriedly gathered enough wood to build a fire in the cold fireplace. The first fat raindrop fell on Duncan's shoulder just as he entered behind Mercy.

Rain fell in torrents and wind whipped around the cottage, shaking the closed shutters, but inside a fire burned brightly in the fireplace and food was spread out on the blanket before it.

"You will like my brothers," Duncan said as they ate.

"Tell me about them."

"Reeve is twenty and six years, a year younger than me and a warrior beyond compare. Lean and tall, many mistakenly believe his slender build makes him weak, but he is stronger than me, than any of us. I've seen him defeat four men on his own without a bead of sweat marring his flesh. His warrior skills are his greatest assets and he much admires courage. He will like you."

"And the others?"

"Bryce lets his actions speak for him, and Trey"— Duncan paused and shook his head—"Trey is hard to define. It's best if you judge him and the others for yourself, though I should warn you about my mother, Mara."

"Why so?"

"She can take a person by storm," Duncan said with a grin. "She speaks her mind when and where she pleases and her barbs, though meant humorously, can often sting."

"She sounds interesting."

"That she is," Duncan said with a laugh.

"And your father?"

"He's a quiet man, though speaks his mind when he feels it necessary."

"You admire him, don't you?" she asked.

"Very much," Duncan admitted. "But what of *your* father?"

Mercy remained silent for a moment and then responded, though reluctantly. "I didn't see much of my father. Tell me more about your home. It sounds wonderful."

It was obvious she had no desire to speak of her father or mother and so he did as she asked and regaled her with stories about his family.

By the time they retired for the night the storm had subsided, the pounding rain turning into a gentle tap against the cottage and the wind dying to a whisper.

"You wish a large family of your own?" Mercy asked as Duncan covered them with a soft wool blanket before lying beside her.

"Aye, I do," Duncan said. "I couldn't imagine growing up without my brothers. When first we met, we knew we were family, even though different blood coursed through us. It was as though we had always known each other, similar to when you and I first met."

"What do you mean?" she asked, her brow furrowing.

Duncan ran his finger gently along the ridges on her brow. "We've worked well together from the beginning. And to do that there had to be a degree of trust, which usually is only given to someone you're familiar with.

Therefore, we were familiar with each other from the start. Don't tell me you didn't feel the same yourself?"

She hesitated only a moment. "You're right. I would have never jumped off the cliff if I hadn't believed in you."

Duncan felt the recognizable catch to his gut. She had a way of doing that to him, stabbing at him, making him feel things foreign and yet somehow familiar. He had spent so much time on seeing that the mission succeeded that he had ignored his own wants and needs. He had told himself that there would be time for that later.

Then Mercy entered his life and later suddenly became now.

He soothed her brow until the ridges were no more. "See, you and I were meant to be right from the very beginning."

"How can you be so sure?" she asked with an ache that tore at his heart.

"Because," he said, brushing his lips over hers, "you believe in me and that takes trust and trust is the foundation that binds."

She shook the chain that joined them. "This also binds, but for a time only."

"But this," he said and kissed her with an intensity that quickly stirred their passion, "binds forever."

"Not so," she whispered breathlessly.

"Aye, it does," he insisted and kissed her again. This time his tongue slipped in to mate with hers in a familiar rhythm as old as time.

She tasted luscious and he couldn't quite get enough of her. While he tasted, his hand drifted beneath her blouse and settled over her full breast that fit perfectly in his hand. Her hardened nipple poked his palm and he was quick to tease it with his fingers.

She groaned in his mouth and her body arched, as if pleading for more and he wanted to give her what she wanted. He lifted her blouse slowly, giving her time to object if she wished. But she didn't and when finally her beautiful breast lay exposed, she shivered.

She needed heat and he intended to give her not only what she wanted, but what she needed. He lowered his mouth to her nipples and with the first lick of his tongue across the hardened nub she groaned and dug her fingers into his scalp.

He didn't stop. He knew she didn't want him to and he didn't want to. He feasted on the rosy orb enjoying it as the special treat it was and lingering in its addictive sweetness.

Her continued assault on his scalp aroused him even more since it felt as if she urged him not to stop and he had no intentions of stopping. They were alone with no threat of discovery and it seemed only natural that they finally consummate what was inevitable . . . their union.

His hand loosened the band of her skirt and eased it down far enough for his foot to grasp hold of and push it away. Then his hand explored traveling over her flat stomach and slipping discreetly between her legs.

When his fingers found her wet warmth he almost lost his patience. Knowing that she grew wet so easily for him had his own passion surging strong, but he had to remember her innocence.

It was all new to her and he didn't want this plunge to be like her plunge into the cold water. He wanted it filled with warmth and gentleness and memories that would forever haunt her mind and make her want more.

His fingers teased her gently before even attempting to penetrate her, though she seemed eager, arching against his hand, as if taking command, as if forcing more from him.

He wrapped his leg over hers to still her some and then he moved to claim her mouth once again. After a kiss that left her chest heaving, he asked, "Tell me this is what you want. Tell me you have no doubt. Tell me this is meant to be between us."

Her dark blue eyes sparkled like the finest sapphire as she said, "Must you ask? Can't you feel how much I want you?"

"I won't take unless you give freely, willingly, lovingly," he said. "It is yours and yours alone to give. The choice must be yours, but know when it is made that *you* belong to me and *I* belong to you. I'll have it no other way."

She hesitated, her blue eyes dimming and he decided then, at that moment, he would not let her escape him, not let her fear prevent her from finding pleasure and love.

His thumb moved to massage the nub between her legs and her eyes turned bright and her breath caught.

"A taste of what awaits you, though I much prefer my tongue in place of my finger."

She gasped and shook her head. "I can't think."

"I don't want you to," he whispered. "I want you simply to enjoy."

She shook her head.

"I'll stop, if that is what you want," he said and slowly drew his hand away.

"No," she protested, grasping hold of his arm. "It's just that—" She stopped as if unable to go on.

He kissed her slowly and let his finger drift over her nub once again, though faintly, a reminder of the pleasure that awaited her.

"What stops you?" he asked softly. "We are here alone with no fear of intrusion. It's our time. Surrender."

It disturbed him that there was a touch of sadness in her eyes. Why would she feel sadness when there was only pleasure to be had? He didn't know, but he did know that he wanted to wipe all her sadness away. He wanted her to see how it could always be between them.

He tenderly kissed her cheek and whispered, "We are meant to be, that's all that matters."

He caught a flash of joy in her lovely eyes and he hated when it vanished as quickly as it had appeared. But then if it appeared once, though only briefly, he could make it appear again and again until finally it remained.

He looked in her eyes and whispered, "Let me love you."

Her breath caught and joy shined once again in her

blue eyes, and for a moment longer than before. His manhood not only swelled, but so did his heart. Damn, but she had worked her way inside him and had taken command of every part of him.

Damn, but he loved this mighty, petite woman like he never imagined possible.

He brushed his lips across hers, then said, "And love me in return."

She cupped his face in her hands. "Always and forever."

His heart swelled near to bursting as did his manhood. But forget them both, for it was her eyes that affected him more deeply than anything. There was a sustainable joy in her lovely blue eyes that made him realize that she loved him. She actually loved him and nothing could make him feel so wonderfully alive.

"I'm going to make love to you all night," he said.

"We'll be too tired to travel in the morning," she said with a hint of a giggle.

"Then we'll spend another day here or, no maybe three."

"As long as I have this night with you, nothing else matters," she said and kissed him.

That was all he needed. His mouth joined hers and the night began.

Chapter 18

Mercy surrendered everything, her heart, her mind and her passion. Remembering her mother's warnings about never surrendering completely to a man had caused her to hesitate. Had caused her to question whether intimacy with this man would be a wise choice. Then Duncan had said the unexpected.

Let me love you.

Not "let me make love to you", but "let me love you", and that had made all the difference, for she had heard the truth of his words and saw it in his eyes. Whether it was only once, or God willing longer—*please, please let it be forever*—then she would surrender and love him as he loved her.

His mouth settled over her nipple and heat rippled over her body. He didn't stop there. His lips traveled over every inch of her, tasting and teasing and making her ache for more.

His hands explored her heated flesh along with his lips. There wasn't a part of her he didn't touch or taste or come to know. She tried to do the same to him, but he had murmured, "Another time. This time is for you."

He was so unselfish and so giving that she knew this was a very special man she had found and she never wanted to let him go.

He captured her mouth in a soul-wrenching kiss as he rose over her and gently nudged her legs further apart.

"Tell me, if at any time, you want me to stop," he whispered.

"I don't want you to stop," she urged.

He smiled. "You might."

"Never," she insisted.

"I like the thought that we'd never stop loving."

Her stomach fluttered and she was overwhelmed with the need for him.

"Then love me," she whispered and wrapped her arms around him and urged him down on top of her.

She was amazed of how smoothly he slid into her and how wonderful he felt deep inside her. And when he moved, she sighed with pleasure. Her body seemed to instinctively know what to do and she let it take the reins. She simply flowed with the rhythm and soared with the passion that surged through her.

She heard him ask time and again if she was all right and she would smile and nod her head and tell him not to stop, please, don't stop.

"Please, please," she whispered. "It feels so very good."

And he obliged, increasing the rhythm, increasing the

pleasure. It grew stronger and stronger and she clung to him more tightly, her hips arching up to meet his every thrust. It was as if she couldn't get enough, couldn't feel enough, and when she felt a small tingle radiate deep inside her she dug her fingers into him and swayed her hips beneath him trying to take him deeper inside her.

His passionate groan excited her and she increased the sway of her hips, and he his thrusts. Her tingle increased, built, grew out of control until her desirous groan matched his and all at once something exploded inside her, throughout her, around her and she called out his name over and over and over.

He continued the rhythm, extending her pleasure until she felt him release, stiffen, groan with his own climax and finally still against her.

His body went limp over her and after a moment his weight was too much for her to bear. He seemed to sense the same and rolled off her and they lay side by side, both breathless.

He regained his breath before her and turned to rest on his side next to her. His hand reached out and brushed strands of her hair off her perspiring face.

"I didn't hurt you, did I?" he asked with concern.

She laughed softly. "If what you did to me constitutes hurt, then you can hurt me anytime."

"You enjoyed?"

She turned to rest on her side facing him. "Enjoyed? It was fantastic, marvelous, brilliant, breathtaking—" She sighed. "I had no idea how wonderful making love could be." She smiled sweetly. "Though I imagine it was due to your prowess."

"More so to you," he admitted.

"Me?"

"Yes," he said and kissed her softly. "I wanted this to be special for you and in doing so it was more than special for me."

Her smile grew. "It was special. I will remember it always."

He grinned. "It's just the beginning for us."

Mercy nodded, that was all she could do, for she feared their time together would be short and after making love with him, the thought pained her heart.

A yawn unexpectedly escaped her mouth and she rolled closer and cuddled against him. It was then she heard the clank of the chain and was reminded of their shackles. Not once during their lovemaking did she recall the chain. While they may have been fettered, they loved as if they were free.

She snuggled even closer to his warmth, slipping her arm over his waist and sidling up against him.

"You know you're a perfect fit, don't you?" he asked, his arm going around her.

"I know," she agreed. "It's as if we were made of the same mold."

"I believe we were."

He reached behind him for the soft wool blanket and settled it over them.

She nestled comfortably in the fit of his arms and

realized that action spoke much louder and broader than words ever could, especially when it came to love. Neither of them may have spoken the words *I love you* aloud, but their actions spoke volumes.

Soon her eyes were closing while her thoughts continued to linger on just how much Duncan and she loved each other.

Duncan woke to the patter of rain and smiled. That the day dawned rainy filled him with pure delight. It meant that they would have to remain where they were and that was no trial at all.

After last night, he knew he would never get enough of Mercy. Every touch and taste only had him hungering for more. And the pleasure he had derived from making love to her had been astounding. He had never enjoyed coupling so much, but then it had been so much more and that was what had made all the difference.

Just thinking about it made him grow hard and while he would have loved to wake her with touches and kisses, she looked too peaceful to disturb. There would be time all day to dally and play.

He grinned at the delightful thought.

But he reminded and reprimanded himself for not thinking of the mission. He needed to return home and see what his brothers had learned. Any bit of information could be vital to their objective . . . to seat the rightful king to the throne.

These were turbulent times in Scotland and only the

rightful king could bring some order and peace to the land. He couldn't let anything stand in the way, though he believed that Mercy would understand once he had a chance to explain it all to her. Unfortunately, he couldn't do that just yet. While he had no doubt she was trustworthy, he couldn't take the chance and explain his mission to her. It had to be kept secret until he was sure of everything; then and only then could he confide in her.

She stirred against him and his thoughts were quickly diverted. She was a beauty in many ways. And he especially favored the way she responded so eagerly to his every touch and kiss.

While he was well aware that it had been her first time, it hadn't seemed so. But then she had already slept naked in his arms more than once, so there was no apprehension when it came to that. And it had been obvious that she was just as eager to love as he had been.

Love.

That was the key, it had to be. It had been the only factor missing in all the times he had coupled. He may have cared for the women he had been intimate with, but there had been no love there on either part. He had purposely kept a distance from falling in love. He had reminded himself over and over again that he had no time for it now. Later when all was settled and done, then he would love.

Love, however, seemed to have a different plan in mind.

And he had to admit that from the very first, Mercy

had enticed him, though he had pictured a far different woman for himself. Larger, stronger, and yet she had turned out to be both. Even though she was petite, she was large in spirit and strong in nature.

She was perfect for him.

Her eyes drifted open and she smiled at him.

He grinned. "It's raining."

She chuckled. "Were you praying for rain?"

"As hard as I could."

"That makes two of us," she said and placed a soft kiss on his chest.

"You're playing with a fire that's already aflame," he warned.

"I don't mind getting burned."

Her sultry voice was enough to tempt, but when her hand closed around him, he knew he was finished.

"My turn," she whispered and began to kiss him all over while her hand explored.

They didn't dress or eat until noon. They snuck outside when the rain grew light to see to their personal needs and hurried back in to sit before the fire.

Duncan was content with the silence between them, talk seemed unnecessary at the moment. It was nice just being able to share the quietude after weeks of trying to survive.

Mercy interrupted the silence with a sigh. "I wish it could always be this peaceful."

"We will have many more such moments," he said,

for he had no intentions of losing her. Life simply would not be the same without her.

"You always sound so confident."

"Because I am," he boasted with a smile.

"Then I should simply believe you?" she asked.

He heard the urgency of hope in her voice and he wanted to reassure her. "If you do nothing else, Mercy, believe in me. I will be there for you."

She laid her head on his shoulder. "I have since the start."

He hugged her and they said no more. They sat and listened to the fire crackling in the hearth, each lost in their own thoughts. Good or bad, it didn't matter, for right now they had each other.

The rain grew in intensity again and the wind whipped at the cottage, but they remained safe and protected inside. When night fell and supper was done they undressed each other and drifted into each others' arms.

They took their time exploring and enticing until their passion demanded satisfaction and they joined together as one. They held tight to one another as waves of pleasure simultaneously racked their bodies.

They slept then, though Duncan woke in the middle of the night with such an aching need for her that he couldn't resist touching her. She responded, in her sleep at first, and then woke as he slipped into her and she accepted him, her own body aching with need.

Surprisingly, they woke early the next morning and

weren't too pleased to see the sun rise bright and the day clear. There would be no reason to delay their journey any longer. And the thought angered Duncan.

He mumbled and groaned and began snatching the food off the blanket and shoving it in the sack.

"Tempermental today?" Mercy snapped.

"You sound the same yourself," he accused.

"I suppose it's contagious."

"Oh, it's my fault now?"

"You've been a grouch since you woke," she said.

"So what if I have?"

"So I don't like it."

"Well, you can't like everything," he snapped.

"I like everything about you."

He stared at her as she drifted closer.

Her delicate hand reached out and slipped inside his shirt to rest against his naked chest.

"I like the feel of you and I like the taste of you."

She nuzzled her face in the opening of his shirt and kissed his chest before drifting over to his nipple and teasing it with her tongue.

He groaned.

She looked up at him as her hand moved down under his plaid and grabbed hold of him. "But I especially like when you're inside me."

That was it. He grabbed her around the waist and swung her up, her legs instantly wrapped around his middle. Then he rushed her backward and braced her back against the door.

He kissed her like a starving man. "You make me crazy with the want of you."

"Then take me, for I want you just as badly."

He didn't waste a minute, he entered her fast and furious and that's the pace they kept. It took only minutes for them both to explode in a blinding fury, not once but twice.

Once his senses returned, Duncan rested his brow to hers. He worried that he may have hurt her since he had thought of nothing but the need that had gnawed at him.

"Good lord, Duncan, that was wonderful."

A wide grin surfaced before he laughed. "And here I thought I may have hurt you."

"Nonsense, you made me feel better," she admitted. "I was feeling a bit grouchy myself. But now I feel great."

He laughed. "Good. Then we'll always know what to do to stop the other from being grouchy."

"Oh my, yes," she agreed and kissed him.

"Now it's time to go," he said reluctantly.

"I know, but I shall never forget this place, this time with you. It's been the best time in my entire life and I will cherish it forever."

"So will I," he said and though he wanted to tell her that he would cherish her forever, he waited. There were things he needed to do first and then . . . then he would make Mercy his wife.

Chapter 19

The day remained clear, though a chill hung in the air. Duncan draped the blanket around Mercy like a shawl.

"What have you to keep you warm?" Mercy asked.

He grinned, and realized he had been grinning more than usual lately, and that made his grin grow even wider. "I have you."

She shook her head.

He hugged her to him. "Just the thought of you heats every inch of me."

She laughed and gave him a playful shove. "There will be none of that, or we'll not get very far today."

He took hold of her hand. "Right now, I'm pleased to be where I am."

"I admit the same," she said, "but all good things come to an end eventually."

"Not with us," he said adamantly.

He didn't like that she didn't agree or that she didn't respond at all. But then could he blame her? It had been a difficult road for them, but more so for her. He at least had his family to return to, she had no one. And though it was different now, she still had faced the prospect of being on her own. Not a good place to be for a woman.

"We can cover much ground today," she said and began walking.

He was right by her side, their hands still firmly clenched as if in fear of being separated even though the shackles made that impossible. It was their way to remain connected and it would always be until the day the heavens separated them and even then he would fight to remain with her, for he had no intention of ever losing Mercy, not even to death.

The day and land proved gracious to them. The terrain was pleasant as was the weather and so they covered more ground than they had expected. A brief meal under a large oak and a few kisses and intimate touches that promised a night of lovemaking and they were off again.

With their thoughts overly occupied they didn't realize that they approached the border of Pict territory. And unknowingly they slowed their pace, their steps more cautious.

Mercy turned to Duncan. "There's something wrong. I can feel it."

"A few more feet past these woods and we leave Pict land."

She shook her head. "I thought we would have another night of peace."

"I hadn't realized we covered as much of a distance as we did, for I thought the same."

"Beyond, we are once again vulnerable to the king's soldiers?"

"Aye, the possibility exists once more."

"How far to your land?" she asked.

"If we kept a good pace we could possibly reach it by nightfall."

Her slim fingers tightened around his. "What if we remained on Pict land for one more night?"

"As much as I'd like that, there is a chance that being this close to the border, the king's soldiers might venture across. And while I have no doubt the Picts are watching, I would not feel as safe as we did at the cottage."

She nodded. "You're right, I but hoped."

"Once home we'll need not worry about it any longer."

She looked up at him. "And the chain will come off."

He nodded, though he knew in his heart that while free of the shackles, their love forever chained them together and he liked the thought.

"Let's be done with this," she said bravely.

"We will finish this, so that you and I can begin."

He didn't like that she didn't smile or verbally agree with him, she simply nodded.

They continued on, drawing ever closer to the border until finally Duncan stopped.

"Not far ahead we leave Pict land. The forest grows thicker, which means more places for the soldiers to hide, and more places for us to take cover. We will need to remain silent and alert, and watch our steps."

"Much like we did before."

"Only this time we are a stone's throw away from my land. Once on it and spotted by the sentinels we should be safe."

"I'm ready."

She sounded to him as she did the day they had jumped off the cliff together, confident even though fearful.

"We'll make it," he assured her.

She smiled then. "I have no doubt."

Her smile and belief in him was reassuring and their next steps began the end of one journey and the beginning of another.

It had been several hours since they had left Pict land and Mercy could feel the difference. The air had chilled considerably and apprehension hung heavy around them. Every crack, squawk and rustle had them stopping to listen and observe, which slowed their pace. But it couldn't be helped. They needed to be more cautious than ever. They were much too close to being free to make a foolish mistake now.

Duncan tugged at her hand signaling her to stop. He crouched down and she followed. He quietly cleared a small patch of earth with his hand, then with a small twig drew a map of sorts. He was attempting to show her the distance until they reached his land.

It wasn't far off and she assumed that he felt that

this was the area that they could be most vulnerable to attack.

She nodded her understanding and they once again were on the move.

Mercy silently prayed for their speedy departure from the area to safe ground as she kept keen eyes on the surrounding forest and the path they traveled. Talk wasn't possible even without the danger of being heard. The rough terrain demanded complete attention.

Thick dead branches lay strewn around and sizable rocks, partially hidden by earth and time, jutted out unexpectedly, catching a foot or scraping a leg. More than once Duncan's quick response prevented her from falling. And each time there was no annoyance or judgment in his dark eyes, simply concern.

She could feel exhaustion begin to claim her limbs and, as before, she ignored it and plodded on. There would be time enough to rest once they reached safe ground.

She was grateful, however, when a short time later Duncan signaled for them to stop and take a brief rest.

She leaned against a thick tree trunk allowing her weary limbs to rest while Duncan busily looked about. She knew she had only a few moments and a nap wasn't possible or wise, but she closed her eyes hoping to pretend when she opened them that she had napped for a couple of hours.

Her eyes sprung open and she tensed when she heard the crack of a branch and immediately looked to Duncan to see if he had heard it too. He had. His eyes were wide and his finger pressed to his lips, reminding her to remain silent.

"Watch where you're stepping, you fool."

The low and angry whisper seemed to surround them and all they could do was remain still and wait.

"We've seen no sign of them," the man said angrily. "I tell you, the Picts got them."

"They better not have," the other man retorted sharply. "The king now wants her alive."

The man grumbled. "What if she's already dead?"

"I wouldn't want to be the one to tell the king that."

Their voices faded along with their footsteps.

Mercy decided that it would be best if she appeared perplexed as to why the king would want her kept alive. So she was surprised when Duncan stepped close to her and leaned down to whisper in her ear.

"I'm sorry."

"No need," she murmured and with light steps they set off again.

The overheard conversation seemed to have upset them both, their thoughts being elsewhere, when suddenly they both stopped and realized they heard the snort of a horse, or were there more than one?

It drew closer, louder and Mercy felt for sure there were several horses and they were about to surround them. Her heart pounded wildly in her chest. They couldn't have traveled this far, have gotten so close to safety only to be caught.

And why in God's name did her father suddenly want her kept alive.

Duncan stepped behind her and pressed his mouth near her ear. "No choice. We must run."

She nodded knowing he was right. It would be harder for the soldiers on horseback to keep up with them through the dense forest. Their only recourse was to run as fast as possible, keep ahead and pray they reached safety and help before the soldiers reached them.

"Ready?" Duncan asked and locked his hand with hers.

She nodded and gave her chin a tenacious tilt.

He grinned, kissed her quickly and nodded.

She took off with him. Her short legs were no match for his long ones and so she had to pump doubly hard to keep up with him. She jumped fallen branches right along with him and while he could easily vault boulders, she couldn't. So he swung her up so that her foot grazed the boulder and then he would see that she landed safely on her feet.

The pounding of the horses' hooves rumbled the ground beneath her feet and she was certain that any second they would be pounced upon and captured. And so she kept up the grueling pace.

They whipped through a grove of trees that surely would slow the horses down and hopefully put more distance between them. The happy thought had her smiling, though it was wiped from her face fast enough when her foot caught the edge of a rock and she went tumbling forward.

She felt her arm jerked back but not before the side of her head bounced off a rock. She didn't know what pained her more, her arm or her head? She had no choice but to ignore both, though it was difficult with the blood that ran from her head wound down her face and over her eye.

She couldn't let Duncan know and was glad it was on her right side, where he couldn't see it. If he saw the blood he would certainly want to stop and tend to it and they couldn't. The distance they were gaining would be lost, and by no means did she intend to be the cause of their capture.

They made it to a small clearing and Duncan halted abruptly and took a quick look around. The sudden stop sent dizziness spinning through her and she thought she would faint.

Don't you dare faint, she warned while trying to keep Duncan from seeing the blood.

"A few feet ahead," he said and tugged her forward.

She ran as best she could, even though her arm hurt terribly and her head wound throbbed. They would be on his land soon enough. Sentinels would spot them and they would be safe. All would be well.

You can do this, Mercy. Stay strong.

She continued to silently encourage herself even though she felt her body grow weak. She refused to surrender to the pain, refused to be the cause of their capture, refused not to conquer the pain.

Her body, however, had different plans and she knew that soon she would collapse whether she wanted to or not. She had to alert Duncan.

"Duncan," she cried out, though not loud enough, for he didn't respond.

She was fast losing strength, not even having enough strength to squeeze his hand. With what little she did have left, she raised her voice and called out to him again. "Duncan."

He turned and she made sure he could see the blood running down the side of her face and into her eye.

She wasn't quite sure since her vision had turned fuzzy, but he looked as if he paled badly and stopped so abruptly that she collided with him.

"My head," she managed to say, and the last thing she remembered was Duncan scooping her up in her arms and running.

Chapter 20

Low chatter surrounded Mercy and she struggled to get past the fog that not only muffled her hearing, but also muted her vision. She tried to move, but the pain that shot through her head brought an abrupt end to her efforts. Instead, she continued to listen.

It took her a moment to recall where she was and what had happened and when she finally did, she grew more alarmed. Duncan was speaking to someone. Had the soldiers caught up with them? Was he bargaining for their lives, or was he biding time hoping she would wake and be ready to help him?

She couldn't let the pain interfere, no matter how badly it hurt. If he still had his sword or dagger, he would need her to help use it. She would remain still, let no one know that she regained consciousness and learn what she could from the chatter.

"I can't believe you tracked us that easily."

That was Duncan, no doubt keeping the enemy engaged

in conversation. She had to find out how many he faced, if only one, they had a chance.

"It's laughable how easy it was."

She didn't recognize the direct, strong voice, but one thing was certain—this man was confident, which meant he believed he held the upper hand. Mercy continued to listen.

"Make fun of me, and I'll see you suffer for it."

Mercy would have smiled at Duncan's terse response if she could, but she still didn't want anyone to know that she was regaining strength.

"You make me laugh."

He certainly wasn't laughing, though she thought there was a hint of humor in the soldier's voice, or was it smugness?

"Get off your damn horse and come over here."

Mercy wondered if Duncan was attempting to get the soldier to move closer so that he could strike. Did he have a weapon ready? Was he prepared to use his free hand, since he most certainly believed her useless to him? Was there some way she could help?

"You dare command me?"

His voice boomed, though not threateningly, but with authority. Whoever this soldier was, he certainly wasn't afraid of Duncan.

"I'm waiting."

Duncan was ready and so was she. She would not fail him.

She heard the soldier's approach and thought to give

Duncan's hand a squeeze, but she was afraid the soldier might see. She waited, relieved that the pounding pain in her head was diminishing, though her stomach tightened in anticipation.

"What the hell?"

Mercy didn't wait to find out what had surprised the soldier, she bolted up, assuming Duncan had plans to attack and needed her help. Pain not only shot through her head, but also her right arm and all she could do was reach out, grasping for Duncan before she began to slip back into the fog.

"Mercy! Mercy!"

Duncan's shouts assaulted her like a blow to the head and she scrunched her eyes against the pounding sound.

Mercy heard the soldier ask, "How badly is she hurt?"

No, she thought, fighting against the fog that attempted to claim her. A soldier would not concern himself with her injures. If not a soldier, then who was he?

"A head wound, and I'm not sure how much damage I have done to her arm."

"Is the arm broken, and why the hell are you chained to this woman?"

"I don't think it's broken, but her head wound needs tending. And I'll explain about the shackles later."

Mercy surmised by the concern and ease in which they conversed that they knew each other. Could that mean they were on Duncan's land? Was this man one of his warriors? If so, that meant they were no longer alone. There was someone there to help them and Mercy squeezed Duncan's hand as she uttered his name.

"You're safe, Mercy," Duncan said. "My brother Trey is here and we're going to get you home."

Relief rushed through her and helped dissipate the haziness. Not wanting to suffer through another bout of pain, she slowly worked her eyes open while remaining perfectly still. It took several moments to see clearly, and though she should be more concerned with her condition, she was eager to meet one of the men Duncan called a brother.

Mercy glanced up at the man. She hadn't expected any resemblance since Duncan had mentioned the men he'd been raised with weren't truly his brothers. So she wasn't surprised to see the difference in the two men. Where Duncan was tall and broad, Trey was tall and lean. And where Duncan's features were strong and rugged, Trey's were decidedly handsome. And both had long hair that fell past their shoulders, Duncan's earthy brown in contrast to Trey's dark auburn.

She also took note of Trey's eyes, the color hard to describe since they appeared to change color as she gazed at them. Were they blue, or green or of a golden hue? She simply couldn't be certain, but one thing was for sure; the ever-changing color was his shield. He was a private man who allowed no one to trespass.

"It's a pleasure to meet you, Trey," she said and smiled, though a grimace fast replaced it. She closed her eyes against the pain for only a moment, not wanting to fall back into a stupor. And opened them slowly, realizing that the pain faded more quickly than before.

"It's my pleasure as well," Trey said and smiled.

His smile dazzled, though certainly not intentionally. He was simply a handsome man whose smile added to his fine features. She doubted this man ever lacked for female companionship and yet . . .

Her gaze drifted to Duncan and her heart soared. Here was the handsomest of men, at least to her. His rugged features bore courage, good-nature and compassion and made him a man that every woman would most certainly find a desirable mate.

"I tried to stop your fall—"

Mercy pressed her fingers to his lips. "You got us to safety. I'm only sorry I couldn't have helped."

Duncan grinned and once again Mercy's heart took flight. She loved his half smile. It played with the senses, making you wonder who you truly dealt with, leaving him an enigma to most, though not to her.

"It was no chore to carry a wee bundle like you," Duncan assured her.

"Then I suggest we tend to this wee bundle and be on our way," Trey said, "before one of the roving bands of soldiers find us."

"Duncan, please help me sit up," Mercy said.

"In a moment," Duncan said. "First, let me cleanse your wound and give you more time to regain your strength."

"I'm feeling stronger," she assured him and as if to

demonstrate, she wrapped her fingers tightly around his. Though if she were more honest with herself, it was because she wished to feel his strength ripple along her fingers and up her arm until it finally settled completely over her.

Sure enough, he returned the squeeze that shot a ripple of strength rushing over her, the intensity causing her to shudder.

Duncan quickly asked, "Are you all right?"

"Just wishing this done," she said.

"It will be done soon," Duncan assured her.

"And we should reach home by nightfall and then your shackles will be removed and you both shall be free," Trey said.

Neither Mercy nor Duncan replied, and Trey took note.

Duncan kept a sleeping Mercy cradled in his arms as the horse plodded along.

"It is good that her wounds are minor," Trey said walking alongside the horse.

"I thought the head wound worse at first, but was relieved it wasn't. The arm, I'm afraid, will be sore for a while longer."

"Mother will be there to help," Trey said. "Now I have waited long enough, tell me how it is that you are chained together."

Duncan would have much preferred to inquire about the mission, but he couldn't take the chance to speak about it in front of Mercy even if she was asleep. No one must know or even suspect. Therefore, he would need to wait until he was home and free of Mercy to speak with Trey and the others.

"Soldiers arrived at a croft that I had just come upon and was gratefully partaking of the water offered me."

Trey nodded. "You didn't want to jeopardize the farmer's life by opposing them."

"Or his wife and two children. They chained me before we left the farm and then a short time later we met up with a large group of prisoners and it wasn't long before I found myself chained to Mercy."

Trey stopped him when he got to the part where the soldiers were ready to kill them. "Wait a minute. It seems that you both were chained together with the express reason of being killed. Now the king may be going crazy killing off men of a certain age that could be a threat to his throne, but why her?"

"I figured that perhaps it was her misfortune to simply be chained to me, or perhaps she had *displeased* a nobleman."

"She's a kept woman?"

Duncan smiled and shook his head, glancing down at Mercy sleeping peacefully in his arms. "No, I discovered she's not."

Trey grinned. "And how did you discover that?"

"With a kiss."

"Just a kiss?" Trey scratched his head.

"Her first kiss," Duncan said with a huge smile.

Trey shook his head. "How is it that a woman as beautiful as she has never been kissed?"

"I haven't figured that out yet."

"What do you know about her?" Trey asked.

"She's courageous, adventurous, determined and"—he grinned—"we fit nicely together."

Trey stopped so abruptly he almost tripped over himself. "You've fallen in love with her."

Duncan wasn't about to admit it to him before he spoke the words to Mercy.

Trey laughed. "You have! Damn, Reeve, Bryce and I are going to have a good time with this."

"I'll kill you if you breathe a word to them."

"About all of it, or just the falling in love part?" Trey chuckled.

"I'm warning you, Trey. I beat your ass once and I can do it again."

"You were eight and I was seven. I think this time it would prove more difficult."

"You're tempting me to prove you wrong," Duncan warned with a snarl.

Trey continued chuckling as he resumed walking. "And the wee woman will be helping you to fight?"

Duncan had to grin recalling all the times over the last week that Mercy had fought so bravely by his side.

"Don't underestimate her," Duncan said with pride. "And aye, she'd be right by my side."

Trey nodded. "Perhaps then she's a good match for you."

Duncan didn't respond, his thoughts lost in the knowledge that Trey was absolutely right. Mercy was a good match for him. Even though they had been forced upon one another, they had adapted to their shackles easily enough. They learned how to work together as one, to depend on each other, to trust each other and under the most difficult of circumstances.

She hadn't shed one tear or complained. She had done whatever was necessary for their survival, even stripping naked on more than one occasion. It had taken a tremendous amount of courage to trust him, let alone share such intimacy with a stranger. And Mercy had done it all without a whimper or grumble.

Mercy woke on and off during their journey, spoke briefly with Duncan and then returned to a peaceful slumber.

"She's exhausted, isn't she?" Trey said.

"It hasn't been easy, but she's proved herself a tenacious warrior," Duncan said.

"We'll stop at Harold the smithy before proceeding to the keep. He'll see to freeing you of that chain."

I'll sleep alone tonight.

The thought disturbed Duncan. He liked falling asleep with Mercy wrapped snugly in his arms and he liked even more waking up with her snuggled against him. He didn't like that his arms would be empty this night and the spot beside him in bed cold.

He glanced down at her and couldn't help but think

that she was right where she belonged, always belonged, and always would belong.

He made the decision fast, as if he needed it confirmed immediately. "The morrow is soon enough for the chain to come off."

"Mercy may think otherwise," Trey said.

"She's exhausted and injured," Duncan said firmly. "I will not make her suffer through having the chain removed this evening."

"She might prefer them removed sooner rather than later."

Duncan glanced at her wrists. The salve that Bliss had put on their wounds made the skin look less raw and certainly eased the pain. But he wondered if perhaps they both would be left with scars, a constant reminder of their time joined together.

She stirred in his arms, her eyes drifting open.

"We're almost home," he said softly.

"Food and bed," she said with a smile.

"I agree," he said and then whispered, "especially the bed part."

Chapter 21

Night had already fallen when they finally reached Duncan's home and though the horse took its time, Mercy wasn't able to see much of the village. She did, however, smell the delicious scents wafting about and she sniffed the air with anticipation and appreciation.

"Something smells good," she said, glancing up at Duncan from where she lay snuggled comfortably in his arms.

"Our hunters and farmers keep us well stocked and our women keep us well fed."

Mercy heard the pride in his voice and she envied it. How lucky for him to be part of a family, a clan. She had often wondered how it would feel to have the support of so many, to have others to rely on and help in times of need and to help those in their time of need. She and her mother had led a restrictive life due to her father being king and her mother his mistress. It had been a lonely existence, and she had never understood why her mother favored it.

"Are you feeling better?" Duncan asked.

"I am," she said and smiled.

"That's good," Trey said. "Duncan worried you would not feel up to having the chains removed tonight. But now with you feeling well, we can stop by the blacksmith and have him remove them."

Free of Duncan.

No, she didn't wish to be free of him yet. *Not yet.* She wanted more time with him, more intimate kisses, touches that lingered and more, so much more before it came time for her to take her leave. But would there be time?

The horse snorted and pawed the ground once before stopping at the keep, and Mercy knew the time had come. It wouldn't be long before she and Duncan were separated.

Trey stepped forward to help, but Duncan shook his head.

And Mercy said, "We can manage."

"I've no doubt you can," Trey said and stepped away, taking hold of the horse's reins.

Mercy relaxed against Duncan as he dismounted with ease, taking her along with him. It was as if they were one, their every movement made in unison. No one led or followed. They were partners, always there for each other, always ready to help or keep safe. How would she ever do without him?

He set her feet gently on the ground and waited a moment. She kept her hand on his arm until she was certain her legs felt strong enough to hold her and then she smiled and reluctantly took a step away from him.

The pain hit her with such intensity that she didn't have time to react, though Duncan did. His powerful hands grabbed her before her limp body could hit the ground and once again she found herself in his arms.

"That's it. You're going straight to bed," Duncan commanded.

Though she was left with a residue of weakness from the jolting pain, her humor had remained intact. And it was with a teasing grin she whispered, "Exactly where I wanted to be . . . with you."

He didn't break stride as he mounted the steps to the keep and said, "You're not well enough for making love tonight."

"I was teasing."

"I'm not."

His tenacious tone warned her that he certainly wasn't, and it was nice to know he was concerned for her. He was a fine man, a good man, a man she could love. And that was the biggest problem of all. But then, how many times had her mother warned her against falling in love.

Love ruins everything. Don't ever make the mistake of falling in love. I promise you will suffer for it if you do.

Her mother's words resonated clearly in her mind, that was how often she had reminded Mercy of it. Many times through the years Mercy had wondered what had happened to her mother that had caused her to distrust love. But no matter how many times Mercy had asked, her mother would always tell her that the past was best left in the past.

The great hall was ablaze with lights when they entered, a plethora of candles, wall torches and a huge stone fireplace being the sources. It wasn't a large room, though certainly sufficient to hold many with its numerous tables and benches lined in rows.

"My son!"

The joyful screech made Mercy smile as Duncan turned with her in his arms to face the woman who rushed over to him.

She was taller than Mercy by at least two heads and thick in body, and with the prettiest face Mercy had ever seen. Creamy flawless skin and large wide green eyes, long, curly auburn hair not touched with a single strand of gray and piled high on her head, and full cheeks flushed pink, while the deep lines around her mouth were evidence that her smile was permanent.

The woman threw her arms wide when she stopped in front of Duncan. "What have we here, my son?" Her bright green eyes twinkled with mischief. "Have you finally brought home a wife and maybe a wee bairn waiting to be born?"

Mercy couldn't stop herself from blushing.

Duncan, however, laughed, shook his head and said, "Not yet."

"Then take her upstairs and see to your business," his mother ordered with a wink.

"If she wasn't injured I might—"

"Injured, you say?" his mother barked. "What's wrong? Take her upstairs. Carmag get my healing basket. Why are you standing there? Move!"

Duncan jumped to his mother's orders and climbed the stairs, his mother in quick pursuit.

"Put her in your bed and leave her to me," his mother said.

"I can't do that."

"Aye, you will," his mother insisted.

He entered the room, his mother scurrying past him to turn down the bed. She moved out of his way and he gently laid Mercy down on the soft stuffed mattress. He then sat on the bed beside her, yanked off the blanket that had hid their chain and held up his hand.

"This is why, Mother."

His mother gasped.

"What the hell?"

"You watch your mouth, Carmag," his mother said, turning to scold her husband as he entered the room.

Carmag shook his head and handed his wife her healing basket. "Why are they chained together?"

"You heard your father. Answer him," Duncan's mother ordered and both parents glared at him.

"Can it wait until after you've seen to her wound?" Duncan asked.

His mother threw her hands up. "Whatever is the matter with me? Of course, this lovely young woman—" She turned wide eyes on her son waiting to be introduced.

"Mercy."

"You can plead for mercy later," his mother warned. "Right now I'd like you to introduce the lady to me."

"Her name is Mercy," Duncan said with a laugh.

His mother swatted his arm and then looked to Mercy. "I'm Mara and it is a pleasure to meet you, Mercy."

"I'm so pleased to finally meet you," Mercy said. "Duncan has spoken lovingly of his family."

Mara chuckled. "I can't imagine Duncan talking *lovingly* about his brothers."

"He did of his mother," Mercy said.

Mara beamed, her plump cheeks stinging red. "He's a good son."

"Because of you," Mercy said.

Mara looked to Duncan. "I like her. She'd make you a good wife."

"See to her wound, Mother," Duncan said with a grin and rattled the chains. "She's not going anywhere."

"Then perhaps the chain should remain," Mara said with a teasing glint and placed her healing basket on the bed and got busy tending Mercy.

"Tell us about the chain," his father said, moving to stand at the foot of the bed.

One glance and Mercy knew he was Trey's father. He was as handsome as his son or rather his son was as handsome as him, only older, though age did not distract from his fine features. He stood a head over his wife and was built broad and solid. But the one thing that she noticed the most was the loving look in his eyes every time he glanced at his wife.

Duncan obliged his father, starting with when he and Mercy were first chained together, though omitting the intimate details.

Mara listened while she busily filled a bowl of water from the pitcher on a stand near the fireplace and rinsed a cloth to cleanse Mercy's head wound.

"The king grows out of control," Carmag said angrily. "Why ever would he commit a young innocent woman to death and then suddenly change his mind?"

Mercy tensed.

"I'm sorry, dear, did I hurt you?" Mara asked.

While she had felt no pain, her wound allowed her to conceal her reaction that the truth about her might be revealed. "Just a little."

"You're safe here," Carmag said firmly.

"And here she'll stay," Duncan said, glancing down at her.

Mercy didn't reply. She closed her eyes while Mara continued to tend her. She didn't want to think of the future, for then she might hope and in the end she would be disappointed. She knew she would. Her mother had and her mother before her. In a strange way, it seemed to be the destiny of all women in her family.

"Her arm was injured, though suffered no wound," Duncan informed his mother after she had thoroughly cleansed the head abrasion and had applied a healing paste.

Mara looked over her arm, moved it about some and when Mercy winced told her, "Time will need to see to this." Then she leaned closer to Mercy and asked, "Anything else you need me to tend?"

Mercy blushed and whispered, "My backside, though I don't know why it should pain me."

"Why didn't you tell me?" Duncan asked.

"And what business is her backside of yours?" Mara snapped.

Duncan leaned closer to Mara. "Since I've already seen it, it is my business."

Mara grinned. "Then it's a wedding we'll be planning soon."

"How is she?" Trey asked entering the room.

"She's just fine," Mara said. "But you and your father have to leave while I tend to a private area." She pointed to the door. "Out. The two of you."

Duncan grinned.

"And you shut your eyes," Mara said shaking her pointed finger at Duncan.

Mercy shook her head at him hoping he'd understand that while there wasn't any part of her he hadn't seen, seeing any part of her naked while in front of his mother would embarrass her.

He winked and grinned at Mercy and she was relieved he understood.

"All right," he grumbled teasingly. "But I do so under protest."

"You can protest all you like. You'll still do what I say," Mara ordered though retained her smile.

Mercy liked Mara. She took no backtalk even from

grown sons, and she obviously loved them since her eyes always twinkled with love and humor whenever she looked at them, especially when she playfully scolded them.

Mara hoisted her skirt after Mercy pointed to where she had felt the dull though constant pain. Mercy relaxed under her gentle probing.

"What's wrong?" Duncan demanded. "You're not saying anything. Is it a bad wound?"

"A bruise that's all, though if you shared Trey's horse to get her here, which I imagined you did," Mara said. "It caused further bruising. This wound, like her arm, will require time to heal."

"Then she'll rest," Duncan commanded.

"Not on her backside she won't," Mara said with a chuckle as she pulled Mercy's skirt down to cover her.

"Can I open my eyes now?" Duncan asked.

"Aye, all done," his mother said and began returning things to her healing basket.

"Are you all right?" Duncan asked running a gentle hand over her sore arm.

"Truly I am," Mercy said, not wanting him to worry but comforted by his concern.

"We'll need to get you two to Harry the smithy," his mother said.

Mercy knew that their separation was imminent, but she preferred to prolong it even if it was just for a little longer.

"Actually," Mercy said, "could we possibly eat first?"

"Good Lord, what a fool I've been," Mara said admonishing herself. "You two must be starving."

"That we are," Duncan confirmed.

"I'll see that a feast is brought to you," Mara said placing her healing basket on the floor near the bed.

"Along with plenty of wine and mead," Duncan said.

"And afterward we'll get you to Harry so he can set to work on freeing you of your chains," his mother said and with a wide grin left the room.

Mercy wished she could have found a reasonable excuse as to why the chain need not be removed tonight, but there truly wasn't one. She wasn't in grievous pain and having slept in Duncan's arms for the better part of their journey, she was no longer exhausted. And certainly after feasting she would have more strength.

So tonight she and Duncan would be free of each other.

"If you're not feeling up to this—"

Mercy shook her head, finally accepting the inevitable. "No, you've been shackled to me long enough."

Duncan rested his brow against hers. "It's no chore being shackled to you."

"We shared a grand adventure, didn't we?"

"I've known no grander," he said and drew back with a smile. "And you haven't forgotten what you owe me, have you?"

Mercy laughed for they had done so much more than kiss. "I've already kissed you."

"But the promise was that when we were free of the chain you would kiss me."

"I cannot break a promise," Mercy said. "Once the chain is off, I will kiss you."

"Then I look forward to the kiss."

She did too, though she knew that once she kissed him she would not want to stop kissing him and then surely she would want to make love and not want to stop making love with him.

Truth was that she didn't want any of this to end with Duncan. She wanted a life with him. A long, happy life, but that wasn't possible. Particularly now that her father was after her and that he no longer wanted her dead, but brought back alive to him.

He was up to something and for some reason she couldn't help but think that it might have something to do with Duncan. That meant the longer she lingered here with Duncan, the more danger he and his family were in.

She would need to leave, but how was she going to do that?

How was she going to walk away from the man she had come to love?

Chapter 22

Duncan sat on the bed beside Mercy taking her in his arms. He was relieved they had finally made it home and though he certainly wouldn't mind spending one more night fettered to her, he knew it was time for the chain to come off.

There was work to be done, work that she couldn't be part of. Not that he planned on letting her slip away. Not now, not when he had just found her, just realized how much he loved her. And that was what he wanted her to learn and see for herself . . . just how much he loved her and always would.

"Ready for the chain to come off?" he asked.

"As strange as it was at first being shackled to you, now it will seem even stranger not to be," she said.

"It didn't take long for us to grow accustomed to it," he reminded.

"No, it certainly didn't," she admitted with a grin. "That was because you were so chivalrous."

He leaned down and stole a quick kiss. "It wasn't easy.

There were times . . ." He stared at her a moment. "That I so badly wanted to do this."

He kissed her strong and hard, as he had wanted to since arriving at the keep. He wanted to remind her how he felt about her, how he forever ached for her, how he simply couldn't resist kissing her, not now, not ever.

Her eager response thrilled and excited him, much too much. She was in no condition to make love. She needed rest and yet he couldn't stop kissing her, didn't want to stop kissing her. It would be so easy to slide into bed beside her and ease his hands under her garments to touch all those intimate places that drove not only her wild, but had him growing hard simply thinking about it.

"Stop that!"

Duncan jumped up at the sound of his mother's scolding voice and once again wrenched Mercy's arm.

She gave a holler and scrunched her face in pain.

"I'm sorry," he said apologetically and hunched down beside the bed. He rubbed away the pain lines on her forehead. "I responded to my mother's voice as I always have." He smiled. "Quickly and with a touch of fear."

"I trained my sons well," Mara said with a laugh that plumped her full cheeks.

"Now I know where you get your humor," Mercy said. "You are much like your mother."

Mara beamed. "I'm getting to like this woman more and more."

"You just want me married and making babies," Duncan teasingly accused.

"Of course I do," Mara admitted. "Lots of babies, but she is in no condition to do that right now, besides the food will be here any moment."

As if Mara was heard, a knock sounded at the door and she opened it to allow servant after servant to enter with laden-filled trays.

"Look at all that food, Duncan," Mercy said and eagerly licked her lips.

He leaned close to her ear and whispered, "And here I thought you only had a taste for me."

Her warm cheek stung his cool one as she pressed it against his. "I'm saving the tastiest, most delicious for last."

"Now you're really tempting me," he warned.

She placed her lips so close to his ear that he thought she would kiss it, but instead she whispered. "Since I must stay off my backside, where then do you suggest I settle?"

Visions of her on top of him had his heart beating madly and his manhood aching.

"Keep teasing me and I'll settle you right on top of me."

"Enough whispering," Mara ordered. "Time to eat, and then time to remove that chain."

Neither of them said a word. Duncan helped her stand and he saw that this time her stance was firm and steady. They settled at the table and they both had barely taken a bite when Trey rushed in the room.

"Soldiers have been spotted at the border and Reeve is but a short distance away."

Mara looked from one son to the other. "What are you waiting for? Go help your brother. And don't dare come back without him, and see that not a one of you gets hurt."

Duncan jumped up and this time Mercy went with him. He shook his head. "I forgot about the chain."

"I can go with you," Mercy offered.

"No," Trey and his mother said in unison.

Duncan felt Mercy tense.

"I have fought beside him more than once," Mercy said proudly.

"It's no longer necessary that you risk your life," Trey said.

"It will take too long for the smithy to free us," Mercy argued.

"She's right about that," Mara said. "Harry told me it might take some time to get even one metal cuff off, since the king's cuffs are forged together, making it impossible to break free without much hard work."

"We're wasting time discussing this," Mercy said.

"You need rest," Mara reminded her firmly.

"I need to help save another, as I was saved," Mercy said adamantly.

"I told you she was like you, Mother," Duncan said with pride.

Mercy smiled at Mara. "I'll make certain to bring your three sons back without a scratch."

Mara laughed. "Then be off with you and be safe."

Duncan didn't like placing Mercy in danger again,

but he also didn't like not being there to help his brother. And he was proud of the way she immediately stood to join him, even though rest had been advised. She didn't even question why he needed to go when one would assume that surely he'd have warriors to look after the matter. Or perhaps she understood that you never leave your brother to fend for himself. Or could it be as simple as her standing by his side? After all they had grown accustomed to it.

Trey mumbled beneath his breath as they descended the circular stone stairwell.

"Speak your mind," Duncan said.

"I don't see what help you'll be chained to her," Trey said.

"I'll prove my worth," Mercy said.

"It isn't that," Trey said and hurried ahead of them.

Duncan held back for a moment. "In time you'll get to know Trey and understand."

"I have patience," Mercy assured him.

"I know and I appreciate it." He would have kissed her then but time was of the essence and so he once again hurried his steps. "Follow my lead and do as I direct."

Mercy nodded.

"Are you certain you feel well enough?"

"I actually feel much better than I was feeling. My arm pains me more than my head."

Duncan winced. "My fault. I'm sorry."

"You prevented my fall and if you hadn't, I could have suffered far worse injuries," she assured him. "And do not let being fettered to me prevent you from doing for your brothers."

"I know you can hold your own."

"Good, then let's get this done. I'm famished."

Duncan laughed and took her hand, the silent signal that once again they would work together as one.

Mercy sat in front of Duncan on his stallion. It was a large black horse and she could feel his power in his muscled limbs and proud prance, and the strength it took to command him. But command him Duncan did and the horse obeyed.

"Warriors have been sent along the border, ready and waiting for orders," Trey said atop his mare that appeared more malleable than Duncan's stallion."

"How far out is Reeve?" Duncan asked.

"Not far from the king's men," Trey said.

"We must be careful. It would be unwise to allow this to erupt into a battle," Duncan said. "No doubt Reeve has seen signs and is aware of the soldiers' presence."

Trey nodded. "No doubt, he has always been good in sensing enemy presence."

"And does he keep safe distance from it?" Mercy asked.

"That's the problem," Duncan said. "Reeve never backs down from a battle."

"He'd take on a whole troop," Trey said shaking his head.

"But he must know the odds are not in his favor," Mercy said.

The two men laughed.

"Reeve would continue fighting to the very end," Trey said. "And even then I wonder if he would defy death and finish the fight."

"It doesn't sound as if he needs your help," Mercy said.

"Regardless," Trey said. "We never leave a brother to fight on his own if it can be helped."

"Which is why you came in search of Duncan?" Mercy asked.

"We received word that he was headed home, soldiers close on his heels and—" Trey quieted suddenly.

"That he had baggage with him?" Mercy asked.

"Something like that," Trey said and then said no more.

"Was there something in particular that drove you to find him?" Mercy asked.

"Last I heard he was journeying through Pict territory, which caused me no worry since we have done that before. It was when I learned that a contingent of men was being sent to patrol the area between Pict land and ours that I knew he would require help."

"Then according to your decision, we should go help Reeve," Mercy said, "since soldiers surely wait his approach."

Trey looked to Duncan and Duncan glared back.

Mercy sighed. "I understand. Duncan had an added burden . . . me, while Reeve is on his own."

"Much better odds of survival," Trey said.

Mercy sat tall and straight in front of Duncan. She would not allow his doubt in her to upset her. She had never faced a fight until Duncan happened in her life. Purposely or perhaps inadvertently he had taught her to embrace her strength and courage and now that she had, she had no intention of stopping.

"I'm ready when you are," she announced with confidence.

"What say you, Duncan?" Trey asked.

"It is quiet except for our chatter. I suggest we wait and listen. Reeve knows we would come for him. He will let us know if he needs us."

"True enough," Trey said.

They waited in silence. The night dark and the air chilled. There was the occasional rustle of trees from the light wind and the scurry of an animal across the land, or the hoot of an owl. But no human sounds and so they continued to wait.

Then when Mercy finally slumped back against Duncan believing nothing would happen, a shout sounded.

"We got him," the man bellowed. "We got him."

"Don't hurt the woman," another man ordered.

Mercy turned to Duncan and he nodded understanding that the soldiers thought they had captured him.

"What wo—"

A scream pierced the night, followed by painful moans, more screams and solid thuds that rocked the ground.

Mercy grew worried that Duncan and Trey made no move to help their brother, but they were seasoned warriors and new much better than she did. So she remained quiet and waited to move when Duncan did.

"Let's go help him," Duncan said to her relief.

She sat up, ready for whatever was to come.

"We fight as we have done," he said to her as he guided his horse through the dark toward the sounds of anguish and suffering.

Mercy wondered if they had waited too long. Would they find Reeve badly hurt? Could the soldiers have tortured him for information about her? She grew more and more concerned, worried that Duncan's brother should suffer because of her.

The disturbing thought actually made her realize that she definitely could not stay here long. She would place Duncan's whole family in terrible danger. She could not live with that thought. She would have no choice. She would have to present herself to her father. At least he no longer wanted her dead, but no doubt he wanted something.

They finally arrived on the scene, soldiers laid strewn about, many moaning in pain and some bleeding badly from their mouths and noses. Some eyes were blackened shut and a few bones protruded at foreign angles. And in the middle of the melee stood a man, tall and lean with long dark hair.

He slowly raised his head, his fingers raking back his long ebony hair and exceptionally dark eyes peered at her intrusively. His face was all sharp angles and lines, as if his features were sculpted by a master craftsman, and he wore a feral smile.

Mercy shivered.

"His bark is worse than his bite," Duncan whispered.

"Now you can clean up the mess, since you waited so long to help," Reeve yelled at them.

"It doesn't look it," Mercy murmured.

"And why the hell have you brought a wisp of a woman to a battle?" Reeve demanded.

"You're complaining that you needed help?" Duncan asked and turned to Trey. "This is a night to remember."

"The night our brother Reeve whined about needing help," Trey said with a laugh.

"Did I say I needed help?" Reeve yelled. "I swatted these soldiers, if you can call them that, as easily as flies."

"Then you can clean them up just as easily," Duncan said.

Mercy watched as Reeve grabbed one wounded soldier struggling to stand by the back of his neck and tossed him into a thicket of bushes as if he was a sack of feathers.

"I've cleaned many of my own messes up," Reeve said approaching them. "Now answer my question that you've so blatantly ignored. Why bring a frail woman to a battle?"

"I may be small, but I'm not frail," Mercy retorted with a sneer.

"Damn, she's got a bite to her," Reeve said and grinned.

Mercy was surprised by the way his broad grin changed

his features. Suddenly he seemed approachable and not so sinister.

Reeve stopped by Duncan's horse. "The answer to my question is?"

Trey laughed. "Why don't you just show him, Duncan?"

Duncan obliged, raising his arm slowly.

Reeve shook his head and laughed aloud. "This wee bit of a woman's got you locked good and sound."

"It's the king who locked us together good and sound," Duncan informed him.

Reeve's grin vanished and he spun around to face the wounded soldiers hurrying to gather their injured and be gone. "Tell your false king that his time has come. Soon he will rule no more."

One soldier grew bold. "Those who follow the mythical king will rue their choice."

"Be gone with you, you fools," Reeve commanded.

The brave soldier stood and bowed. "M'lady, your father the king wishes your safe return. Please come with us."

Mercy couldn't see Duncan's face, but she felt his body tense solid and if the glares Reeve and Trey sent her were any indication of Duncan's reaction . . . she was in trouble.

Chapter 23

Mercy had hoped she could slip away before her identity had become known. Now that it had she had no choice but to bargain for Duncan and his family's safety. She kept her courage strong as she told the young soldier, "Tell my father that unless he can guarantee the safety of this family and land that I will not be returning home."

Duncan's voice suddenly boomed from behind her. "Tell the king his daughter will never be returning home. She belongs to me now . . . Duncan MacAlpin."

"You wish to ransom her?" the soldier asked.

"Clean your ears out, you fool," Reeve yelled. "Did you hear any mention of a ransom?"

"I don't understand," the soldier said.

Duncan wrapped his fingers around Mercy's and raised their chained wrists high. "The king gave her to me and I plan on keeping her."

"The king did no—"

Duncan didn't let him finish. "The king wanted her

dead. Now he changes his mind and wants her back." He shook his head. "No. She stays here with me."

"I shall inform the king," the soldier said.

"Make sure you do," Duncan warned.

The soldier turned and helped one of his fallen comrades to his feet before disappearing into the woods. Warriors arrived then, following the ragtag bunch to make certain not one lingered.

When Reeve and Trey lowered their heads and walked away, she knew it had been by Duncan's silent command. She had expected he would want to speak with her about this right away and she couldn't blame him. She only hoped he understood.

She wanted to face him and discuss the matter and he must have had the same idea for his hands settled snug on her waist and with a lift and a twist she was suddenly sitting sideways in his lap, his arm snug around her.

She spoke first. "I'm the king's bastard daughter."

"And you didn't think it was important to tell me that?"

There was no anger or accusation in his tone. However, Mercy thought she heard disappointment.

"You were a stranger—"

"Not for long," he said.

"True," she agreed, "but I believed it best for us both if my identity remained unknown."

"Perhaps at first I could see the reason in that, but not later," he said. "You should have trusted me."

"I did—" She shook her head. "I do trust you."

"Not enough to tell me who you really are."

"You know who I am better than anyone."

"I thought I did," he said.

She tensed and raised her chin. "Being the king's bastard daughter has little to do with who I really am. I revealed my true self to you. If you cannot see that, then you are a fool." She had to stop a moment and swallow down the catch in her throat. And then with courage she wasn't sure she had, she said, "It's time for this chain to come off."

They exchanged not a word on the return ride and when they stopped at the smithy, a mix of emotions rose up to choke her. She wanted to be free of the chain, but she didn't want to be free of Duncan and she feared that just might happen.

Harry, the smithy, was short and round and strong as an ox. He examined the metal cuffs and the thick chain, scratched his partially bald head and looked them over again.

"This is best left until tomorrow," he announced.

Mercy almost laughed at the sense of joy that assaulted her, though it was mixed with apprehension of what was to come.

"Are you sure of that, Harry?" Duncan asked.

He scratched his bald spot again, then nodded toward Mercy. "It's her I worry about. She's a wee wisp of a thing and if I don't take my time and I'm not careful, I could break her wrist."

"Then tomorrow it is," Duncan said and after a brief

chat about how Harry's family was doing, they left.

They walked back to the keep alone. Trey and Reeve had gone ahead taking Duncan's stallion with them. She wished he would say something and then again she was afraid of what she might hear. And then part of her was angry with him for not understanding and another part understood why this troubled him.

Her emotions so overwhelmed her she felt as if she was about to burst.

They entered the keep, his parents along with Trey and Reeve sitting at one of the long tables and benches. They all looked over at them and it was Mara who waved them over to join the family.

While Mercy understood that his family was probably concerned about this matter, she felt that she and Duncan should first discuss it privately, and so she told him just that.

"I wish to go upstairs and talk."

"And I wish to speak with my family first."

His decision disturbed her and she bristled.

"This affects them as well," he said.

She shook her head annoyed and a slight dizziness assaulted her, though she ignored it. "Don't you think I know that? Don't you think I was concerned how my presence here would affect you and your family's safety?"

"Then you should have told me the truth," he said through gritted teeth.

"And what would you have done?" she asked slapping her free hand to rest on her hip.

His eyes narrowed and he brought his nose to within an inch of hers. "I would have—" He stopped abruptly.

She glared at him. "Go on, tell me what would you have done when you discovered the woman you were chained to was the bastard daughter of the king?"

Mercy could have cringed when she realized she had raised her voice to a near scream. Everyone stared at them and she simply shook her head at her own foolishness. Not a smart reaction since it caused a wave of dizziness to wash over her. Her stomach turned queasy and her head grew foggy.

She couldn't faint now, she just couldn't. It would make her appear weak or needy and she didn't want either. She had survived much these last few weeks and she would survive more and she would fight. Yes, she would fight for Duncan.

Her hand felt heavy but she managed to lift it and rest it on Duncan's chest. She couldn't remember what it was she wanted to say.

"Mercy?"

She heard his concern and she wanted to smile. That was her Duncan, the man who worried about her, the man who protected her, the man who fought to keep her safe.

It came to her then. She wanted him to know that she loved him but for some reason her thoughts and mouth weren't working as they should and only one word spilled out. "Help."

* * *

Duncan scooped her up into his arms and yelled, "I have you. Do you hear me, Mercy? I have you. You're safe."

"Stop screaming at her," his mother ordered as she reached his side. "She's just fainted. She needs rest, not charging into battle."

"Then why didn't you stop her?" Duncan asked accusingly.

Reeve joined them, slipping an arm around his mother's shoulders. "So are you going to take a stick to him now or later?"

"Watch it or I'll take a stick to you," Mara warned. "And as far as you—" She pointed to Duncan. "Not only does Mercy have a mind of her own, but you had it in your head that you wanted her to go with you. So you both got what you wanted."

Reeve grinned and went to say something, but his mother cut him off.

"Not another word, Reeve. Mercy needs tending." With that she was shoving Duncan toward the stairs. "Get her into bed. She needs food and rest to restore her strength."

Duncan had her up the stairs and in bed before her eyes began fluttering open.

"You best wake up," he encouraged. "We have much to discuss."

Mara swatted his arm. "Not tonight. She's had enough."

"But—"

Mara placed a gentle hand on her son's shoulder. "Let it be. She needs your caring right now, not your anger."

Duncan nodded and gave his mother a hug.

Mara smiled and patted his arm. "It will all work out in due time. Now let's get her out of these cumbersome garments and into something that will help her rest. You start undressing her while I go get what we need."

Mercy opened her eyes just as Mara left the room.

"I've orders from my mother to disrobe you," Duncan said with a grin.

Mercy nearly sighed. There was her old Duncan, the one she was familiar with, the one who she knew cared for her beyond reason.

"Then what are you waiting for?" she asked, though when she tried to smile, her head pained her and she winced.

"You're not feeling well."

His concern comforted her, but she wished to reassure him. "Just a bit out of sorts."

"You'll rest tonight," he insisted.

"You'll stay with me?"

He rattled the chain. "I'm not going anywhere."

"But do you want to?" she asked, her eyes focused on his.

"I'm right where I want to be."

He sounded certain enough, and besides, he squeezed her hand and locked his fingers with hers. That was a sure sign he didn't want to go anywhere and that they would fight this battle together.

"You've done nothing," Mara scolded as she rushed into the room.

Mercy corrected her. "He's done everything for me."

Mara looked to her son, smiled and then turned to Mercy. "Well, he's about to do more."

Duncan worked alongside his mother and in no time they had Mercy out of her garments and into a white, soft wool nightdress and tucked beneath an even softer wool blanket. Mara then took a couple of platters of food from the table and placed them on the chest next to the bed where Duncan sat. She added pitchers of wine and mead. When she was finished she gathered Mercy's discarded garments.

"I'll repair these garments so they'll be ready to wear when you are," she said. "Now it's time to get some food into you and then time to rest."

"And Duncan too," Mercy said.

Mara nodded. "Sleep well and I'll see you both in the morning." Mara stopped at the door and turned and though she spoke to Mercy, she looked to her son. "One thing, Mercy, our parents don't define us. We define ourselves."

Mercy looked to Duncan ready to talk, but he silenced her with a gentle finger to her lips.

"No more tonight," he said. "There's time enough tomorrow or the next day or the next."

She smiled as his finger slipped away. He was letting her know that he didn't intend for her to go anywhere. He wanted her right there with him. And so she gratefully let it be for another day.

While the food was appetizing, she found she wasn't hungry, which seemed to concern Duncan.

"Just eat a little," he cajoled offering her a small piece of hard cheese.

She was about to tell him she just wasn't hungry when she realized that if she did he would stop eating so that she could sleep.

"Maybe a little," she agreed.

He smiled as she took the cheese from him. "A little will do you well, while a lot will do me even better."

She nibbled on the cheese as they sat in bed, his back braced against the thick, hand-carved headboard and her head rested on his shoulder. She thought about how irritable they had been tonight and then about their first bout of grouchy angriness and how it was settled.

She laughed softly. "You and I were grouchy tonight."

"And you find this humorous?"

"I recalled how we decided how to handle such a situation," she said and cuddled in the crook of his arm.

He lifted her chin and planted a soft kiss on her lips. "If only you were up to it, I would make love, oh slow and gentle to you, until sunrise."

She sighed knowing she didn't have the stamina, already sleep was creeping over her. "I wish it could be so, but sleep will soon claim me, though I would prefer your touch to claim me."

He quickly disrobed using the knife on the table to cut away his shirt from the shackle. Then he slipped beneath the blanket easing her down on the mattress with him.

"Close your eyes," he whispered, "and my touch will take you into dreamland."

And it did.

Mercy slipped into a gentle slumber as Duncan's fingers worked their magic on her warm skin.

Chapter 24

Duncan hadn't expected to sleep so soundly but he had, his eyes drifting open with the sunrise. Mercy didn't stir, hadn't all night, since they were in the same position they had fallen asleep in.

He stared at her, the bastard-daughter of the king. He had never given such a possibility thought. That she was daughter to the king had stunned him, especially since he was fighting for the true king to claim the throne.

What did trouble him was why the king had changed his mind about wanting his daughter dead. He couldn't help but think that it might have something to do with him. Had the king discovered their mission? Did he think his daughter could provide him with information? And how did he confide the truth to Mercy when he'd been sworn to secrecy?

Also while it had disturbed him that she hadn't told him of her identity, he could understand why. It was just that he wanted to know that she trusted him enough to confide anything to him and yet . . .

He couldn't offer the same . . . he had taken an oath.

Falling in love with her had come so naturally and he had assumed the rest would follow just as naturally, even though he had his mission to tend to. But now it was all different.

Now he had fallen in love with the king's daughter. A king he intended to dethrone.

She stirred in the crook of his arm and then settled once again.

He brushed a strand of her dark hair away from her face, a face so lovely that he never tired of looking upon it, and never would.

Today they would be free of each other, though not truly. It wasn't these metal cuffs and chain that bound them. No, love had somehow sneaked in and fettered them more than any shackle could.

He only hoped that the chains of love were strong enough to overcome the obstacles they were about to face.

A soft rap on the door drew his attention and he called out in a relatively low voice, "Enter."

He wasn't surprised to see his mother, garments draped over her arm and her stitching basket on the other. She had never missed hearing a thing he and his brothers had said through the years, even if she had been across a room or field. For awhile they had believed that she had possessed magical hearing, but then her sight had also been magical, since she had caught them at just about every trick and tease.

"She slept well?" his mother asked.

"Aye, as did I," he said knowing it would be her next question.

"Good, I'm pleased that last night's troubles didn't keep the two of you from sleeping," Mara said. "I thought it best if you both ate with the family this morning."

Duncan knew it was a summons rather than a request.

"I'll help Mercy get into fresh clothes when she's ready and then we'll eat and then it's off to Harry to free you of these chains."

"You have it all planned do you?" Duncan grinned.

Mara retained her smile, but her words warned, "There's work that needs doing."

Duncan's grin faded and he nodded. "I know."

"Can I help?" Mercy asked.

They both turned to see her waking with a yawn and a stretch.

"That's if you don't mind," Mercy said. "There's much I've been taught to do."

"You can help with the stitching," Mara offered.

"Oh, I can do much more than stitch," Mercy informed her. "I can run every aspect of a keep and I am excellent with numbers."

"You read and write then?" Mara asked.

"Aye, Latin, French and most of the Gaelics."

Mara looked to Duncan and nodded. He knew what she was thinking. Mercy would be a good one to have on their side, but then that would mean betraying her father. And though her father might have wanted her dead, would she want the same for her father?

He also wondered why she hadn't told him of her many talents before this, but with his mother present he wasn't about to broach the subject. Then again, perhaps he should remember what she had told him last night.

You know me better than anyone.

"I'll help anyway I can," Mercy said.

"Well, for now that would be getting up and dressed so that you can join my family for the morning meal," Mara said.

Duncan not only sensed, but he saw her hesitation as she struggled to sit up. He reached out, wrapped an arm around her waist and lifted her up to sit. She leaned against his arm and he had easily come to realize that it was her way of seeking protection and comfort. He knew what troubled her and what she needed from him.

She glanced up at him with pleading eyes.

Damn if her glistening blue eyes didn't do him in. They mesmerized and he'd about do anything for her when caught in their beauty.

He had to shake his head. "If you can battle soldiers and emerge victorious, then you will have no trouble sharing a meal with my family."

"I wouldn't be too sure," Mara said and laughed. "Now let's get you dressed. And you—" She pointed to Duncan. "Get your plaid on and be quick about it."

Duncan obliged and in no time the three were leaving the room, delicious scents growing stronger as they descended the stairs.

They never reached the table. A young lad hurried into the room with a message from Harry. "He's ready for you."

"We'll take a bite with us," Duncan suggested.

"Suddenly I'm not hungry," Mercy said clinging tightly to Duncan's arm.

He felt the same, though made no mention of it. Soon they would be able to walk away from each other. After spending every moment with her for the last several weeks, he wondered how it would be without her. He'd find out soon enough.

"Freedom!" Trey and Reeve yelled, jumping up off the bench with broad smiles and tankards high.

"They tease," Duncan said to Mercy.

"But who? You or me?" She smiled and walked away, forcing him to follow.

He was surprised by her sudden, determined gait and that she remained a few steps ahead of him, not beside him or with her hand clasped in his. Once outside her steps took on a more rapid pace.

"Anxious to be free?" he asked curious as to her sudden rush.

She didn't stop or turn around. "I have a promise to keep."

"A promise?" he asked rubbing his chin.

"You don't remember?"

It struck him then. "I get my kiss."

He rushed forward, with no doubt what looked like an idiot's grin on his face, and scooped her up into his arms. "I can get us there faster."

They laughed, and though Duncan was eager for her to kiss him, once the chains were removed, everything would change.

Mercy turned her face away as the hammer came down on the edge of the metal cuff braced on the anvil. She thought her wrist would shatter from the vibration, but she kept her fear to herself. Duncan had withstood the ordeal without complaint or grimace and he was free, his metal cuff gone. She intended to do the same, though she was glad he remained by her side, not leaving her to face this on her own but to share his strength.

Harry had insisted that he remove Duncan's cuff first, explaining that it would be safer for Mercy.

She braced herself for another blow and this time she couldn't help but wince.

Harry grumbled beneath his breath.

"What's wrong?" Duncan asked, stepping forward, though Harry had warned him to keep a distance.

"This cuff is heavier than yours," Harry explained. "I've seen it used before on prisoners the king wants to make certain can never escape, can never be free."

"You can get it off, can't you?" Duncan asked.

Harry rubbed his bald spot repeatedly.

Trey suddenly appeared, a bit out of breath. "We need to talk now."

"I can't leave her," Duncan said and looked to Harry. "Can you?"

Harry examined the cuff again and again rubbed his bald spot.

Reeve arrived. "Father's waiting."

"He won't leave her," Trey said.

"You're free, she's brave, so say you. What's the problem?" Reeve asked.

Duncan ignored them both and focused on Harry. "Tell me you can get the damn cuff off her."

"I can get it off, but I can't promise I won't damage her wrist doing it."

Duncan turned to his brothers. "Tell Father whatever it is must wait. I will not leave Mercy to go through this alone."

"It sounds important," Mercy said, not truly wanting him to go, but not wanting him to think that she couldn't handle it on her own. She didn't want to think she couldn't handle it alone. She might have Duncan right now, but there was no telling what the future would bring, especially with her father wanting her to return home. He was a man who always got his way and didn't care what he had to do to get it.

"It will wait," Duncan said, sending his brothers a sharp look that had both of them taking a step back.

"Is there anything we can do?" Reeve asked.

Harry stared at Reeve a moment, then he looked down

at the metal cuff on Mercy's wrist, then back at Reeve again and nodded. "There just might be."

"What can he do?" Duncan asked, slipping his arm around Mercy's shoulder.

"I've seen no one with the strength of Reeve," Harry said. "There's not a one of us fool enough to go up against him, except you and Trey and Bryce of course."

Reeve laughed. "I always knew my brothers were fools, but it's good to hear that someone agrees with me."

"I didn't mean it like that," Harry grumbled.

Duncan sent his brother another scolding look and Reeve quit laughing, though retained a grin. Mercy was beginning to see just how close these men were for in the short time she had been introduced to them, they had without question or hesitation been there for each other.

"Explain, Harry," Duncan said.

"Reeve's arm strength goes far beyond mine," Harry said. "It's possible that with one blow he could crack the cuff making it easier to remove. Of course if he used too much strength he could shatter the cuff and her wrist along with it."

Duncan turned to Reeve, though spoke not a word.

Reeve stepped forward. "What say you, Mercy?"

He was so lean one would never expect that he possessed such strength, but having witnessed how he had disposed of the soldiers, she knew otherwise.

"I trust you," she said and smiled.

"Good lord, you're a beauty," Reeve said. "And lord knows I could never damage such beauty."

"Enough," Duncan said irritably. "Get to work and you *better not* damage her."

"Or what?" Reeve teased.

Duncan's grin spread slow and confidently. "I'll tell Mother."

"That's cruel," Reeve said and the brothers laughed.

Mercy joined in the laughter. She had never known such close family ties. Family that you could depend on no matter what and who accepted you for who you were, not who you were expected to be.

Harry demonstrated to Reeve what he needed him to do. And Mercy was relieved to see that Reeve displayed not a hint of doubt that he could manage it.

Reeve approached Mercy, hammer and pin in hand. "Turn your head away in case any metal splinters go flying."

Duncan stepped to her side and positioned his body as a shield between her and Reeve. "Keep your face pressed against me."

Mercy didn't argue. She much preferred burying her face against Duncan's naked midriff, since he had yet to slip on the shirt he had brought with him, than watch Reeve battle the cuff.

A fine sheen of perspiration covered Duncan's skin, the familiar scent filling her nostrils. It brought back memories of their journey and the many times they faced the possibility of capture and death together. And the times they had lain naked in each other's arms, not yet loving, but protecting. And she felt safe once again, protected and this time loved.

She waited with much less worry, confident in Reeve.

The blow came quickly, sending a vibration up her arm and throughout her body. Duncan's arm had instantly wrapped around her and she knew he had felt the blow along with her.

"Perfect shot," Reeve cried out.

Mercy had to see for herself, though she knew the metal cuff was gone. She felt the weight gone from around her wrist. She peeked past Duncan and sure enough her wrist was bare, free of the metal constraint that had joined Duncan and her for weeks.

The skin was no longer raw, thanks to Bliss's salve, though it continued to heal, and she wondered if it would leave a scar, though she needed no reminder of the time she had spent with Duncan.

She felt a swell in her chest. They were separated, free of each other. No longer would they spend every moment together. The thought made the swell grow until Mercy thought it would consume her.

"Are you all right?" Duncan asked.

She lifted her head with some difficulty, though she didn't let him know that. "Aye, I'm fine.

"And you're finally free of my brother," Reeve said, giving Duncan's arm a slap.

"Can we go now? Father's waiting," Trey reminded.

Mercy didn't want Duncan to go. She felt as if he was being ripped away from her and though it was foolish, she felt that once they separated they might never be together again.

"Are you sure you're all right?" Duncan asked, his hand resting on her cheek.

She wanted to tell him that she was far from fine, that she was frightened now that they were apart, worried that her father would come claim her, concerned that they would never ever be joined so solidly again.

"Go. I'm fine," she assured him while trying to believe it herself.

Chapter 25

Duncan kept turning around glancing over his shoulder to look at Mercy. It felt odd being separated from her, leaving her behind and walking away with his brothers. He thought to take her along, but couldn't. When Trey had announced their father wanted to speak with them, it was a signal that a messenger had arrived with news and they were to meet him in the woods behind the keep.

He didn't like leaving her right after having the shackles removed. He felt as if something needed to be said between them, and yet he wasn't sure what it was. Did he tell her he loved her, or was it fair when he wasn't sure of his own future? Or did he brave the unknown and to hell with what lay ahead?

He wasn't sure of anything at the moment except that he missed having her by his side. Instead of feeling lighter, freer with the chain gone, he felt as if he were missing a part of himself.

He didn't share any of this with his brothers. He didn't need to. He was sure they knew how he felt about Mercy, or they wouldn't have remained at the smithy to help him.

"She's a brave one." Reeve grinned. "And a beauty."

"Don't make me beat you," Duncan said.

"I think our brother has fallen in love," Trey said with a laugh.

"I think the two of you should get your mind back on the mission," Duncan scolded.

"Ours never left it," Reeve said. "Can you say the same about yours?"

Duncan knew this discussion was inevitable. When the mission began the four of them swore that nothing would interfere with it, especially women. A dalliance here and there didn't matter, but love had a way of intruding and it was agreed it should be avoided at all costs.

"You doubt my commitment?" Duncan asked.

"No," Reeve said and laughed. "Your sanity."

"While there was always a chance that one of us, the most foolish one, would fall in love," Trey said with a grin. "Never would any of us have imagined it would be with the present king's daughter."

"I didn't know and I never intended to fall in love with her or anyone until this mission was completed," Duncan said.

"Then what now?" Trey asked.

"I have no idea. Let's meet with the messenger and see what he has to say, and as for the rest?" Duncan shrugged. "Only time will tell."

They didn't have to go far into the woods to meet with Neil, a wiry little fellow who appeared quite agitated by the time they arrived. Their father was with him and simply shook his head as they approached.

"What kept you?" Neil demanded, pulling at his mouth, a habit of his when he was nervous. "I took a chance coming here now with the king's soldiers swarming the land."

"Why?" Duncan asked, though he knew the answer.

Neil leaned closer to Duncan as if he feared being heard. "The king searches for his bastard-daughter."

"Why?" Reeve asked.

"No one knows," Neil said, shaking his head vigorously. "Though they're all wondering what he intends for her."

"He had wanted her dead," Duncan said. "Why the change of heart?"

Neil shrugged. "Some believe he feels guilty for acting so rashly when he discovered that her mother, his longtime mistress, had betrayed him. He flew into a rage and ordered both their deaths. He succeeded in taking his mistress's life, but his daughter got away." Neil nodded, bobbing his head repeatedly. "Some think that the king discovered that her mother left vital information about the true king with her and he wants that information."

"This is all speculation?" Trey asked.

Neil continued bobbing. "All except the death of his mistress. That's true. Her daughter survived because her mother sent her away with plans to meet up with her later. Her delay cost her her own life, but saved her daughter's life . . . though for how long is anyone's guess."

"Is this the important news you brought us?" Reeve asked.

Neil's bobbing turned to shaking. "No. I have uncovered some dire news." His voice turned low. "I have learned that there is a spy amongst you."

"Who?" Duncan demanded.

"I don't know," Neil said. "I only know that the person has recently arrived."

"Man or woman?" Trey asked.

"Again I don't know," Neil said. "It is being kept hushed and I was lucky to have learned of it. Be careful. Do not let anything happen to the true king. The people are praying for his safety and that he takes the throne soon."

"He's in safe hands. Don't worry," Reeve said.

"I will try to learn all I can about the one who has come to spy on you," Neil said.

Duncan reached out and placed a firm hand on the thin man's shoulder. "You serve the true king well. He is pleased and looks forward to meeting you one day."

Neil smiled and tears gathered in his weary eyes. "I pray I live to see him crowned king."

"Be careful and be safe," Duncan said.

They left Neil with their father who, along with six warriors, escorted him to the border where one warrior would trail him until he was safely away.

The three brothers returned to the keep and went straight to the solar where all mission matters were discussed. It occupied the second floor of the keep, the doors kept lock. It was known that none could enter without permission and none dared.

"Neither of you have to say what you're thinking," Duncan said, sitting in one of the wooden chairs in front of the hearth.

Reeve said what Duncan wouldn't. "That Mercy's a spy. Problem is that it just doesn't make sense. I'm more concerned with the thought that Mercy could possess information about the true king."

"He's right," Trey said, sitting in the chair beside Duncan and stretching out his booted feet to the fire. "I could see why some might think it, she being daughter to the king. But if anyone knew of what you two have gone through, it just won't be a thought. However, I too, wonder if she knows something that she does not share."

"I'm glad you two see how improbable it is that she would be a spy," Duncan said.

"We're the only ones that matter," Reeve said. "Besides, this news can't be known, this has to remain between us."

Duncan nodded. "We let whoever it is set his own trap."

"And we're there to capture him," Trey said.

"As for Mercy having information about the true king," Duncan said, "if she does, she hides it well. She even eluded that it was simply a myth and nothing more."

"What if she doesn't know she carries information?" Reeve asked.

"That's a good possibility," Trey said. "Her mother never would have risked her status unless she had positive proof about the true king."

"Has Mercy spoken of her mother at all?" Reeve asked.

"No, she hasn't," Duncan said.

"Has she said where she was to meet up with her mother?" Reeve said.

Duncan shook his head. "I'm going to need to learn more about her mother and whatever plans she had for them."

"Probe carefully and quickly," Reeve warned. "Mercy may not know she carries vital information."

Duncan nodded, not happy with the thought. What had Mercy's mother been up to and just how much did Mercy truly know?

For the next couple of hours they discussed the matter and what each had learned on their prospective missions, until finally Duncan asked about Bryce.

"I saw him two days ago," Reeve said. "He's almost done forming plans with the western contingent. He should be home in a day or two."

"I have a thought," Duncan said. "I spent some time in Pict territory. I believe it would wise of us to befriend the Picts more than we have."

"They would fight with us?" Reeve asked.

"I believe they would. I don't think they're foolish enough to believe they are safe from this king," Duncan said.

A rapid double knock sounded at the door, the signal that it was someone known to them. Trey unlocked it and his father entered.

"How goes the news?" Carmag asked.

And for the next couple of hours the men talked, though through it all Duncan kept glancing at his chafed wrist. He wondered what Mercy was doing and worried that she felt a stranger in her new surroundings. And then there was the information she may know. He not only needed to speak with her, he needed to be with her. He needed to hold her hand.

Finally he asked his father, "Is Mother showing Mercy around the keep or the village."

Carmag shook his head. "Mara is busy delivering Brena's baby."

"Have you seen Mercy around?" Duncan asked, moving to the edge of his chair.

"I saw her walking in the village and waved, but didn't have time to stop since I wanted to come here and see what has been learned."

"I'm sure she's fine on her own," Trey said.

Duncan stood. "We've been shackled together for weeks and then I suddenly thrust her out on her own in a place where she knows no one. That's not very chivalrous of me."

Reeve grinned.

"Don't dare make a remark," Duncan warned and walked to the door.

"Go rescue your fair maiden in distress, but—"

"Shut up, Reeve," Duncan warned again and walked out slamming the door behind him.

Reeve laughed. "Damn, but if he isn't in love."

Trey and Carmag agreed with nods and laughter.

Mercy didn't remain at the smithy after Duncan had left. Finally being on her own, she wasn't certain what to do with herself and oddly enough she wasn't looking for company. She preferred time to think. Something she had done much of when she was home with her mother, or mostly when her mother wasn't home or otherwise occupied.

She had learned at a very young age to entertain herself, and when her father had insisted she be educated, she took to her lessons eagerly. After that, she explored everything she could. There was no holding her back. She wanted to learn everything about everything.

While she would have preferred to avoid her stitching lessons, her mother hadn't allowed it. She had told Mercy that there may come a day that she needed to stitch more than a garment. Her mother introduced and stressed the knowledge of numbers. She had insisted that Mercy know how to keep tally of what belonged to her and how to bargain for better prices with traveling merchants. And most importantly, how to hide money so that no one knew your true worth.

Her mother had established a small fortune while mistress to the king, but unfortunately she had spent much of it trying to locate the true king in an attempt to make Mercy his queen.

But all that was behind her now. Life had changed suddenly, in the blink of an eye, and Mercy had never had the time to consider the ramifications. She had been on the run since her mother had sent her away with a quick kiss and a promise they would be together soon.

She was shackled to Duncan soon after and only now

was she truly on her own. And she momentarily felt lost, adrift without oars and no shore in sight. She would love to believe that Duncan was her knight to the rescue, but there was her father to consider. And what man would truly wish to defy the king?

Though Duncan had, recalling how he had informed the soldier in no uncertain terms that she belonged to him now. She had told him once that she had belonged to no one, and yet she didn't argue when this time he claimed that she belonged to him. Perhaps it was because she felt that he belonged to her.

Mercy drifted through the village returning a frantic wave from Mara who was hurrying behind a man.

"A birthing," Mara called out and waved for her to join her.

Mercy declined with a vigorous shake of her head and a smile. She preferred to be alone right now.

She smiled, thinking about the baby about to be born. Babies were something she wanted. Being an only child was much too lonely, so she wanted to have a slew of babies, even though her mother had warned her against it. She had claimed that a man would lose interest in her after awhile, where one child would tie her to him, but not take the woman's attention away from the man.

She glanced around the active village. Many stared at her, but few approached or offered welcome. She wondered if they had already heard that she was the bastard daughter of the king. It would certainly explain the distance they were keeping from her.

The gawking and whispers continued as she explored and finally it became too much for her. No one greeted her pleasantly or hospitably and so she sought the only sanctuary where she would feel safe . . . she went to Duncan's room.

The bed had been freshened and the fire stoked. There was also a dark blue skirt and pale yellow blouse draped over the wooden chair. She assumed Mara had left them for her.

She yawned and thought a nap might due her well, and then she was suddenly seized by a reminder from her mother.

You must protect yourself at all costs.

Of course, her mother hadn't meant that she should physically protect herself, but suddenly it seemed like a necessity. And so she hurried out of the room and out of the keep and made her way back to the smithy.

He greeted her a bit apprehensively, but she didn't let that bother her.

"Harry," she said with a smile. "What type of weapon would be relatively easy for me to use in order to protect myself?"

Inquiring about his area of expertise brought a huge smile to his face and he was quick to reach for a weapon. It was a dagger, the blade slim, the metal handle light and a perfect fit for her hand. He explained the basic fundamentals of using the weapon. He also explained that the only way to attain any skill with it was endless practice.

He demonstrated a few moves and gave her much

advice, then offered the dagger to her as a gift. She insisted that there must be a way for her to repay his kindness.

"Someday perhaps there will be a way," he said and folded her fingers around the blade. "For now, I am pleased to know that you have a way of protecting yourself. Just promise me that you will practice."

She raised the dagger. "I will start this very moment."

She thanked him again, and with renewed spirit headed for the woods to practice.

It was more fun than she had imagined practicing with her new weapon. It felt right and fit particularly well in her small hand. She thrust and jabbed as Harry had shown her and paid mind to her feet as Harry also had warned.

It is a synchronized dance, he had told her, and you must learn the rhythm.

She was more than willing to learn, and so she listened to the melody in her head until her steps matched her thrusts and jabs. And she bent and stretched and bowed and swerved in a dance that if anyone saw would think her crazy.

She smiled as she continued practicing, feeling at ease for the first time since she and Duncan had parted. The first hour apart had been the most difficult. She had felt as if a part of her had been missing, as though a limb had been severed. It had been the strangest feeling and one that had not completely dissipated.

She didn't believe her head wound had pained her half as much as separating from Duncan and that worried her, for what if she had no choice but to leave him in order to protect him.

Her concerned thoughts directed her thrusts and they turned more powerful as her rumination grew more intense. She needed this, the knowledge that with practice and purpose she could learn to defend herself and the ones she loved.

If she had learned this along with her other lessons, perhaps she could have saved her mother. Instead, the soldiers had laughed when they had told her how they had watched as her mother's blood soaked into the ground around her and that how with her last breath she said—

"Mercy."

She spun around ready to jab, the voice not her mother's.

He attacked before she could turn, locking his hand over hers that held the weapon. While his other hand grappled with hers, though not for long since his strength overpowered and forced her arm tight against her waist, pinning her back against him.

In mere minutes she found herself weaponless and defenseless against him.

Now what did she do?

Chapter 26

The solution was simple.

"I've missed you," Mercy said, having known from his first touch that it was Duncan. A true foe would have been harsh. His touch had combined strength and passion, and besides, the scent of him was all too familiar.

He leaned down and nuzzled her neck. "And I you. But what is this you do here?"

She waggled the weapon in the air, though his hand remained firm around hers. "I asked Harry for a suitable weapon for me."

"Why? You have me and my family to protect you."

"But who protects you?"

He laughed. "I think I'm capable of doing that."

She titled her head back until it hit his chest and looked up at him. "That might not always be so. I want to be prepared for you and for me."

Duncan released her hand, keeping her pressed against him. He ran his hand up her exposed neck, until his fingers played along her chin. "I will always be there for you, Mercy."

She struggled to smile. "As much as I'd like to believe that, I know it may not always be possible."

"Then I will teach you how to defend yourself," he stated emphatically.

Her smile came easily. "I would like and appreciate that. Can we start now?"

"A brief lesson for now, for I wish to talk with you."

She nodded, glad for the time with him and glad he wished to talk with her, for she felt the same.

Duncan took the dagger from her and they stepped apart.

"A dagger is basically a companion to the sword. Its thrust span is limited, meaning unless you know how to move and avoid someone who attacks with a sword, you will not survive a fight. Remember that," he cautioned.

She nodded and listened intently, wanting to learn everything he could teach her.

"You were doing well, finding a good rhythm. It is important in any blade fight. You must know when and where to step to avoid injury and to do damage." He held his arms out to her. "Come, we will move together so that I can show you areas you must pay close attention to."

She went into his arms without hesitation. She knew she always would and the reason made no difference. She simply wanted to be there.

His large hand devoured her small one; she fit so snugly in his hand. And his arm went around her waist easing her back against him.

"Move with me."

That would be easy, since she had become so very familiar with his moves. Chained or not, they seemed to have a natural rhythm to them. She liked to believe it was born of love since it seemed so normal, so right.

He detailed various attack scenarios and demonstrated how she should approach them. He was also candid about ones that could prove fatal far more easily than others. But it was the thrusting and jabs he emphasized and warned, as Harry had done, that only practice would make perfect.

He worked with her over and over, admonishing and praising her efforts, and her confidence grew, and so did her passion. Their bodies moved in unison with each thrust and jab, and each time, her bottom bumped against his groin. And she was well aware that his passion had been stirred along with hers.

"Very soon you're going to find me inside you if we continue this," he said, keeping her flat against him just before a thrust.

"Then perhaps it is time for that kiss I promised you," she said.

He spun her around to face him. "It won't be just a kiss you give."

She rested her hand to his cheek, and his heated flesh tingled her palm. "I know."

"Then kiss me," he said impatiently.

Apprehension suddenly assaulted her, and she felt unsure. Would she do this right? Would her kiss please him? Then she almost laughed. He already desired her. She had nothing to worry about. She only needed to enjoy.

She ran her hands inside his shirt and slipped along his warm, hard chest until her arms circled his neck, and though she tugged at him to lower his head to hers, he did not budge.

"I cannot reach you if you don't lean down."

"Can't you?" he challenged.

She grinned, knowing exactly what he had in mind and holding tight around his neck she jumped up wrapping her legs around his waist. His hands quickly dipped beneath her skirt and grabbed firm hold of her bottom.

"Better?" she asked.

"Perfect," he said.

"Now can I kiss you?"

"By all means do."

She didn't know what took hold of her. Whether it was passion, rare need or pure love, but once her lips touched his, she kissed him like she had never done before. Her mouth took complete control and without thought or reason she found her lips making love to him and her body seemed to follow. She rubbed against him with wanton desire that soared beyond anything she had known.

"Love me," she whispered between kisses. "Just love me."

She thought she heard faint, distant thunder, but then realized it was that low rumble of his that started deep inside him and rose slowly, and she smiled, a tinkle of laughter spilling into the kiss.

"What do you find funny?" he asked after easing away from her lips.

"Not funny," she said, returning to his lips to brush across them. "Happy. I'm so very happy when I am with you."

A brilliant smile burst forth from him. "I'm glad, for I am very happy when I am with you, and I am about to make us both even happier."

"I can't wait," she said. "I don't want to. I want you now."

He obliged her, walking them over to a large oak tree and bracing her back against it. He lifted her to rest over him and entered her slow and easy, until she thrust her hips against him and took all of him inside her.

It went quick after that, their need great, their passion powerful and their climax explosive.

When sanity returned Duncan said, "That was a kiss worth waiting for."

"Truly?" she asked with a smile.

"The best kiss I've ever had, or doubt I'll ever have again," he teased.

"You challenge me to do better?"

"If you think you can," he teased.

"You'll just have to wait and see," she said.

A rustle of leaves had them scurrying to right themselves, and Mercy was retrieving her dagger when a young boy, no more than four years, suddenly appeared.

He burst into tears as soon as he saw Duncan and ran up to him throwing his tiny arms around Duncan's thick leg. Duncan scooped him up into his arms.

"What have I told you, Rand, about wandering into the woods by yourself?"

He sniffled through his tears. "Alida lost me."

"It is your big sister's fault, is it?" Duncan asked.

Rand nodded, his tears subsiding and pointed at Mercy. "She's pretty."

"Yes, she certainly is pretty, but we need to find your sister," Duncan said. "Where did you leave her?"

Rand twisted round in Duncan's arms, smiling and jabbing his tiny finger in all directions. "That way, that way, that way."

Mercy had to chuckle. He was so adorable, red curly hair, round, chubby face and the roundest green eyes she had ever seen.

"What were you and your sister doing when she lost you?" Mercy asked.

"Picking sticks."

Duncan explained. "His mother, Cora, crafts most of our baskets."

"Big," Rand said, swinging his arms wide, then bringing them back together. "Small." He grinned. "Ma makes them all."

She grinned. "He is so cute."

"He is a terror, forever getting lost and getting into something."

Rand giggled as Duncan tickled him, and then he threw his small arms around his neck. "You found me."

"More like you found me, little one."

"We should find his sister," Mercy said. "She must be frantic looking for him."

"It's happened so many times, I'm surprised she didn't tie a rope around him," Duncan said.

Rand laughed, tossing his head back. "Alida tie me. I broke fee."

Mercy had to laugh. Rand may be a handful but she wouldn't mind a son like him, full of life and inquisitive enough to explore on his own.

Suddenly frantic shouts ripped through the air. "Rand! Rand!"

"Alida!" Rand shouted back.

"Rand!" the young girl yelled.

"I have him, Alida," Duncan called out.

"Thank God," Alida shouted and within moments burst past the trees.

She looked barely ten years, pretty and with the same red hair and green eyes as Rand. The small lad stuck his arms out as soon as he saw her. She took him, though how she managed to hold the squiggling child was beyond Mercy.

"I'll see you two home safe," Duncan said.

"Thank you, but I must go retrieve my bundle of branches. Mother is expecting me to bring them home and will be disappointed if I don't."

"I'll go with you to get your bundle," Duncan said.

Mercy wasn't surprised that he wouldn't leave Alida and Rand on their own. She believed that Duncan didn't realize just how much of an honorable man he was and how very proud she was of him.

Mercy stepped forward and extended her hand to the girl. "Hi, I'm Mercy and I'll help too."

"That's very kind of you, m'lady," Alida said with a bow of her head.

Mercy caught her smile before it faltered, not wanting the young lass to think she had said something wrong. She hadn't expected to be addressed as a noble woman. After all, she was the bastard daughter of the king, not his legitimate daughter, though she was his only child.

To Alida's relief, Duncan took the restless Rand and hoisted him up to sit on his shoulders. The child giggled with glee and they were soon off to help Alida.

When all was done and the children deposited safely at their parent's cottage, and a beautifully crafted basket given to Mercy in appreciation for her help, Duncan surprised her with a suggestion.

"We'll go gather some food from Cook, put it in your basket and find a private spot to eat and talk."

She was thrilled with the idea and let him know. "I would love to do that."

And so they hurried off.

Cook was Etty, more round than tall and with a curt nature.

"You're disturbing me," she yelled at Duncan and Mercy took a step behind him.

Duncan cajoled her with a smile and sweet talk. "You make the best bread. I can't resist it. And your meat pies?" He rubbed his stomach. "Mmm, delicious."

"Go on with you." She shooed at him.

"Not without some of your tasty treats."

She capitulated, though Mercy hadn't expected her to.

"I'll give you a few," she said waving a wooden spoon at him. "No more."

"Whatever you give me I'll appreciate," Duncan assured her.

To Mercy's amazement they left with a full basket.

"I didn't think she would give you anything," Mercy admitted once outside.

"You have to know how to handle Etty if you want to get food from her," Duncan said. "The real problem is keeping it from others once you've got it. We need to find a place fast before Trey or Reeve gets a whiff of it."

He placed a hand to the small of her back and hurried her forward while on the alert for his brothers.

"We can share—"

"Absolutely not," Duncan said.

Mercy was surprised at his adamancy. "Why?"

"To the victor goes the spoils."

"That doesn't sound at all like you."

"Listen, I was the only one who could cajole Etty into giving us food, and each time I did, my brothers wound up eating it all. If they get a whiff of this, there'll be nothing left for us."

"Duncan!"

"Damn," Duncan muttered and looked to Mercy. "Don't turn around and look at Reeve, just keep walking."

Mercy laughed and did as she was told delighted by and envious of the brothers' antics. How she wished she had siblings growing up.

"Wait up," Reeve yelled. "I know what you've got in that basket and you have to share."

Mercy laughed as she hurried her pace alongside Duncan.

"He doesn't understand the meaning of the word share," Duncan said.

Mercy continued to find the whole matter amusing. She could just imagine them as young lads running off with a basket of Etty's food and fighting over the contents. They must have wonderful memories of earlier times together.

"I know you can hear me, Duncan, and you're not sneaking off with that basket without me."

"What basket?" Trey called out.

"Damn," Duncan mumbled again.

"Get him, Trey, he got a basket of food from Etty," Reeve shouted.

Mercy was now running to keep up with Duncan, though she didn't know how long she would be able to keep pace with him since she was laughing harder.

It didn't matter though, because within the next second a horn sounded so suddenly and so sharply, that she stopped dead and so did Duncan.

He grabbed her arm and shoved the basket into her hand. "The king's soldiers approach. Go to the keep and stay there until I come for you."

She nodded and hurried off as his brothers joined him and they disappeared in the opposite direction.

"Rand! Rand!"

Mercy heard Cora and Alida calling for the young

lad as she was passing their cottage. The look of terror on their faces made her stop.

"What's wrong?"

"We can't find Rand," Cora said, clearly upset. "He was here a moment ago and now he's gone."

"I should have watched him more carefully," Alida said through tears.

Her mother took her in her arms. "Nonsense. Rand has a mind of his own. There is no stopping him. He knows to go to the keep when the horn sounds. He's probably there already."

"Let's go see," Mercy suggested, knowing the women should be seeking shelter there.

Once inside they searched frantically for Rand but couldn't find him.

Mara approached them. "What's wrong?"

"Rand is nowhere to be found," Mercy explained.

"I'm sure he's fine. He's a smart one. We'll find him after this is done."

Cora looked ready to protest and Mara slipped an arm around her. "You know the men are needed. Rand will do fine. He always does. We will find him later. This will be done soon enough."

Cora nodded, though clearly she didn't agree.

"We can't just leave the lad out there on his own," Mercy protested.

"We can and we will," Mara said. "There are no men to spare to search for him now."

"Then I'll go," Mercy said.

"I believe Duncan ordered you to remain in the keep as all women do," Mara challenged.

"If he had known Rand was in need of help—"

"You don't know if Rand is in need of help and even if Duncan knew he would still have ordered you to remain in the safety of the keep."

"I cannot remain here when a small, helpless child is out there alone," Mercy argued.

"I'm afraid you'll have to," Mara said sternly.

Mercy tossed her chin up. "No, I won't. You hold no authority over me. I do as I please." She turned to Cora and Alida. "I'll go find Rand and bring him here. Is there a particular place he might go?"

"You will not leave here," Mara ordered.

"You cannot stop me."

"There's a small grove not far from the cottage where he likes to play. A worn path leads the way there," Alida said. "I'll go with you."

Mercy shook her head. "No, you must stay here. I'll bring your brother back."

"I forbid you to leave here," Mara said.

Mercy simply smiled and said something she never ever thought she would. "You cannot forbid me to do anything. I am daughter to the king."

Silence settled over the hall and Mercy didn't care how loud she had said it, or who had heard. She turned and hurried out.

Chapter 27

Mercy had no time to think of what she had just done. Later she could ponder it and most certainly offer an apology to Mara, but right now she needed to find Rand. She maneuvered through women and children running to the keep and headed to Cora's cottage. She entered the woods just beyond and stilled for a moment listening.

The soldiers could be anywhere, and if they found her, she would be returned to her father, and she wasn't ready for that. And besides, she had to find Rand. He was out there alone and needed help.

She glanced down and realized that she had kept hold of the dagger all this time and was relieved she had. She could protect herself and Rand if necessary. Not that she was by any means skilled, but she knew a little and could possibly make it appear she knew a lot more.

She found the trail Alida had spoken about and with careful, though speedy, steps she followed it. She didn't allow herself to think. She kept her mind free and eyes and ears alert.

It didn't take her long to find the groove, though Rand wasn't there. She stood amongst the spreading oaks and could see why the young lad would come here. The many lush trees were perfect for climbing . . .

She looked up and there was Rand, eyes closed tight and his little body curled up in the crook of a thick branch.

"Rand, it's me, Mercy."

His eyes sprang wide and he peered down at her. "Mercy, you come for me?"

"Yes. I've come to take you to your mother." She heard a distant rustling noise and with a finger to her lips, she cautioned Rand to be silent. He nodded and hugged the tree tighter.

She didn't know what produced the sound and not wanting to take any chances, she decided to climb the tree and join Rand. If soldiers were afoot they may have heard her and Rand talking and would comb the area in search of them.

The tree was the safest place for them right now.

Her mother would have disapproved if she had ever known that her daughter climbed trees. Not only climbed them, but loved climbing them. So it was with little effort that Mercy grabbed hold of a branch and climbed up.

Once she reached Rand, she decided it was best if they climbed a bit higher. Having tucked the dagger in her boot, she took Rand in her arms and climbed two branches higher to nestle quite comfortably in the crook of a solid branch.

She cautioned silence again with her finger to her lips

and Rand nodded and cuddled closer against her. Mercy wrapped her arm around him and held tight. She'd let no one harm this child. *No one*.

They waited and it wasn't long before she heard . . .

"Have you seen her yet?" a man's voice asked.

Rand grabbed tighter to Mercy and she felt his little body tremble. She squeezed him close, letting him know he was safe with her.

"I've seen her from a distance."

Mercy barely heard the other man's reply, his voice no more than a whisper.

"You have three days, no more. Get her and bring her to the border."

"But—"

"Three days," the man repeated.

Footfalls drifted off, but Mercy remained where she was, again warning Rand to remain quiet. She didn't know if it was safe just yet and intended to wait awhile. Besides the brief exchange upset her. She knew they spoke about her, and she wondered how they had gotten one of their own men into the village. And why didn't her father simply attack and be done with it?

He had gotten to be king because he had let nothing stand in his way, not even claims that no true royal blood ran through him. He had defied the kings who ruled various areas of Scotland and through bloody battles claimed victory and dominance.

Why not do again what he had done once before?

And why did he seek her return so tenaciously?

The questions troubled her and she would need to find the answers.

"I think we can climb down now," Mercy said softly to Rand.

"Safe?" he asked.

"I think we'll be safe, though we should be as quiet as we can be."

Rand nodded and Mercy smiled.

It took less effort to climb down than it did up and in no time they were on the ground. Rand remained clutched to Mercy and she took quick steps to get them away and closer to home.

She took no more than a few steps when a man stepped out from among the dense trees. Startled, she stumbled back, righted herself and then realized he looked familiar.

"Bailey?" she asked.

"Aye, it's me."

Rand hugged her neck tight.

"It's all right, Rand. I know this man and he won't harm us," she said, glaring at Bailey as if defying him to deny it.

Bailey reached out and tickled Rand under the chin. "I'm a friend."

Rand laughed, though kept firm hold of Mercy.

"Are you?" she asked.

"We should return to the keep. It's not safe here," he said.

Mercy nodded and began walking, Bailey following beside her.

"I climbed trees when I was a lad," Bailey said.

"Like to climb," Rand said and yawned.

They walked a bit in silence and when Rand's head finally hit Mercy's shoulder in sleep, she said, "You knew we were in the tree when you spoke with the soldier."

Bailey nodded.

"The noise I heard. You purposely made it to warn us."

Bailey nodded again.

"I don't understand." Mercy shook her head. "You helped Duncan and me once and you warn me now. Why then do you help the soldiers?"

"They have my wife."

Mercy gasped.

"We left shortly after you and Duncan stopped at our cottage. Though we were cautious they found us and claimed us enemies of the king. Of course they had no proof of anything, but still they took us prisoners along with others they had taken captive for various reasons. All I could think about was the safety of my wife and unborn child."

"Where is Kate?"

"I'm not sure where they took her. When I was told I could save her and my child, it didn't matter to me what I had to do. I knew I would agree to anything and so did they. I was told that if I found you and brought you to them, Kate and I could go free." He shook his head. "I had no choice."

"Of course you didn't," she said.

"I picked up your tracks fast enough, but lost you when you entered Pict territory, since I would not dare go there. Your earlier tracks gave me a good indication of your destination, and I knew if I kept going that way, it would eventually lead me to the stronghold. And I had no doubt Duncan would get you safely home. So I came here and waited. Everyone was so good and generous to me, and then you arrived and I saw how you and Duncan looked at each other." He shook his head again. "You two love each other as much as Kate and I love each other. And I knew the only way I could save my wife was to ask you."

"Ask me?"

"To return with me so that they will set my wife and unborn child free. You could do this. You're daughter to the king."

Mercy stopped walking and stared at him.

"I don't know what else to do," he pleaded.

"We could talk with Duncan. A rescue could be planned."

"They are too busy planning for the king's return," he said.

She looked at him oddly.

"You don't know where you are?" Bailey asked.

"Duncan's land."

He shook his head. "You're in the stronghold of the true king of Scotland."

She took a step back startled by his remark. "Duncan fights for the true king?"

"He and his brothers were raised to protect the true king and to succeed in seeing that he claims the throne."

"How do you know this?" he asked.

"There are men who cross the land recruiting others to join the fight. I heard one such man speak, and after hearing him tell of the brothers, who from the time they were young, trained to help seat the rightful king of Scotland, knew I wanted to be part of that fight."

"How did Kate feel about your decision?"

"She agreed, wanting a better and freer life for our child. And after you and Duncan showed up, and I realized he was one of the brothers, I knew I could dally no more. Kate and I had to journey to the stronghold, and besides, I knew my wife and child would be safer there."

"How did you know where it was?"

"That was simple. I only needed to track you and Duncan."

"You followed us?" she asked.

"I'm a good tracker and can track from a distance, but enough of this. Will you help me?"

Mercy didn't know what to say. She certainly couldn't be responsible for a mother and unborn child's death, and yet she knew Duncan would never agree to her returning to her father. It was a quandary and the solution not an easy one.

"I will not let your wife die because of me, but I know not how to approach this matter. I must think on it."

"You won't tell Duncan, will you?" he asked anxiously.

"It will be difficult for me not to do."

"He will never permit you to leave."

"He cannot keep me against my will," she said.

"No, but his love can keep you here, just as my love brought me here."

He was right about that, which made the situation all the more difficult. She had no idea what she would do.

"Let me think on it," she said again.

"Please don't take long. I have but three days," Bailey pleaded. "And I fear for my wife's life."

When they reached the edge of the woods, Bailey insisted that it was better if no one saw them talking and pleaded that she meet him at the groove tomorrow at dawn.

She shook her head. "No. I do not know if I will have an answer by then and I do not trust that you will not turn me over to the soldiers."

Upset, Bailey said, "I wouldn't do that."

"You told me you would do anything to save your wife and unborn child, and I believe you. I will be in touch when I decide." With that Mercy left him and walked out of the woods.

Upset herself, Mercy didn't know what she was going to do, though if she intended for Kate not to suffer because of her, her actions were clear. She would need to return to her father. That would mean losing Duncan, but then if he fought for the true king of Scotland and she was the daughter, bastard or not, of the reigning king, how safe was she with the true king?

The chain wasn't even off a day and she felt more trapped than ever.

When she rounded Cora's cottage she could see men and horses loitering in front of the keep's steps. As her steps took her closer she could see that it was Duncan and his two brothers, their horses prancing in agitation as Mara spoke to her sons.

It wasn't long before Mara pointed in her direction, and Duncan didn't waste a moment; he rode straight for her.

When he reached her, she didn't let him speak first. "I found Rand."

"So I see," he said curtly. "But you should not have left the keep."

"I needed to," she insisted. "Rand was missing and with soldiers lurking about, his safety was of concern to me."

"So you defy my orders and leave?"

"I did what I felt was right," she said.

Rand woke then, lifting his little head in a stretch. As soon as he saw Duncan his eyes flew open and he smiled. "Mercy climb tree. Save me."

He glared at her. "You climbed a tree?"

"I did," she admitted proudly and spotting Cora and Alida running toward her, began walking in their direction.

Duncan followed and said nothing until after Cora

and her children had taken their leave, though not before they had thanked Mercy profusely.

The agitation in his dark eyes told her that a fight was brewing, though she wished it was a grouchy look she had seen for then the solution would be easy. She wondered if perhaps it would work anyway.

"I think we should settle this in your bedchamber," she suggested.

That brought him off his horse to stand in front of her. "You think coupling will settle this so easily?"

"No, but it might ease your agitation, which will allow us to discuss this more reasonably."

"You think *me* unreasonable?"

"No. *You're* agitated. I want *us* to discuss it reasonably," she clarified.

"So we couple and all of a sudden we're reasonable?"

She placed her hand on his chest, though did not slip it beneath his shirt. She simply let it rest there. "Perhaps not, but I doubt you'll be agitated anymore."

Her tender touch had the desired affect she had hoped for. He smiled.

"I suppose you could be right," he said.

"We won't know if we don't try."

"That is a good point," he agreed.

"And afterwards we'll talk, which we have been trying to do all day," she reminded him. "Perhaps it would be best if we had food brought to your bedchamber so that we won't be disturbed. After all, we have much to discuss and I have yet to eat."

"That might be wise."

Finally, she ran her hand beneath his shirt, her fingers crawling along his muscled chest. "So then we'll give it a try and see how it works?"

"Aye, we'll give it a try."

They approached the keep steps, his brothers, father and mother stood waiting, obviously wondering what had gone on between her and Duncan, and if he would do anything about her defiance of his order.

He threw the reins of his stallion to Reeve and said, "See to him." Then he turned and scooped Mercy up, flinging her over his shoulder and giving her bottom a slap. "I have to see to Mercy's punishment."

He was demonstrating his authority over her and it annoyed the heck out of her. She'd been the one who handled the matter and rather wisely, proposing a settlement that worked for them both and now he goes and makes it seem like he's handling the matter his way.

What to do about it?

The solution came quick and it was simple. As he walked up the steps to the keep, she raised her head and sent everyone a victorious grin.

Chapter 28

~~~✦~~~

Duncan lay spent, Mercy spread naked over him.

"It certainly worked," he said with a laugh. "I'm not agitated anymore, but I am famished."

Mercy raised her head off his chest and grinned at him. "So am I."

He slapped her naked bottom gently. "Then let's eat."

They scampered out of bed, Mercy reaching for her blouse. He snatched it out of her hands.

"I like you just the way you are."

"The room holds a chill," she protested rubbing her arms.

He grabbed his plaid and wrapped it around her shoulders, though left her breasts partially exposed. "Better?"

"Much," she said and hurried to the table.

They took seats opposite each other and Mercy began munching on a variety of foods. Duncan poured them wine, then rested back in the chair. He had much he wished to discuss with her, but for the moment he simply wanted to enjoy the sight of her.

Her dark hair was tousled from their vigorous love-making and her neck and breasts were dotted with love bites that already were beginning to fade. God, but he loved this woman.

"Eat," she urged with a sweet laugh, shoving a thick piece of cheese at him. "You claimed you were hungry."

"I am," he said snatching it from her, though he didn't tell her that it was she he hungered for all the time.

"What did the soldiers want?" she asked.

He was glad she asked for they needed to talk. "You."

"But you already told them I wouldn't be returning to my father."

"For some insane reason they thought I might have changed my mind."

"I wonder what my father wants from me," she said.

"I was thinking the same. Perhaps you have something that belongs to him."

"No," Mercy said, shaking her head. "I left with only the clothes I wore. And Mother had no intentions of bringing anything more than a satchel. Mother always planned everything. So I knew when she frantically began throwing things in a satchel and demanding I leave and wait at the river's edge, a favorite place of mine, that her decision had been made in haste and out of necessity."

"You didn't ask her why?"

She rolled her eyes. "I never dared question her authority. Repercussions could be swift and painful."

"Do you know if she angered your father and worried over the consequences?"

"I know they had recently argued over me, and while I wasn't privy to the heated discussion, my mother's mumblings gave me a good indication as to why she was upset."

"Why?" he asked, eager to know.

"I believe my father had made arrangements for me to become mistress to a nobleman of not very high status or wealth."

"He intended to give you away to a man?" Duncan asked, slowly moving forward in his seat.

"I imagine it was a lucrative agreement for my father."

"He intended to just give you to a man without thought or consideration?" he said, anger building with every word he spoke.

"I am his bastard daughter. He can do as he pleases with me. Ignore me if he wished. I'm sure he felt he was doing best for me."

"You defend him?"

"No. Not at all. I didn't want to be mistress to a man I never met. I never wanted to be a mistress at all. I saw what it had done to my mother and I did not want the same for myself. But truly what choice did I have? I had no money."

"What of your mother? She sounded like a wise woman. Surely she had managed to tuck away extra coins."

Mercy nodded. "She did, but spent most of it on her own plan for me."

"And what plan was that?"

"She would not detail it for me, but I surmised that she searched for the true king with intentions of seeing that I became his mistress."

"Did she find him?" Duncan asked anxiously, believing that the pieces of the puzzle were about to fall into place.

"From her excitement and fear I believe she discovered something, but what I don't know."

"Who did she fear?"

"Since she rushed me away from the house, I'd say she feared that she had learned that my father had discovered her betrayal and that soldiers were on the way."

"How would she have known?"

"My mother had many spies in various places," Mercy said. "There wasn't much she couldn't find out."

"And she gave you no indication of what she may have discovered?"

Mercy thought a moment. "Come to think of it, just as I was leaving the cottage, she grabbed my arm and said something odd to me."

Duncan felt every muscle grow taut, worried that somehow her mother had uncovered secret information concerning the true king.

"She said, 'You will see it in his eyes and know.'"

Duncan rubbed his chin, trying to make sense of it, but unable to. "Know what?"

Mercy shrugged. "I have no idea what she was referring to. She traced a symbol in the palm of my hand and muttered something."

"Show me," Duncan said and held his hand out to her.

She cupped it in hers and faintly drew a cross in the palm of his hand, then pressed her thumb in the center. "I remember," she said softly. "When two are one, it will be done."

Duncan eased his hand out of hers and refilled his tankard. He didn't trust himself to speak. How Mercy's mother had discovered the secret symbol and words known only to the true king, and those few known to him since he was young, astounded him.

She could have only learned them from one in the inner circle. But who? Who would betray the true king? And why to this woman?

"I had forgotten that, but then everything had been done in such haste and confusion. I was sitting looking over a piece of hide with drawings on it I had found in mother's sewing basket when I went looking for thread and needle in her sitting room. That's where mother found me when she had rushed into the cottage and told me that we were leaving right there and then. We had not a moment to waste."

"A piece of hide with drawings on it?" Duncan asked.

"Yes. It was strange and old. Mother grabbed it from me and threw it into the hearth. The flames consumed it with haste."

"Do you remember the drawings?"

"No," she said and reached for an apple.

Duncan turned silent. He was sure the old piece of hide was where it had always been, safely tucked away in a chest in the solar. But she had called the hide strange and old and that was always how he and his brothers referred to it.

"You have asked me many questions and I have answered them. Now it's my turn," Mercy said.

"Ask," he said and fought the urge to go see if the piece of hide was where it had always been.

"Why do the soldiers not attack?"

"We outnumber them and they know it. Besides the king to the north holds no favor for your father and would send his sizable forces to help us."

"But he had accepted my father as ruling king."

"He had no choice. Your father claimed the ruling throne and there was nothing he could do unless he declared war and shed his clansmen's blood. He did what many chose to do. Wait for the true king to appear and claim his rightful title."

"You fight for the true king?"

"Aye, I do."

"This land," she said. "Who does it belong to?"

"I am told the true king of Scotland. It is here the warriors are trained and made ready for battle."

Mercy stared at him, her eyes turning wide. "And you brought the daughter of the present king to the true king's stronghold?"

"No. I brought the woman I love there."

He hadn't expected complete silence from her. She seemed to freeze, and he had to admit he hadn't planned to blurt it out like that, or admit it just yet. But for some insane reason, it had simply spilled from his lips.

It seemed that the more they had talked, the more he felt her slipping away from him and he wouldn't have it. He wouldn't lose her, he couldn't. He loved her, loved her beyond any reasonable breath of sanity.

"Say something," he demanded.

"I know you love," she said softly. "And I love you. I never doubted that we loved each other even though we never spoke the words. It took me a moment to realize that you actually spoke them aloud. I usually hear you say them in my thoughts and dreams, and so hearing you say it aloud shocked me."

He smiled. "I shocked myself."

"Why did you choose to tell me now?" she asked reaching her hand across the table to him.

He quickly took hold of it. It fitted so comfortably, so right as it always did, as if the heavens had crafted them that way.

"With all that has happened between us and all that is yet to come, I didn't want to waste a moment. I wanted you to know how I felt. How I would always feel about you." He grinned. "You stole my heart."

She laughed softly. "No. You gave it to me as I gave you mine."

He stood, though didn't let go of her hand and walked

around the table. He lifted her in his arms, kissing her, and then walked to the bed. He placed her down, covering her with his body.

"I'm going to make love to you," he whispered in between kisses.

She smiled and wrapped her arms around him. "All night. Make love to me all night."

A couple of hours later exhaustion claimed Mercy, but not Duncan. He eased her out of his arms and slipped on his plaid. He quietly closed the door behind him and made his way down to the solar.

The piece of hide hadn't left his mind. It had remained in the recesses of his thoughts and had risen to torment him after Mercy had fallen asleep. He had to make certain for himself that it was still there. It was important to the king and only he knew its hidden meaning.

It was late and no doubt all were in their beds. Still, he took cautious and quiet steps down to the solar, a chill running up his legs from his bare feet, since he hadn't taken time to slip on his boots.

When no one was in attendance the room was kept locked, the key hidden beneath a stone in the stone floor. Duncan retrieved it, unlocked the door and slipped in, easing the door closed behind him.

He took a candle from atop the mantel and held it close enough to the hearth's flames for the wick to light. He then walked over to the corner where a large chest was tucked. He opened it and rummaged around until he found a small chest. He lifted it and tucked it beneath his arm to carry over to the table, where he sat it and the candle.

The chest had no lock. There was no need. Few people knew of its existence. He hesitated a moment, his hand on the latch.

Two raps sounded at the door, causing Duncan to jump, though he bid the person enter since he had given the appropriate signal.

Duncan grinned and left the chest to go greet his brother Bryce.

They grasped hands and hugged, Duncan slapping him on the back.

"Did you only arrive?" Duncan asked and seeing the fatigue in his eyes, he knew that his brother had pushed to get home, just as they all did.

"Aye, though the journey was long, it was fruitful. I have much to share, though it will wait until morning. I was seeking the peace and comfort of my bed when I approached the second floor and thought I heard someone at the solar door."

"And you were right."

"What are you doing here at this late hour?" Bryce asked.

"It would take me too long to explain what brought me here and you are tired. But I have good reason to be here this late. I wish to make certain that the strange and old piece of hide with the drawings is still where it has always been."

"Why would you think—"

Duncan shook his head. "Don't ask. I'm probably wrong, but I need to prove it to myself."

"Then let's do it."

The brothers walked over to the table, the flickering flames casting shadows over the small chest, making it appear as if claws were laying claim to it.

Both stood for a moment staring at it, as if neither wanted to open it. The piece had always been treated with reverence, even though only one knew its true worth.

Bryce nodded to Duncan, as if telling him that it was time to be done with this, and Duncan agreed with a nod of his own.

Duncan opened the latch and threw back the lid.

Both men stood staring.

The chest was empty.

Chapter 29

Mercy woke alone and with scattered thoughts. Her musings jumped from delight to worry and she had no idea what she would do. Her heart soared and she laughed, recalling how Duncan had told her how he loved her. He had blurted it out so unexpectedly that he had not only shocked her, but himself.

She loved that he had done that, not giving thought, simply saying what he felt. It meant so much more hearing it like that from him. Making love just afterward made it seem as if they sealed their love, claiming it forever theirs.

That moment was forever etched in her memory, and while she would have preferred to have it followed with thoughts of a happy future together with Duncan, there were too many things that stood in the way.

She, being daughter to the present king, and he fighting for the true king were the largest looming threats to their happiness, not to mention Bailey's dire situation. So while it was grand being in love, she worried that their love would never see fruition. That they would never wed, never have children, never share a life together.

Mercy stretched herself out of bed, concerned by what step she should take next. Having spoken last night with Duncan about her mother brought back memories more clearly. She had forgotten what her mother had said and done, though she certainly couldn't berate herself over it.

It had been a day she would have rather not remembered. She had never seen her mother look so frantic. Her eyes had been wide with fear and instead of her usual impeccable appearance, she appeared disheveled, her brow perspiring, almost as if she had run a distance.

She had never thought her mother had ever run, but that day it looked as if she had run out of fright, or perhaps for her life.

Mercy shivered and hurried to dress, though she couldn't get her mother's wide-eyed, glaring expression out of her mind. She even recalled her mother shaking her and insisting that she obey every word. That Mercy was to go and stay at the river's edge and not move, *dare not move*, until she came for her.

She hadn't told Duncan all her mother had said to her after she had drawn the symbol on her palm. She didn't want to. She felt her mother's words were meant for her and her alone and she intended to keep it that way.

After her mother had drawn the symbol she had said, "I'm sorry, Mercy. I'm so very sorry."

Mercy had assumed her mother's apology had been

for her plan that had gone terribly wrong and placed her daughter in harm's way. And she was grateful her mother had acknowledged her regret, since it made Mercy feel that her mother truly had loved her.

She only wished that her mother hadn't suffered for her own folly. But that was behind her now, in the past, and her mother had told her that the past was best left in the past. Right now she had to consider Bailey's predicament and what to do about it.

She could keep silent and simply return to her father, but somehow she wondered if that was the right choice. Her father had never shown her any particular favor, let alone love. She had learned at a very early age that if she did as he asked, he treated her well. Do something that displeased him, and he wasn't so kind.

Had her father assumed she had joined in her mother's plan, or had he found out that she had no knowledge of it? And could he truly be trusted to free Bailey's wife Kate? Or had she already suffered her fate?

There was a rap at the door just as she finished dressing.

Mercy bid the person entrance as she slipped on her boots.

Mara entered, shutting the door behind her.

Mercy stood. She liked Mara and she wanted no bad feelings between them. So she offered an apology.

"I am sorry for the way I spoke to you," Mercy said. "And very sorry for claiming power I do not have."

Mara grinned. "But you do have it, lassie. You are

daughter to the king, bastard or not, and you have the power to speak as you did."

"I meant no disrespect."

"I know that, or else I would have handled it differently," Mara said with a twinkle in her eye.

"I want us to be friends," Mercy said. She truly liked Mara and admired how she combined her blunt nature with a smile.

"We are," Mara claimed, "and always will be."

"Then you forgive me?"

"Noting to forgive, lassie," Mara insisted. "I came to fetch you for breakfast."

"I haven't missed it then?" Mercy asked. "I feared I slept through it and I'm famished."

"Then you best hurry. Those lads of mine usually don't leave a single scrap."

Mercy smiled and followed Mara out the door. It felt good being included in the family. There was more than enough reason for them not to want her around, reason to be rid of her, and yet they welcomed her. Even with all the problems she presented, they treated her kindly. She may have arrived here only recently, but it was easy to see that these were good people.

And people her father would sooner see dead.

Mercy spotted Duncan as soon as she and Mara entered the great hall. To her, he stood out among the men. It wasn't merely his size, which was considerable, there was much more. He had a commanding presence about him and a sharp intelligence. Combine both and it was obvious to see that leading came easy to him.

A crack of thunder sounded outside and a fierce wind whipped around the keep in a whistle-like sound, causing Mercy to rub her chilled arms.

A storm brewed, not a good omen at all, Mercy thought, and so she wore a tentative smile, not sure that it fit the moment. The brothers and their father were gathered around a table not far from the hearth.

She was familiar with all who were there except one man. His back was to her and it was wide, his shirt taut as if it didn't quite fit him. Long dark hair fell past his wide shoulders and when he raised his heavy tankard, she saw that his thick hand palmed it and held firm, not an easy feat without strength.

The men stood when they saw the women approach and moved, offering them seats, and then the men settled around the two women, though not before the stranger gave Mara a kiss.

"You should have woken me last night when you got home," Mara scolded with a grin, then turned to Mercy. "This is my son Bryce."

Mara claimed the four her own, though Trey was the only son she had born. And the way her eyes brightened when she looked upon all four would make an observer think she had labored to bring each one into the world, her love was that obvious.

"Hello," Bryce said.

Mercy took a moment to respond since there was something about this man that captured the attention.

He certainly had fine features, even handsome ones, but it wasn't that, or the size of him, which was quite large. He was a fine specimen of a Highlander warrior, and yet he seemed much more.

"A pleasure to meet you," she finally said.

"The pleasure is mine," he replied. "You truly are a beauty."

"Thank you," she said a bit flustered and leaned against Duncan, who slipped his arm around her.

"Aren't you going to threaten to beat him?" Reeve asked Duncan.

"Why?"

"You threatened me when I called Mercy a beauty."

"You say it differently than Bryce," Duncan said.

"I do not," Reeve protested.

"Duncan's got you on that one," Trey said.

"I agree," Bryce said with a laugh.

"Enough," Mara scolded. "You'll have the poor lassie thinking that you do nothing but argue."

"They argue," Reeve said pointing at his brothers. "I don't since I'm the one who's always right."

"Shall we refresh his memory?" Bryce said, looking to his brothers.

"You'll not be talking of your antics in front of Mercy," Mara warned. "You'll have her running in fright."

Mercy chuckled, enjoying the teasing banter that continued through the meal as stories were exchanged about when the four were just young lads. She didn't know how Mara had ever dealt with the many things the four had gotten themselves into, though the woman's huge smile certainly indicated that she had enjoyed the challenges her sons had presented.

She wouldn't mind having a similar experience, whether sons or daughters, it would be nice to have her own family. She had no doubt that Duncan would make a good father.

Bailey would too.

The sudden thought wiped the smile from her face. She quickly forced its return, not wanting anyone to notice that something had disturbed her. But it did and deeply. Here she sat, sharing funny and endearing stories about family while Bailey sat worrying over the safety of his.

Mercy waited for a loll in the conversation and asked, "Have the soldiers taken their leave yet?"

"No, they intend to wait a few days to see if we change our minds and hand you over to them," Duncan said and laughed. "Something that will never happen."

"What if they force your hand?" she asked.

"How so?" Bryce asked.

Mercy shrugged, not sure, but knowing her father a shrewd man. She saw it in his dealings with her mother, who was just as shrewd. And she worried that they were sadly misjudging him. He certainly hadn't gained the throne through stupidity.

She finally voiced her concern. "He is king, isn't that enough?"

"This area of the Highlands did not fall under his rule

easily," Bryce explained. "Unrest has continued since he took reign and he's wisely left it be."

"Why?' Mercy asked.

"His armies were needed on the southern borders," Trey said. "The English are seeking help."

"It allowed the north time to regroup and grow strong," Reeve added. "And now we are a force to reckon with, while his armies remain scattered."

"Your father knows he does not have the troops he needs to conquer us," Bryce said.

"That is why he searches for the true king," Carmag said. "He is the hope of the people, and if your father kills the true king, he kills that hope and seals his rule."

"But what do I have to do with all this?" she asked, shaking her head, more confused than ever over her part in it all. "I am merely his bastard daughter. Why be adamant about my return when he had previously wanted me dead?"

She noticed that Bryce and Duncan exchanged a knowing glance and gooseflesh prickled her skin. They knew something.

"That is something we need to find out, and we will," Carmag assured her. "But right now it is time for daily reports."

"Go," Mara urged. "I shall show Mercy around the keep since it storms outside."

Duncan looked to Mercy as if he questioned leaving her and it lightened her heart. "Go," Mercy said. "I'd like to see more of your home."

"Not only beautiful, but compliant," Reeve said grinning.

"I'm going to beat you, Reeve," Duncan warned.

Reeve laughed. "I'm shaking with fear."

"You better be," Duncan said and leaned down to give Mercy a quick kiss, then walked off with his brothers, the four of them bantering about beauty and beatings.

The bantering stopped once the solar door was closed. Duncan didn't waste a minute. He informed them all of what he and Bryce had learned last night, this being the first chance of privately discussing it.

"The piece of hide with drawings on it is gone."

"What?" Reeve shouted.

"What do you mean?" Trey demanded.

"Are you sure?" Carmag asked.

"We discovered the theft last night," Bryce explained.

"How?" Trey asked shaking his head. "We rarely view the piece. It is for the king's eyes."

Duncan spoke up, explaining the exchange between him and Mercy, and how for some unexplainable reason, he immediately had thought about the hide buried at the bottom of the chest in the solar.

"I don't know why I thought the two connected, but I did," Duncan said. "And to assuage my concern I came here and looked for myself."

"And discovered it missing?" Reeve asked.

Duncan confirmed once again. "Yes, it's gone."

"This is a problem," Trey said. "The four of us and mother and father are the only ones who know where it is kept."

"Do you suggest one of us a traitor?" Reeve barked.

"Nonsense," Carmag said, stepping forward. "We have all worked hard toward a common goal and there is not one among us who would jeopardize that."

"Then who took it?" Trey asked.

"That is something we will need to find out," Carmag said.

Chapter 30

Mercy settled in a small room on the third floor after the tour of the keep was cut short. She had tried to show interest, but Mara, being as astute as she was, suggested that perhaps the tour was better left for another day. She had then brought Mercy to this pleasant room. Two wood chairs faced the hearth that kept the room toasty warm and a large chest sat between them, several candles sitting atop. A basket of embroidery sat to the side of one chair and Mara had explained that this was where she snuck off to on occasion.

It was her place of solitude, a place where she simply could be and not let anything disturb her.

Mercy appreciated the time alone. She truly needed to think. She needed to find an answer to her dilemma, though if she were honest with herself she would realize that there was only one conceivable answer.

She would have no choice but to trade herself for Bailey's wife.

She would have never believed herself capable of such

decisive action. Things had always been determined for her. It was the way of things, meant, she supposed, to protect her. But since sharing this unexpected journey with Duncan, she realized she had grown strong and somewhat self-sufficient.

Duncan had given her that and more, and while she would have much preferred to remain here in the safety of his arms, she couldn't.

And it wasn't only Bailey's wife who concerned her. It was Duncan's family as well. She feared for their safety no matter how Duncan and his brothers tried to reassure her. She might not know her father all that well, but she knew enough to know that while he had shown her kindness, he had also shown his wrath. There was no trusting the man.

And with his sovereignty threatened, he would certainly do whatever was necessary to retain his power.

Briefly, very briefly she considered telling Duncan about Bailey and letting him help her sort it out. But on closer consideration she knew that in the end, if there was no other choice, he would not allow her to be traded for Bailey's wife. And she would never be able to live with the fact that her father had killed a woman simply because his daughter had refused to return to him.

Besides, what future did she truly have with Duncan? She certainly could dream of one, but that was all it would ever be—a dream.

He had a mission, and her fate had been decided the day she had been born the bastard daughter of the king.

And like her father she was no fool. She would find Bailey and give him a message to give the soldiers. If they wanted her to return with them, they would have to bring his wife to the meeting place. There the exchange would be made, otherwise there would be no exchange.

The one last thing she would do was to ask Bailey to deliver a message to Duncan. She wanted him to know why she had made the decision she did and that she loved him and always would.

Tears pooled in her eyes and she laughed as she wiped them away before they could fall. Her mother had been right about love. It brought tears, pain and suffering, but she would not have given up knowing and loving Duncan for anything. She would suffer it all again, without hesitation.

She rested her head back against the chair and allowed her eyes to drift close. She wanted a few moments of quiet and peace before she went to find Bailey and meet her fate.

When he was finally finished in the solar, Duncan went in search of Mercy. The sudden look of worry that had flashed across her face at breakfast had haunted him the whole time he had been talking with his brothers and father. Something had suddenly troubled her, where only before she had been smiling. He wanted to know what had intruded on her thoughts, robbing her not only of her smile, but her peace of mind.

He covered a good portion of the keep and couldn't find her, so he looked for his mother.

He found her in the kitchen talking with Etty, or rather arguing. The two could never agree on anything, and if truth be told, he knew his father much preferred that she leave Etty alone as did he and his brothers.

Etty was the god of food to them and you didn't mess with a god.

"I'll be making what I've planned and that's that," Etty said as he approached.

"But Carmag mentioned to me how much he likes roasted boar—"

"And he'll be getting it soon enough, but not today," Etty declared, kneading the dough with white-hard knuckles.

"I want it cooked today," Mara said.

"And I want it to taste its best and that won't be until tomorrow."

"Well, place the meat closer to the flames," Mara demanded.

That was all Duncan needed to hear. He wasn't about to suffer through charred meat, which happened when his mother decided to cook herself. Something he, his brothers and father had no desire to experience ever again.

"Mum, I need your help," he said, walking over to her and slipping his arm around her shoulder.

She smiled at him and he easily guided her out of

the kitchen. And from the huge smile and nod Etty sent him, he knew he'd be well rewarded.

"What is it you need, love?" she asked.

"I can't find Mercy."

"Did you look in my resting room? That's where I left her."

Duncan furrowed his brow. He wouldn't even think of treading on such hallowed ground.

His startled expression had her laughing and she said, "Come with me and we'll see if she's still there."

He walked alongside her through the great hall. "Did Mercy enjoy the tour?"

"We never finished it," Mara said. "There seemed to be something on her mind, but then with all that has happened to her in a relatively short time, it's no wonder she's preoccupied. It certainly can't be easy for her."

"She has me," Duncan said.

Mara stopped before starting up the stairs and placed a gentle hand on his arm. "Of course she does, but think about it, Duncan. She loses her mother, her father, the ruling king, wants her dead and where does she end up? In the heart of the true king's troops. Who then does she truly trust?"

"Me!" he said with an adamant pound to his chest. "I love her and she knows it."

Mara's constant smile faded and it startled Duncan to the point where he felt a chill run through him. Never had he seen his mother without a smile. Angry or not, she wore her smile, as she insisted it helped keep her sane.

"Love sometimes isn't always enough for some," she said.

"It is for Mercy and me. Our love will see us through this," he insisted.

Her smile returned and chased away his fearful chill. "I'm sure it will."

He was certain of it and would let no one tell him any differently. Their love was strong and would survive any and all obstacles. Hadn't it already? And it would continue to do so, no matter what the turmoil. It was that strong and he that certain.

Duncan followed Mara into her private sanctum, pleased that she favored Mercy enough to share her private retreat with her.

"She's sleeping," Mara whispered as she peered around the chair. "This room can do that to you; take away your worries if only for a time."

Mara gave Duncan's arm a gentle pat. "Take your time."

"I can stay here?" he asked teasingly.

"Not if you sass me," she quipped and playfully slapped his arm before leaving.

Duncan crouched down in front of the chair and stared at Mercy. She looked so content and he was glad that she could escape her concerns for awhile. He couldn't say he wasn't worried himself. Though his family agreed that Mercy shouldn't be returned to her father, he knew if her presence here ever threatened the mission that there was a chance she would have to leave. Not return to her father, but seek asylum elsewhere until the true king took the throne.

He didn't want that. He wanted Mercy where he could protect her and keep her safe, but he also knew that might not always be possible. That was one reason he taught her how to use a dagger. She had been right when she had suggested that there might not always be someone there to protect her. He felt better knowing that at least she had a minimum of skill.

He reached out and gently took a strand of her long black hair between his fingers. He loved the feel of it, so soft and silky, just like her skin. He let it fall back to rest on her chest and he continued to drink in her beauty.

She stirred then and he hoped she would wake, though his thoughts were no longer on talking with her, but rather making love. Damn, but he couldn't resist her. He was already growing hard when he was around her and that wouldn't do. He needed to talk with her, needed to know what troubled her . . . needed to kiss her.

He was in trouble, big trouble, since there was no way he could make love to her here in his mother's private sanctuary.

It didn't take him long to make a decision. He eased her into his arms without waking her, her head falling to rest on his chest and her body cuddling against him. Even in sleep she seemed to know he held her.

It didn't take him long to get her to his bedchamber and as he placed her on the bed, he couldn't stop himself from kissing her or touching her. His hand slipped beneath her blouse. Her skin was warm and so very soft. His hand gently explored her plump breast, repeatedly teasing her nipple with his fingers until it grew stiff. He eased her blouse up, his mouth hungry for her hard nipple when a sharp knock sounded at the door.

Duncan jumped and Mercy's eyes sprang open.

"Duncan," Reeve called out.

He lowered her blouse covering her up and whispered, "I was attempting to make your dreams come true."

She smiled. "You always make my dreams come true."

The second pounding shook the door before it sprang open.

Reeve barged in, not looking at all contrite. "You're needed now!"

Duncan sprang out of bed and sent Mercy an apologetic glance.

"I'll see you later," she said and waved him off.

Duncan raced down the stairs behind Reeve.

"The mission comes first," Reeve reminded.

"I know that."

"Lately, it doesn't appear that way."

Duncan didn't need a lecture. He knew Reeve was right, but he also knew how he felt about Mercy.

"I love Mercy and I intend to make her my wife."

Duncan pulled back to avoid colliding with Reeve, he stopped so abruptly.

"The mission comes first," Reeve reminded again.

"You don't need to keep reminding me."

"Don't I?" Reeve asked. "There's no time for love right now."

Duncan shook his head. "I didn't plan on falling in love."

"Then put it on hold until the king takes the throne."

"I can't put love on hold, but I will not see the mission suffer for it," Duncan said.

"Your word on that?"

"We all gave our word, I need not give it again," Duncan said. "My word is my honor and you should know that."

"Just making sure," Reeve said.

"Enough about me, why the rush?"

"The messenger has returned."

"So soon?" Duncan said. "It must be important."

The two men bolted down the stairs, grabbed cloaks from the pegs by the door and ran out of the keep into the storm.

Trey, Bryce and his father were waiting along with Neil in the stables when Duncan and Reeve arrived.

The wiry little man sighed with relief and delivered his news in a rush. "The king *knows* that his daughter has vital information pertaining to the true king, which is why he wants her kept alive."

"How does he know for sure?" Trey asked.

"Evidence was found at the cottage," Neil confirmed.

"What evidence?" Duncan asked.

"I don't know for sure, though I heard mention of a burnt piece of cloth or hide and a servant who shared something she saw," Neil said.

"What about this hide?" Bryce asked. "What importance does it hold?"

"No one knows for sure," Neil answered.

"But there must be speculation," Duncan said. "People must be talking. It is the way of things around the king. People talk. What are they saying?"

Neil shrugged. "It's only gossip."

"Then let us hear it," Bryce said.

Neil lowered his voice. "It is said that it holds a secret."

"What secret?" Duncan asked.

Neil leaned in closer. "The secret of his birth. The proof that makes him the true king." He shook his head. "But it is only gossip."

"Tell me what happens to the king's daughter if she should return and he finds out what she knows. What becomes of her then?" Duncan asked.

Again Neil shrugged.

"Speculate," Duncan suggested quite firmly.

Neil lowered his head along with his voice. "She dies."

Chapter 31

With a hooded, heavy wool cloak to protect her from the rain, Mercy hurried through the village searching for Bailey. She didn't know how much time she had before Duncan returned and she wanted this done. It wasn't that she worried that she would change her mind. She had made her decision and knew it was the right one, especially after hearing the conversation between Duncan and his brother Reeve.

She had gone to find him shortly after he had left the bedchamber. She had wanted to tell him that she'd be waiting in the great hall for him. She hadn't wanted him to search for her and discover her meeting with Bailey. She had heard Reeve accuse him of not tending to the mission because of her and she felt responsible for causing dissent between the brothers and for having been the cause of Duncan neglecting his duty.

It seemed that no matter where she went her presence presented a problem. She wished there was somewhere she could sneak away to and be safe. The thought struck her so fast that she halted in her tracks.

She would have never even considered the possibility that popped into her head, if she hadn't gained the courage from surviving her ordeal. She had been in the hands of soldiers who intended her dead and had escaped. And if she did it once she could do it again. As long as she knew that Bailey and Kate were safe with Duncan and his family, then there was no reason for her to return to her father. She didn't believe that her father wanted her returned alive because he wished to make amends. He wanted something from her and once he had it, she would meet the same fate as her mother.

Her biggest obstacle was where to seek safe shelter and not bring harm to anyone. And the answer came easily and felt so very right. She would go to Bliss. After all, the woman had told her that they would see each other again, so she would be expecting her return, though perhaps sooner than she had anticipated.

Mercy grew more excited. If she could accomplish this, then someday there might be a chance for Duncan and her. But for now her absence would give him the time he needed to concentrate on his mission and prevent anyone from being harmed.

She felt relieved, for fate no longer had hold over her. She had taken control and would forge a new path of destiny for herself. She felt proud. Never had she thought she would have the courage to take control of her life, seek her own direction and make her own decisions. It felt so very good and so very right, and she doubted she would ever want it any differently.

She spotted Bailey huddled against the corner of a cottage, it and a hoodless cloak his only defense against the harsh wind and rain. She sent him a nod, letting him know it was time for them to talk. He drifted off into the woods and she followed. Thanks to the inclement weather no one was about, so she wasn't worried that someone would see her entering the woods behind him.

He stood under the spreading branches of a thick oak, the rain finding it hard to make its way through.

Her heart went out to Bailey when she got close enough to see how the worry had etched its way into his face in such a short time. She didn't waste a minute in telling him of her plan.

"I will trade myself for your wife, but only if you do as I say."

"As long as I get Kate back safe, I will do anything, even if it means forfeiting my life," Bailey said.

"Your death would defeat the purpose," Mercy said firmly. "What we need to do is to keep our wits and see that we all survive."

"What do you want me to do?"

"You must tell the soldiers that I have agreed to return to my father and that we will meet them tomorrow at dawn. And tell them I insist that they have Kate with them to make the exchange."

"What if they refuse or ask why you hadn't simply agreed when first asked?" Bailey asked anxiously.

"They won't," she assured them, "especially if you tell them I've been held against my will. If they do refuse to bring her that means—" She didn't finish. She didn't want to think that this all would be for nothing.

Bailey nodded. "You're right. I can't just hand you over to them and trust them to return Kate."

"There is something else I wish you to do," she said.

"What is it?"

"I want you to give Duncan a message from me."

"I will take it directly to him," Bailey said.

"No, you can't do that," Mercy said. "Duncan would surely follow with a troop of warriors and now is not time for the true king's troops to battle, especially over me. You will wait until evening. That will give me the time I need."

"Time for what?"

"To escape."

"You will return then?" Bailey asked.

Mercy shook her head. "I cannot return. Not now."

Bailey nodded as if he understood. "Tell me the message. I will repeat it to him exactly as you tell me."

"It is brief. You will have no trouble recalling it," Mercy said.

He nodded and Mercy gave him the message.

"There is no more?" Bailey asked.

"Duncan will know," she said confidently. "But it is better no one else does."

They parted then, their plan firm for dawn tomorrow.

Mercy made her way back through the pouring rain thinking that tonight would be the last time that she and Duncan made love for awhile. She refused to think that they would never love again. After all, she had taken charge of her destiny and Duncan was her destiny. They would be together someday; she refused to believe otherwise.

She intended to make love with him tonight like never before and then sneak away in the morning and do what she must. Do it for Duncan, for Bailey and Kate, and oddly enough for her mother.

Mercy wanted her father to know that he may have succeeded in killing her mother, but that the woman he had once claimed to love beyond belief had raised her daughter to be strong—and to survive.

She hurried out of the rain into the keep and almost collided with Mara.

"What were you doing out in such horrid weather?"

For a moment Mercy didn't know what to say. The only word she thought to murmur was, "Duncan."

"You looked for Duncan?" Mara shook her head, snatched her wet cloak off her and ushered her to the hearth. "He's busy with his brothers at the moment. You need to sit and get warm, or God forbid you catch a chill."

The woman fussed over her like a mother hen and Mercy had to admit that she enjoyed it. Her mother had rarely fussed. She had expected certain things from Mercy from when she was young and like a dutiful child she had obeyed. But every now and then her mother would be different. She would picnic with her at the river's edge or tell her a story and tuck her into bed. Of course that was when she was very young. As Mercy matured those special moments she had cherished with her mother had dwindled until they completely disappeared.

"I'll fetch us each a tankard of mulled cider and we'll chat," Mara said after she finished pulling a chair near the hearth and gently pushing Mercy into it, then tucking a soft wool blanket around her.

Mara returned in no time and pulled a chair up alongside hers after handing Mercy two tankards to hold.

Once she sat, Mercy returned one of the tankards to her. "Thank you for this."

"Nonsense," Mara said. "I'm pleased beyond belief that one of my sons has finally brought home a woman he loves, especially when I can see that love shining brightly in both their eyes."

"It's that obvious?" Mercy asked, not a bit sorry that she and Duncan wore their love so openly and so proudly.

"From the first," Mara said. "I don't believe you could have hidden it if you wanted to."

"I didn't want to."

"It is good you feel so sure about your love for my son," Mara said.

"I have not a speck of doubt that I love Duncan."

"No matter what?" Mara asked.

Mercy thought her question odd but answered it without hesitation and with more truth than Mara would realize.

"If I should have to leave here tomorrow, my love for Duncan would remain strong in my heart always. And no one or anything could change that."

"You are strong. You will survive this."

Mercy wondered if Mara realized that perhaps she was speaking the truth and encouraging her, but that wasn't possible. No one knew of her morning departure, though she wondered if Mara knew more that went on in and around the keep than she let anyone know.

The two women sat in silence for several moments before resuming the conversation.

"Loving someone can be difficult," Mara said.

"Loving someone is easy," Reeve said rounding his mother's chair and giving her a kiss on the cheek.

"Shame on you for sneaking up on us like that, be gone with you now," Mara scolded, shooing him away. "Besides what do you know about love?"

"All I need to know to stay away from it." He grinned and hurried off, out of reach of his mother's swatting hand.

"I fear Reeve will have the most difficult time with love since he takes it so lightly," Mara confessed.

"I never thought much of love," Mercy admitted.

"Why?"

"My mother raised me to believe it served no true purpose and that in the end it brings nothing but tears and heartache," Mercy said. "I've often wondered if perhaps my mother had been deeply hurt by love and that was why she felt the way she did. But I never got the chance to ask her."

"Love can leave scars," Mara said.

"That never heal," Trey said as he walked passed them, though never stopped.

When Trey was out of sight, Mara said, "He loved and lost and has yet to heal."

"I'm so sorry. How terrible for him," Mercy said, her stomach quivering from the thought. Leaving Duncan of her own free will was one thing, but having him taken away from her, knowing she would never see him again was something she didn't know if she could live with.

"Time is the only thing that will help him," Mara said, shaking her head. "Sometimes the wound is too deep to ever heal."

Mercy wondered if that was what happened to her mother. Had she been wounded so badly by love that it never healed? She wished she had asked her mother about her past when she was alive. Now she would never know.

"Though sometimes love can heal any wound as long as the heart is willing to take another chance," Mara said.

"You know your sons well," Mercy said. "Am I what you expected for Duncan?"

Mara shook her head, though smiled. "You are so much more. I knew Duncan would be the first to fall in love. He has known for sometime what he wanted."

"Which was?" Mercy asked eagerly.

"To fall in love, marry and raise a family. He may have enjoyed the favors of women now and again, and probably be horrified that I said so, but he knew once the right woman appeared he would know and never let her go. It seems his dreams have come true."

"Mine certainly have," Mercy admittedly happily.

"I'm the fulfiller of dreams," Duncan sang out and came up behind Mercy, leaned around and kissed her cheek.

"Mercy's just being nice," Bryce teased and slapped his brother on the back. "Come, we have more work to do. You can fulfill dreams later."

Duncan kissed her cheek again and whispered, "Later."

Mercy smiled and watched the two men laughing and bantering as they left the keep. "What of Bryce? How does he feel about love?"

Mara shook her head. "In some ways he's the easiest of my sons to understand and in other ways he is the most difficult. I can only pray that he will find a woman who understands him." Her smile grew wider. "But the most important part is that all four of them make certain that they give me lots of grandbabies to spoil."

Mercy laughed and prayed that she would eventually be part of this loving family. She would miss them all and would be relieved when she finally returned. She had to keep telling herself that she would return. No matter what happened, she had to find her way back here—her way back home.

* * *

Supper was a delightful affair, but then perhaps it was because this was her last night here and she wanted to enjoy every moment of it. The brothers laughed and teased and Carmag regaled everyone with Scottish tales until finally one by one they began drifting off, Reeve first and then Trey.

Then Bryce turned to Duncan and said, "I thought you were the fulfiller of dreams."

"You knew what I was thinking," Duncan said and took Mercy's hand and bid everyone good-night.

She giggled when he scooped her up in his arms and carted her up the stairs. Her heart swelled with love and sadness. She looked forward to this night with Duncan, but knowing she was leaving afterward made it bittersweet.

Once inside their bedchamber he fell down on the bed with her, smothering her face with kisses. She laughed, though it faded to sighs when he began kissing her in earnest.

The sighs soon turned to moans as his hands explored beneath her skirt with such erotic tenderness that she thought she would climax. But his hand slipped away before she did.

"No," she whispered in his ear. "That felt so good."

He kissed her quick. "I'm about to make it feel even better."

He sat up and shed his shirt, and before he shed his plaid, his hand once again dipped beneath her skirt and favored her with gentle strokes that ignited her already burning passion.

"I like that you melt to my touch so easily."

"How can I not when it is such a loving touch," she said. "Now hurry and please me so that I may do the same for you."

He worked fast at his plaid. "And then—" He grinned. "We'll start all over again and I will ride you slow and easy until you cannot stand it a moment longer."

"I already cannot stand it." She laughed softly. "You must hurry."

The solid rap at the door sounded just before Duncan was about to toss his plaid aside.

"This better be important," he shouted aloud.

"It is," Reeve shouted back. "We're all needed in the solar."

"I'll be right there."

"Don't dally," Reeve warned.

Duncan grumbled while he quickly dressed. "One day I'm going to beat him."

Mercy smiled. "No you won't."

"But he deserves it."

She shook her head. "He does what he must do as do you."

"I'll be back soon," he said and kissed her quickly. When he reached the door, he looked back. "I hope to be back soon."

"I'll be waiting," she said and as the door closed behind him, she prayed that it would be so. That he would return shortly and they would have this night together, all of it, not merely an hour or two, but the whole of it.

Please. Oh please. Let me have this night with him.

She had thought about this night all day and how the memory of it would help sustain her in the coming days, weeks, months. She didn't know how long it would be before she and Duncan were reunited.

What if they never were?

No. She would not let herself think that way. Duncan was her destiny and she would have it no other way. She would believe no other way.

She would stay strong for them both. He had his mission for the true king of Scotland and she had her mission. Once done, their lives would be theirs.

But for now she simply wanted this one night.

She had until just before dawn and then she'd have to leave. She laid there awake, sleep unable to tempt her and the hours ticked away.

Chapter 32

Duncan stood with his brothers and father on the battlements and watched the flickering lights in the woods.

"What do you think the soldiers are about?" Duncan asked.

"We don't know," Reeve said. "We've watched them for the last hour, since a sentinel reported their obvious movement, but we've still to figure it out."

"Their movement makes no sense," Trey said. "It's as if they move from here to there for no apparent reason."

"They do it to distract," Bryce said and the others stared at him. "It's the only sensible reason. They want our attention focused on their actions while something takes place elsewhere."

"But where?" Carmag asked.

"That's just it," Bryce said. "With all the activity, where is the spot that we should know about."

"We'll need to send men—"

Bryce interrupted Reeve before he could finish.

"Where? Where do we send them? " He pointed at the woods. "They look as busy and numerous as bees."

"Keeping anyone from discovering their hive," Duncan said.

"Then what do we do?" Trey asked. "There certainly aren't enough sentinels to keep watch over all of them."

"We wait," Duncan said. "We know they haven't the men to wage a successful attack against us. Besides, the king isn't foolish enough to attack us just yet. He's gathering support and warriors just as we are."

"So we hold firm, wait and be ready?" Reeve asked.

"It seems the wisest choice for the moment," Duncan said, a feeling of unrest churning in his gut. Something wasn't right, he could feel it. He stood with his brothers and watched the woods sparkle with light as though hundreds of stars had dropped out of the heaven and sprinkled across the forest.

It was a strange sight to look upon and even more so because he knew it wasn't an attacking army that approached. It was a diversion. And he worried over the reason for it.

After several hours past, Mercy left the bed and dressed quickly. She sensed that Duncan wouldn't be returning to bed this night. And she intended to find him and at least kiss him good-bye.

As soon as she entered the great hall she knew something was amiss. Warriors were coming and going after filling themselves with food and drink that the women kept rapidly replenishing.

Mara burst into the hall directing the women behind her to keep the warriors' tankards full. When she spotted Mercy she hurried forward as did Mercy.

"There is much movement amongst the soldiers in the woods. We don't know what is afoot, a diversion of sorts or so it is believed, and we must remain alert for any possibilities. Everyone is on guard and prepared to fight if necessary."

"Where is Duncan?" Mercy asked.

"On the battlements with his brothers." Mara took hold of her hand. "Do not disturb him now. He needs his wits about him."

Mercy felt her heart plummet. She had so wanted to see him one more time.

"Later, child," Mara said. "He will need you later, be there for him."

Mercy knew her disappointment was obvious and that Mara tried to ease it for her.

Someone called out to Mara and the woman turned and hurried off. Mercy stood there for a moment. All this distraction and worry, she assumed, was because of her and that disturbed her just as much as not being able to see Duncan again.

But there was nothing she could do but carry out her plan. She rushed up the spiral staircase to her bedchamber and quickly gathered what she needed, tucking the dagger Harry had given her into her boot. She added an extra blouse over the one she wore and slipped a vest on over that. With autumn's chill baring down on them and no Duncan to keep her warm this time, she wanted to make certain that she was prepared for her journey.

She intended to snatch some food off the tables in the great hall before leaving and grab her warm cloak that hung by the door. With one last look around the bedchamber and tears gathering in her eyes, she hurried out of the room.

No one paid her heed as she made her way through the great hall, grabbing what she needed as she went. They were much too concerned with their own duties and the uncertainty of the situation.

Once outside, she flipped the hood of her cloak up and over her head, pulling it down far enough so that it and the night helped conceal her identity. With rushed steps she hurried through the village and into the woods.

She didn't stop, didn't look back, couldn't look back. Somewhere high on the battlements Duncan stood looking out over the land, worried for his people, worried over his mission, and she was sure he was missing her just as much as she missed him.

"Mercy."

The whisper made her jump and her rapid heartbeat settled, though just a little when she saw that it was Bailey.

"Dawn is hours away," Bailey said.

"So why are you here now?" she asked of him what he wondered of her.

"I thought it wise with all the commotion that I leave," he explained. "And I worried that perhaps the soldiers were forcing our hand."

Mercy nodded. "A diversion to keep the sentinels and all eyes busy, giving us an easier chance to escape. And of course, avoiding any possible traps that we may have had planned."

"You think like a warrior."

Mercy smiled, thinking how often Duncan had called her a warrior woman. "A necessity forced upon me."

"Warriors are often conceived in battle," Bailey said.

"If that is so, then I am nothing more than a toddling warrior."

Bailey disagreed. "No. You are a mighty warrior for only a mighty warrior enters battle knowing he may not come out alive, but enters anyway."

Mercy placed a sturdy hand on his arm. "No, Bailey, a mighty warrior *knows* he'll come out alive. Now we must hurry, since I assume they wait for us."

They hastened their pace as best they could as they made their way through the dark.

"I need you to give Duncan that message as soon as you return," she said, "since I fear he may discover my absence sooner than I anticipated. And please, Bailey, please, convince him to pay heed to it."

"I will," Bailey said adamantly to Mercy's relief.

They no sooner reached the designated spot than the soldiers appeared, Kate tucked in the middle of them.

Bailey looked ready to call out to her, but Mercy silenced him with a strong grip to his arm and moved closer to him.

Mercy raised her voice and with confidence commanded, "Let the woman and her husband go and when they are on safe soil, I will be yours."

Laughter circled the group and she felt Bailey tense. She was quick with her reply.

"Be foolish and this man who wants nothing more than the safe return of his wife will see me dead."

Thankfully, Bailey went along with her ruse.

"Send my wife to me and after we are safe, I will set the woman free."

The soldiers hadn't expected the husband's bravery and there was muffled chatter before one spoke.

"The king's daughter is given to us first and then your wife is returned."

"Fool!" Mercy shouted. "You think my father would have you taking a chance with my life?"

Rumblings circled the soldiers once again.

"What will you have us do?" a soldier asked.

"As you have been directed," she commanded. "Or suffer my father's wrath."

One of the soldiers gave Kate a shove and she stumbled forward into her husband's arms.

"Be quick about it," the soldier ordered. "We will be on your heels."

Bailey hugged his wife and Mercy heard him whisper, "She helps us."

Kate reached out and squeezed her hand gratefully.

Mercy returned the squeeze as she called out for the benefit of the soldiers, "Let's go, I'm anxious to return to my father."

It wasn't long before Mercy watched as Bailey and his wife disappeared into the safety of the village, clinging to each other as if they would never let go. She turned then and joined the soldiers who treated her differently this time. She wasn't chained and she was shown respect. Obviously her father had sent orders that she be brought to him unharmed. It told her that he considered her no threat, and while he was not foolish when it came to his enemy, he was when it came to her. He would think her frightened and incapable of taking care of herself, and so he would play on her weaknesses until he got what he wanted from her and then he would rid himself of her.

That he underestimated her was to her advantage, and it would help her in her plan to escape. She hurried along with the soldiers, knowing that their torches mingled with the other torches, creating confusion. No one knew what truly went on and that was all right with Mercy.

It gave Bailey time to talk with Duncan and gave her time to escape. She would need to do it soon, before the sun rose high and before they traveled too far away from Pict territory. She would need to time it just right if she was to succeed and she prayed all would go well and that Duncan would heed her message.

If so, then there was a chance, a good chance, that one day they could be together again.

* * *

Duncan grew restless watching the torch lights wander aimlessly about the forest when he knew there was a reason to their madness. It was perplexing. What were they up to? What did they want?

Mercy? Could they possibly want Mercy?

Duncan shook his head trying to make sense of the sudden thought. The king wasn't a fool. He wouldn't attack this far north without support from ruling chieftains, and a far vaster army than these troops.

"What's wrong?" Bryce asked.

"Mercy," Duncan said as if breathless. "They want Mercy."

"Roaming with torches in the woods isn't going to do that for them," Reeve said.

"Where is Mercy?" Carmag asked his son.

But it was Mara who answered her husband's query as she approached with a basket of food and drink. "Last I saw her was in the great hall."

Duncan stepped forward. "I left her in our bed-chamber."

"She was looking for you," Mara said.

"Did you tell her where I was?" Duncan asked, worry fast taking hold of him.

"I told her you were busy and would see her later."

"Damn," Duncan muttered and hurried past his mother, taking the stairs two at a time and running down the hall to his bedchamber. He flung open the door and saw that it was empty.

His brothers arrived as he pilfered the room.

"Her dagger is gone," Duncan said and the four brothers hurried out and down the stairs to the great hall.

Mara and Carmag were already there.

"She's left," Duncan announced.

"Are you sure?" Carmag asked.

"She's taken the dagger that Harry gave her. She intends to defend herself if necessary."

"Or does she intend to return to her father?" Reeve asked.

Duncan ran at his brother with a fist and his father stepped between them.

"Enough," Carmag shouted with such commanding intensity that the two stopped and backed away.

"Mercy loves me," Duncan said.

"The reason she could be returning to her father," Bryce said, "is to protect you. To protect all of us."

"I can't let her endanger her life to save ours," Duncan said.

"You must," a man shouted out.

Duncan narrowed his eyes, studying the couple that approached them. "Bailey?"

"Mercy went to the soldiers to free my wife, Kate," Bailey said, holding on tight to his trembling wife.

Mara hurried over and directed the woman to a chair, though she refused to let go of her husband's hand.

"Mercy was so brave," Kate said through tears. "Much braver than I could ever be."

"Nonsense," Mara said. "You are here safe and sound

so therefore you endured as any brave woman does."

"Where is Mercy?" Duncan demanded, knowing in his heart, but needing to hear it.

"With the soldiers," Bailey said.

"She's returning to her father?" Bryce asked.

Bailey shook his head. "She plans to escape."

"What makes her think she can?" Reeve asked.

"She doesn't think she can," Bailey said. "She *knows* she can."

"That's my Mercy," Duncan said proudly.

"She'll be returning to us then?" Mara asked.

Bailey looked to Duncan, shaking his head. "She has other plans."

"Damn if she does," Duncan said and looked to his brothers. "You'll help me retrieve her."

Before they could reply, Bailey spoke. "You can't go after her."

"Who are you to tell me that—"

"Not me," Bailey said. "Mercy. I have a message from her to you."

"Tell me," Duncan demanded.

Bailey delivered the message. "She said to tell you that she loves you and always will and that she is safe and that you are to come for her when the time is right."

"Did she say where?" Trey asked.

Duncan shook his head. "I know where she is."

"She said you would know and that it was better that no one else did," Bailey said.

"She is a wise woman," Bryce said. "She gives you

the freedom to pursue your mission without worry over her."

"Bryce is right," Reeve said. "What Mercy did was selfless and in the best interest of the true king. She showed how much she can be trusted and how much she loves you."

"That is all well and good," Duncan said. "But what if she can't escape the soldiers?"

Chapter 33

Mercy never thought much of being her father's daughter. He had been remote most of the time, paying her little heed, consumed mostly by his own needs and wants. He had a harsh, berating nature at times and was often impatient with those who served him. And being she was her father's daughter, wouldn't the soldiers expect her to be similar? Besides, she wanted the soldiers to grow annoyed listening to her demands and whines so that they would ignore her soon enough, giving her time to make her escape.

"You're all idiots to think that I would remain with the enemy," she said for the hundredth time and had to keep herself from smiling when she caught several soldiers rolling their eyes. "My father shall hear about how you treated me, chaining me to a foe and threatening to kill me," she yelled. "He will see you all punished."

One of the soldiers mumbled something, and while she had heard him, she pretended she hadn't. "What did you say? Speak up, if you dare."

The soldier grumbled an apology and trotted his horse several feet in front of her.

His remark should have disturbed her, but it hadn't. He simply confirmed what she had believed.

Your father will not suffer you for long.

And she not need suffer her father's soldiers for long.

"I am hungry. I demand you get me food now, or I shall tell my father that you all purposely starved me."

In minutes she was handed several food items, which she gladly concealed in the small satchel attached to her waistband. It would provide her with larder until she reached Bliss.

Mercy continued her complaints until nearly all of the soldiers kept a wide berth around her. And the few stragglers were already drifting ahead of her.

"I need to stop and seek the privacy of the woods," she called out.

The soldier in charge waved at her. "Do as you must." He continued on, not paying her a bit of attention.

She thought to take her horse with her, but she feared it might be trained to return to the soldiers, so she dismounted and tethered her to a branch, then made her way into the woods.

She noticed that not one of the soldiers paid her heed and she knew she had time to make her escape. If she could at least reach Pict territory before the soldiers discovered her gone, then she knew she'd be safe. And there she could wait for Duncan.

The thought of him conjured memories and hopes of the future. She loved him so very much. She had hoped to love but never imagined she would love anyone as strongly she did Duncan. It wasn't easy leaving him. Her heart ached as if it had been broken and yet she knew it had been the wisest thing to do.

The true king needed him and while she had once thought him merely a myth, her journey with Duncan had made her realize that he was no such thing. He was real and Duncan was one of many who fought so that he could claim the throne.

How could she stand in the way of destiny?

Besides, Duncan and her fate were entwined and she would need to be patient, for when the time was right he would come for her and all would be well. She would believe no other way.

She was meant for Duncan, as he was meant for her and that thought gave her courage and helped her keep a pace that might be grueling, but to her was a run for freedom.

Her only regret was that she had been unable to see him, touch him, kiss him one last time before she left. She did not know how long it would be before they reunited; she hoped not long. She already missed him, but knew her decision had been for the best.

She shook her head and cautioned herself against ruminating about what was or might be. She had to reach her destination before the soldiers discovered her gone, or her plan would be for naught.

Mercy hurried through the woods, dawn having broken on the horizon hours ago, and since there had been no sign of Duncan following her, she knew that Bailey had been successful in delivering her message.

The thought hastened her pace. Nothing would stop her from reaching Pict land. She would do whatever it took to seek a safe place and wait for Duncan. He would come for her; she had no doubt. And no matter how long it took, she would wait for him.

"No need to tell you how important it is that this message gets delivered," Carmag reminded Duncan. "Your brothers deliver the other messages. Time draws near, we cannot fail. This is what has been planned and what you and your brothers trained for all those years. And it is what you all pledged—to see that the true king sits the throne."

"I know that, Da," Duncan said. "I will do what I must just as Mercy did."

"She is a brave woman. Not many women would have sacrificed as she did."

Duncan swung his fur-lined cloak around his shoulders, as he made ready to mount his stallion, the weather having taken on a considerable chill. He had tried hard to accept the truth of his father's words, but it was difficult. The woman he loved, who he would die for, was out there facing perils on her own. It may have been difficult when they had been shackled together, but at least she had him beside her. Now there was no one for her to rely on.

His father laid a firm hand on his shoulder. "Mercy will survive, she's counting on you to do the same."

Duncan hugged his father. He always knew the right thing to say and this time was no different. If Mercy had the courage to do what was right, then he had to do the same. Then he would go collect the woman he loved and never let her go.

He mounted his stallion, the horse snorting, eager to be on the way.

"I will see the message delivered and then go get Mercy."

His father grabbed the reins to steady the stallion. "Will you then confide the truth to her?

"I owe the woman I will soon wed the truth," Duncan said.

His father nodded and stepped back and Duncan rode away, intent on remaining true to his mission and intent on retrieving Mercy and making her his wife as soon as they returned.

Mercy kept to her grueling pace. She knew once the soldiers realized her gone they would stop at nothing to find her, for fear of suffering the king's wrath. She believed that they would either assume that she got lost, in which case they would not extend their search too far, or that they would believe she was attempting to return to Duncan. In which case they would search in the opposite direction of where she was going.

However, she intended on taking no chances. The

soldiers might not and extend the search for her. So she remained cautious and kept her pace at a steady speed, hoping to stay ahead of anyone who might be tracking her.

She had not stopped for nourishment, but ate as she walked and now with dusk not far off, her limbs were beginning to complain. She ignored them though, since she was not far from Pict land. She intended to reach it so that when she finally rested she could do so without worry.

She soon approached the edge of the woods, a meadow lay beyond, and she knew that once she crossed it, she'd be on Pict land. She'd be safe until Duncan came for her.

She took a cautious step forward, though did not leave the protection of the woods and glanced around. Dusk was not far off and she thought to wait.

"I must say you are braver than I thought."

Mercy froze, shutting her eyes briefly, then opening them and turning around to face her father.

He stood with two soldiers flanking him. He was a tall man and thick in size, his hands especially so. She remembered how it had hurt when he would squeeze her cheeks whenever he visited.

She noticed that his long brown hair had grayed considerably and while she always remembered a face marred by numerous wrinkles and lines, now they seemed to be abundant.

"You still are a beauty," he said.

"And you have grown old," she said with a toss of her chin.

He laughed. "You've gotten courageous. I'm proud. It's a shame you must die."

She intended to buy herself time and keep distance between her and her enemy, for if they grabbed hold of her she had no chance, but if she could move into the meadow and make a run for it, she might have a chance of surviving. If not, she would not go down without a fight.

"Like my mother?" she asked, taking a step away from him.

"Your mother betrayed me," he said angrily. "She had betrayed me from the beginning, that piece of hide proves it."

Mercy had no intention of admitting that she knew anything. "What are you talking about?"

"Don't lie to me," her father said through gritted teeth. "A servant saw you looking at it. And saw your mother snatch it from your hands and throw it into the fire. She also saw your mother trace something on your hand."

Mercy didn't want to believe that one of the servants she had come to trust had betrayed her mother and her, but then they did truly serve the king, so what had she expected?

"The piece of hide is lost to me, however the symbol isn't and it is what I need to defeat this imposter who claims himself the rightful king."

"My mother gave me no such symbol," she lied and drifted further away from him.

He lurched forward and she skittered quickly away. "Don't lie to me. You'll give me the symbol. You'll be begging to give me the symbol when I am done with you."

"You have such love for your daughter, Father," she said caustically.

"How can I even be sure you are my daughter?"

Mercy hadn't expected that and oddly enough it made her smile. "That truly would be joyful news."

His face grew red with fury. "Tell me now and be done with it."

"So that you may kill me?" Mercy shook her head. "That wouldn't be very wise of me." She moved again, attempting to gain more time and space between them. "And actually it wouldn't be very wise of you to travel all this way just to find me. Why are you truly here?"

He shook his head. "Intelligent and courageous. Perhaps you are my daughter."

"You're here to meet with someone, aren't you?" she asked, hoping whatever she learned could be helpful to Duncan and his mission.

"That is no concern of yours," he barked, obviously annoyed that she guessed correctly. "Tell me what I need to know."

She stepped back away from him and felt the ground change beneath her booted feet. She stood at the entrance of the meadow. Could she run fast enough to avoid being caught? Her limbs were tired and ached from her day's journey when more than likely her father and the soldiers had ridden horses. But what other choice did she have?

"I have nothing to tell you," she said firmly.

"You will tell me," he said, clenching his fist and vigorously shaking it at her. "You tell me what I want to know." With that he lurched at her, his fist opening and his thick hand reaching for her neck.

She turned and took off, forcing herself not to look back. She ran as if the devil chased after her, but then he did. She was surprised when she didn't hear any footfalls close behind her, and she hoped that she had gained enough ground to leave them in her wake.

She was halfway across the meadow feeling that she would make it to safe soil when she was suddenly and forcefully knocked to the ground, her face bouncing off the thick grass. It took her a moment to regain her wits, and when she did, she felt a searing pain in her left shoulder. She knew then that an arrow had taken her down.

"Get up and you'll suffer another one," her father's shout echoed across the meadow.

She refused to lay there defeated, and so she struggled to stand, and though the pain pierced her like a hot iron, she managed to make it to her feet and turn to face her foe.

They were further away from her than she expected and she suddenly felt some hope. If she could avoid being struck again, perhaps—she grew lightheaded and stood stock still, calling on all the strength she had to keep from fainting.

"Stay as you are and you will suffer no more."

Her father's warning shout gave her the strength she needed and she began walking backwards.

"Don't move," he shouted once again.

The soldiers started running toward her, their bows drawn and she knew they would soon stop and take aim at her, and at closer range, they could very well hit their mark.

She had no choice. She turned and began to run in a zigzag pattern, making it harder for the soldiers to take a true aim. One arrow barely missed her and another flew over her head and she kept running while her father's shouts grew louder.

The end of the meadow drew closer and closer. But the pain grew worse and worse, tearing through her like a sharp hot dagger.

Suddenly she heard a voice call out. "Drop. Drop."

It wasn't a familiar voice and she believed it came from in front of her, perhaps the woods itself. If so, that meant it came from the Picts. She didn't consider it for one second more. She dropped to the ground and into unconsciousness.

"Lie still. You're safe."

Mercy recognized the voice. "Bliss."

"Yes, it is I and you are at my cottage. You are safe, though the arrow must be removed."

"It hurts so very much," Mercy said, her breath catching as she lay as still as she could on her stomach.

"Removing it will hurt even more."

"I will survive?" Mercy asked.

"That is up to you," Bliss said.

"I will," Mercy insisted through the pain. "Duncan knows I wait for him. I will be here when he comes for me."

Mercy slipped in and out of consciousness after that. Once when she was a bit lucid, she thought she heard a familiar voice and someone saying that Duncan must be told, and she was quick to speak up.

"No," she moaned, though that was all she could manage.

It was a long and painful night and Mercy wasn't certain if she would truly survive it, but she fought. She refused to surrender. And finally when dawn broke on the horizon it was done and she lay resting on her stomach in Bliss's bed. And after a brew that Bliss insisted she drink she fell into a much needed slumber, the last thought on her mind and the last word to spill in a whisper from her lips, "Duncan."

Duncan sprang up from a sound sleep and jumped up, peering into the dark. He could have sworn he heard Mercy call his name. But nothing but the night's darkness greeted him. He had taken cover in a dilapidated cottage. There was no roof and only three walls, but it provided enough cover for him for the night.

He settled back down on his makeshift pallet, pulling the warm wool blanket over him. However, sleep refused to return to him. He could not get Mercy off his mind. He worried about her, even more so since he had woken hearing her call out to him.

Could she be in trouble? Or worse hurt?

He cursed his troubled thoughts and almost cursed the mission, but stopped before doing so. While he loved Mercy and would prefer to be with her, his mission had to take precedence, and she had understood that and had removed herself so that he could do what he must. He could not insult her courage by not doing the same.

Not that it made it any easier for him. She may be courageous, but she was petite and ever so vulnerable. He shook his head. He couldn't think that way. He had to believe her more than capable of surviving on her own. And he had to acknowledge her bravado in doing it all on her own. If she had approached him with such a plan he would have outright refused to allow her to do such a dangerous thing—surrender to the enemy?

He shook his head. He would have laughed at her, while his brothers probably would have recognized the wisdom of it.

But at least he could have offered her help, though in so doing he would have delayed his own mission.

There was no easy answer to any of this and it was already done, so what was the purpose of lingering on it? What was done was done. It would take a good month for him to see this mission complete. He and his brothers had to make sure who was friend and who was foe to the true king, not an easy task, but a necessary one.

Then when he was done he would go get Mercy. He knew as soon as Bailey had delivered her message where she had planned on going. And he was pleased she had chosen a safe place. She would be looked after there and he looked forward to joining her.

He wouldn't waste a minute retrieving her from the Picts.

Chapter 34

❦❦ "I feel fine. After all it has been two months," Mercy assured Bliss as they took their evening walk to the cave. "If it hadn't been for you and your friends, though, my father and the soldiers would have gotten me."

"Duncan wisely paid heed to your request and did not come after you, but that didn't mean he couldn't make certain that you were helped. As soon as we received his message we went in search of you."

Mercy should have known that Duncan wouldn't just sit back and do nothing. He had reminded her many times that he would be there for her. And it seemed that even when he wasn't there, he still found a way to help her.

"I shouldn't be surprised by his actions; they speak boldly of his good nature. And that Trey had ventured here to see if I had arrived safely also surprised me, though it shouldn't have."

"The path he took crossed ours and as he had told me, it would ease his brother's mind to know you made it here safely, though I saw how worried he was for you. And I dare say I saw admiration in his eyes for you."

"At least, he heeded my request not to tell Duncan of my injury," Mercy said.

"What makes you think he didn't?"

"Duncan didn't return right away."

"If he had, wouldn't then your injury have been for naught?" Bliss asked. "From what I understand you sacrificed yourself so that he could accomplish his mission. If he had returned right away he would have dishonored you."

"You have a way of seeing things more clearly than most," Mercy said with a smile.

"Sometimes it's more a curse than a gift."

"I believe it is a gift and I am grateful for it," Mercy said, "and grateful to call you a friend."

Bliss grinned. "I knew when first we met that we would be lifelong friends, like sisters really."

"I would love that," Mercy said excited. "I had always wanted a sibling, and now to have a sister—" She stopped walking and turned and gave Bliss a hug. "Thank you. You have no idea how much this means to me."

Bliss returned the hug and said, "I am glad that we have met, that our destinies are entwined."

Mercy sensed that Bliss knew more than she said, but if she had learned anything in the last two months with her, it was that Bliss told you things in her own good time.

"That's understandable since so much had happened

to you," Bliss said. "Besides some things are obvious to me, while others see nothing at all."

They entered the cave as they did every night just after dusk. At first Bliss had remained by Mercy's side and had encouraged her as she struggled to learn to swim. But it hadn't been long before her strokes turned natural and she was swimming as if she had been doing it forever.

"I believe the swimming helped tremendously in healing my shoulder," Mercy said.

"Your tenaciousness is what healed your shoulder," Bliss said. "I am amazed at how well and quickly you have healed in just two months."

"It is all because you tended me with as much tenaciousness as I wanted to heal. And as soon as I was well enough to walk, you walked with me here to the pool. You understood without me saying a word how important it was for me to be here."

"You wait for him here, don't you?" Bliss asked.

Mercy nodded, feeling a tightness grab at her heart as it always did when she thought of Duncan. She knew she would miss him, but she truly had no idea how much. Being separated from him tore at her heart daily and the nights were so much worse, especially waking alone in bed. She had grown so accustomed to having him beside her that she felt empty without him.

Her hand went protectively to her stomach. She was far from empty. Duncan had given her a gift she would forever cherish. He had left her with child and that was the one saving grace. She carried part of him with her.

"It will be another couple of months before you round," Bliss said.

Mercy laughed. "If it hadn't been for you I wouldn't have even realized that I was carrying a babe."

"You were too busy recovering from your wound to notice the other signs. Luckily they were minor to some that women experience."

Mercy patted her stomach and smiled. "He is good-natured like his father and will give me no trouble."

"That he is," Bliss agreed, grinning, and Mercy wondered if perhaps she knew it to be so.

Mercy shed her clothes, eager to enjoy the water's warmth, autumn's chill having given way to winter's cold, though it was still a few weeks away.

When she saw that Bliss wasn't doing the same, she asked, "You're not swimming tonight?"

"I have a yearning for honey buns."

"You've set my mouth to watering," Mercy said.

"Then you'll be all right if I return to the cottage?" she asked. "And as soon as I set a pan to bake I'll come fetch you."

"Take your time. I'm lazy tonight and just intend to float in the water's warmth."

Quiet descended over the cave once Bliss left and it gave Mercy a chance to reflex. She was so grateful that Bliss felt like they were more sisters than friends. She had always wanted a sibling, someone she could talk with, confide in, someone to trust.

When she was very young, she had asked her mother

about having a brother or sister and her mother had gotten angry with her and she had never asked again. Her mother was also very careful of who Mercy was allowed to befriend. And so she merely had limited acquaintances.

She had trusted Bliss immediately and she had grown more trustful of her every day since. She had tended Mercy with a gentle touch and a caring heart. She was a unique friend, and now someone she could call sister, just as Duncan did with his brothers.

Bliss had remarked many times how Duncan would come for Mercy, she only need be patient. Mercy wondered how Bliss could be so sure when she didn't know Duncan that well. Bliss had explained that she had seen love in Duncan and Mercy's eyes when she had first met them. And a strong love such as theirs could never be separated for long. Their deep love would always reach out and reunite them whenever apart.

Mercy hoped she was right and prayed that she and Duncan would be reunited soon. She missed him terribly and had come to realize that though their shackles had been removed, they were bound more firmly by love than any metal chains. And that nothing, not the king or a smithy's hammer, could separate them permanently.

She floated peacefully in the warm water, knowing she had not only regained her strength but had become stronger than before. She knew that Duncan would insist she had gained her courage on her own, but he had taught her the true meaning of valor, for he lived it every day.

Mercy quickly turned as she heard footfalls and as

soon as she saw Bliss, she knew something was wrong.

"Come quick, Duncan is in danger."

Duncan sat around the campfire with his brothers, glad they had all successfully delivered their messages and that all was going well with the mission. Troops were being mounted, comrades being made and more plans being drawn. These past two months had served the mission well, and he never thought he would have been grateful for Mercy's departure, but he had. Though he would have preferred she had not suffered a wound because of it, Trey had assured him she was well and in good hands. And that Mercy herself did not want him to know of her injury until his mission was done.

He had thought he had known courage. After all, he had been in many battles, faced death a few times, but he had never really known true valor until he had met Mercy. Petite and not having the body strength to truly defend herself, she didn't let that stop her. She hadn't even let not being able to swim stop her from jumping off that cliff, and damn, if that hadn't taken courage. But what he admired the most about her was her audacity in not allowing the fact that she was bastard daughter of the king to stop her from fighting to survive, when truly the odds were against her.

She was quite a woman and she would soon be his wife.

"So do we celebrate a wedding soon?" Reeve asked with a grin.

"As soon as I return with Mercy," Duncan confirmed.

"I bet Mother already has the whole thing planned," Trey said.

"She's been waiting for one of us to bring home a bride," Bryce said and gave Duncan a jab in the side with his elbow. "She'll be wanting grandbabies soon."

Duncan grinned wide. "I can oblige her on that."

One of their warriors suddenly approached from out of the darkness.

"Something wrong?" Duncan asked, standing along with his brothers.

"The messenger approaches."

"Here? Now?" Reeve asked, surprised.

"Something is definitely wrong," Duncan said.

Bryce nodded. "Neil would never take the chance of meeting us anywhere but the designated spot."

The four men waited anxiously and when the wiry little man appeared, they all tensed. He was sweating from head to toe and they knew he had run a distance.

Trey grabbed a blanket and wrapped it around him, his body trembling.

With labored breath, Neil said, "A trap has been set for the king's daughter and Duncan."

"Tell us," Duncan said, walking over to him.

"Word has been sent to her that you are on your way to her, but that a trap awaits you before you can reach her. The king knows you will learn of it and assumes you will go to her rescue and his plan is to capture you both."

"He has to be a fool to think we'll let our brother go alone," Reeve said.

"No," Duncan said, shaking his head. "He's counting on it."

"That he is," Neil said. "He believes it is a way of seeing for himself who defies him and being rid of all of you in one full sweep."

"We'll rescue Mercy and be gone before the king even knows we were there," Reeve said.

Neil shook his head. "There isn't time. By morning Mercy will have left Pict territory."

"I'll go myself and bring Mercy home," Duncan said.

His brothers strenuously voiced their objections—all but one.

"The hell you will," Reeve shouted.

"Absolutely not," Trey said.

Bryce nodded slowly. "Duncan's right. We can't chance having all of us caught or starting a battle with the king's men now. It's not time yet."

"At least one of us can help him," Reeve said.

Duncan shook his head. "No, this is for me to do. Mercy is my woman."

"Soon to be our sister," Trey reminded him.

"I'm pleased that you accept her as such," Duncan said, "but it is best that I do this on my own. Besides, you all need to report back to father. It is important that he receives the information. The movement grows bigger and stronger. And I wouldn't be surprised if the king realizes it."

"He does," Neil confirms. "And truthfully, it is the information that his daughter has that he wants so badly. The soldiers gossip about how bravely she confronted her father. How she ran across the meadow and was slammed to the ground by an arrow through her shoulder and she struggled to stand, refusing to surrender."

Duncan turned to Trey. "You didn't tell me this."

"I didn't know," Trey said. "The arrow had already been removed when I got there, and Bliss told me that Mercy would heal well. No one spoke of how she received the wound and I had no time to ask."

"From what I hear, a few arrows missed her," Neil said, "but she kept on running, and after getting hit and standing she zigzagged and stumbled to avoid more arrows. If it hadn't been for the Picts . . ." Neil didn't finish, he simply shook his head.

"Damn, our sister was brave," Reeve said.

Duncan fisted his hand so tightly that his knuckles protruded like sharp talons. "I'm going to kill her father."

Bryce slapped a firm hand on Duncan's shoulder. "Keep your wits about you and save your revenge for another day."

Duncan reluctantly relaxed his grip and nodded, realizing the wisdom of his brother's words, though he had every intention of one day seeing Mercy's father dead.

Bryce turned to Neil. "It's become too dangerous for you to return. You'll make your home with us now."

Neil tried to protest, but Bryce wouldn't have it.

"You know much about the king and his strategies. I don't want to risk losing your knowledge."

Neil nodded. "I will do whatever is best for the true king of Scotland."

"You have served the true king well and he will not forget," Trey said and guided the man to sit by the campfire.

Bryce and Reeve joined them, but Duncan remained standing.

"What do you know of this trap set for Mercy?" Duncan asked.

Neil smiled. "Everything."

Chapter 35

Dawn was near on the horizon and with it Mercy knew she'd be leaving Pict land and once again vulnerable to attack and capture. But it made no difference to her; her only concern was saving Duncan.

Bliss's friend Roan, the one who had saved her from her father, had information that Duncan was in danger, though he believed it a ruse to draw her out. Not trusting the source, he had urged her not to go.

She understood his concern and thought the same herself, but she couldn't take the chance. What if Duncan truly was in danger and she didn't go to help him? She couldn't live with the thought.

Bliss hadn't argued with her even though Roan had begged her to. She simply had nodded and explained that Mercy had to do what was right for her. She and Bliss had hugged long and hard before Mercy departed. And Bliss had warned her that all was not what it seemed and that the truth would be the only thing that truly freed her. Then she had told her they would see each other again.

And that when the time was right they would not part, but actually be like true sisters.

That pleased Mercy though she wondered how that could be when Bliss lived with the Picts and she would be with Duncan. But Mercy hadn't questioned it; she had simply bid her good-bye after one last hug and had set out to save Duncan.

Mercy knew she took a chance and placed not only her life in danger but that of her unborn babe. Unfortunately she knew no other way. Whether a ruse or not, she needed to know that Duncan was safe.

Dawn hit the horizon as she stepped away from Pict territory and she proceeded with cautious steps and alert ears. If it was a trap, then her father would certainly pick an area where he would feel he could easily contain her. And so she tried to avoid such areas.

Somehow she sensed that Duncan was on his way to her, and if they could meet and avoid her father and his soldiers, then they could return home and be safe.

Home.

She truly had a home with Duncan and his family, and now she had a sister in Bliss and would be a sister to three brothers. She was thrilled with the prospect, and though fate still held her in its hand, she believed all would go well. It had to. Love had to prove the victor in all of this.

She walked until the sun was high in the sky, and while she was cautious, she couldn't help but feel as if she was being followed. At least she was drawing closer and closer to Duncan's land, which made rescue that much more possible.

Feeling a bit nauseous she stopped to munch on some food that Bliss had packed for her. Leaning against a large boulder she rested, though only for a moment.

"I knew you wouldn't be able to resist warning him."

While she was annoyed at being caught by her father, she refused to show defeat. "What makes you think it isn't a trap I set for you?"

Her father laughed as he stepped from behind the cover of bushes.

Mercy noted that only two soldiers followed him and while she was sure more lingered nearby, there were only two present. She had bested two before, perhaps she could do it again.

"Really, Daughter, do you think I don't scout ahead?"

"Do you think me foolish enough to come alone?"

The soldiers cast wary glances around.

"Stop it, you fools," her father ordered, "she but tries to frighten you."

"Do I?" she asked, her deep voice dripping with such coldness that it made the soldiers shiver.

"Enough, Mercy," her father ordered.

She laughed. "You mean you finally surrender?"

"Chain her," her father commanded.

"Take one step toward her and I'll kill you."

Mercy grinned at the sound of the familiar voice, though didn't turn around to face Duncan. "I told you I wasn't alone."

"One man," her father laughed.

"No, Father," she said, "one *gallant* warrior."

She heard Duncan walk up behind her and waited as he took his place beside her.

"You're late," she teased.

"And you're early, though pleased I am to see you," Duncan said.

"And I you," she said, though wished to say so much more, but it would have to wait. First they had to extract themselves from this dilemma.

"Finally," her father said with a satisfied grin. "I have you both where I want you."

Just as he finished, Mercy felt the tip of a sword to her back and Duncan motioned with a nod that he felt the same. He reached out his hand to her and she grasped hold of it. His long fingers wrapped tightly around her small ones and gave a squeeze as if letting her know all would be well. And she believed it so, for as long as they were together, she had no doubt they would survive.

"Shackle them," her father commanded, and the soldiers behind them had them in chains in no time.

"Now," her father, said stepping forward. "You'll—"

"Step back or I'll kill you," Duncan warned.

Her father laughed. "You are a fool."

"You're the fool," Duncan said. "If you think that

I won't seek revenge for making the woman I love suffer."

"Need I remind you that you are in no position to dictate to me," her father said.

"Need I remind you that there is no way in hell I'm going to let you hurt Mercy ever again?"

"I have no intentions of hurting my daughter," her father said. "It is you who will suffer until she gives me what I want and then you both will meet death together."

Duncan swept Mercy into his arms, and though it looked as if he kissed her, he actually whispered in her mouth.

"Grab your dagger; we run for it."

They parted and she smiled. "I'm ready."

With that, Mercy and Duncan moved so swiftly that chaos ensued. They both had daggers in their hands before the soldiers could reach them.

"Grab them, you fools," her father shouted, but Mercy and Duncan wounded the two soldiers that charged them, which caused the other soldiers to approach more cautiously.

Their hesitation gave Duncan and Mercy the time they needed to run and they did. They took off through the woods like arrows being shot from a bow.

"Don't stop," Duncan warned.

And Mercy didn't. She kept pace with him, ducking out of the way of branches, jumping over fallen logs and not slowing down even to look back and see if the soldiers were gaining on them.

They traveled at such speed that when they broke through the trees and saw they approached the edge of a cliff, they didn't have time to stop. They went straight over.

The two soldiers halted just in time, though it was the one who lagged behind who prevented the other from going over the edge by grabbing his shirt and yanking him back.

The two stared over the edge and watched the couple plunge into the raging river below.

Duncan instantly wrapped his arms around Mercy as they plummeted down to the river. She, in turn, tucked her head against his chest, though not before telling him . . .

"I carry your child."

"Now you tell me," he yelled and did all he could to wrap himself around her and protect her and his child from the fall.

They hit the water and plunged down, and Duncan immediately went to wrap his arm around Mercy to help her swim to the surface. To his surprise she pushed his hand away and began swimming to the top, and he joined her. With them both working together, they surfaced in no time. And together they made it to the bank of the river not far away.

"Our child?" Duncan asked when finally they stood on the bank, his hand splaying across Mercy's stomach.

"Aye, our child," she said and shivered.

"We need to get you home and warm in bed," Duncan said.

"How I wish, but we are too far—"

Duncan shook his head. "Do you really think my brothers would let me come entirely alone?"

Mercy looked around. "But there is no one here."

"There will be soon enough. My men watched from a distance and they will see what has happened and come for us."

And they did, and with dry clothes, blankets and horses.

They made it home by nightfall and retired to their bedchamber shortly after their arrival, after informing everyone that they were fine. They cared naught about the shackles. Tomorrow was soon enough to be rid of them. Tonight they simply wanted to be together, to hold each other, touch each other, love each other.

With hot cider heating their innards and their naked bodies keeping them warm, they snuggled together beneath the blankets. Though it wasn't long before simple touches turned desirous and passion claimed them.

It was a gentle mating, soft and considerate for all Mercy had been through, though when he slipped into her, she took over the pace and they were soon lost in a frantic joining that had them exploding with an intensity and had them both calling out each other's names.

They laughed afterward and cuddled close.

"I can't believe I'm to be a father," Duncan said, his hand resting gently on her stomach.

"You didn't tell anyone," Mercy said.

"I wanted to savor the news," Duncan explained. "I'll tell them all tomorrow.

"You feel well?" he asked and then shook his head. "You must. You have survived another plunge off a cliff." He kissed her. "You know how to swim."

"After I healed, I practiced every day."

His hand drifted to the scar on her shoulder and his fingers brushed over it ever so lightly. "I am sorry you suffered."

"It wasn't your fault," she assured him. "My father is to blame. He wanted to know about the symbol my mother traced on my hand."

Duncan released Mercy and plopped flat on his back. Her chained wrist followed his and came to rest across his chest. She turned with it and slipped her leg over his.

"What's wrong?" she asked propping her elbow beside his shoulder and resting the side of her head in her hand.

"I need to tell you something."

"This will upset me?" she asked, her eyes widening.

"No. Well, I hope not," he admitted.

"Then tell me and be done with it."

"That piece of hide your mother showed you belonged to the true king of Scotland and the symbol she traced on your hand is a secret code, only the true king can decipher.

"How do you know this and how did my mother ever come by it?" Mercy asked, confused.

"I don't know how your mother came by the piece since it has long been stored in a chest in the solar," he said. "My brothers and I assume that someone from here stole it and gave it to your mother."

"Why?"

Duncan shrugged. "We don't know, though if we can find out who stole it, we can find out why it was given to your mother."

"This piece of hide is important?"

"It holds the proof of his birth. It is what makes him the rightful king."

"Then he can no longer claim the throne?" she asked, worried.

"He will take the throne, he knows how, so do not worry."

"How do you know so much about the true king?" she asked.

"That's what I need to tell you," he said. "You know the first part of the myth?"

Mercy nodded and recited it. "Four warriors ride together and then divide, among them the true king hides."

"My brothers and I are the four warriors," Duncan said.

Mercy stared at him for a moment, shook her head, opened her mouth to speak, closed it and then shook her head again. Finally she said, "That makes one of you the true king of Scotland."

Duncan nodded. "And I cannot reveal his identity."

He took her hand in his. "So I need to know if you will marry me knowing that I may or may not be king."

Mercy leaned down and kissed him. "I love you, Duncan, and I would be proud to be your wife, king or not." With a smile she raised the shackles that bound them. "Chained or not, I am bound to you, but it is love that binds us and forever will."

At Avon Books, we know your passion for romance—once you finish one of our novels, you find yourself wanting more.

May we tempt you with . . .

- **Excerpts** from our upcoming releases.

- Entertaining **extras**, including authors' personal photo albums and book lists.

- Behind-the-scenes **scoop** on your favorite characters and series.

- **Sweepstakes** for the chance to win free books, romantic getaways, and other fun prizes.

- Writing **tips** from our authors and editors.

- **Blog** with our authors and find out why they love to write romance.

- **Exclusive content** that's not contained within the pages of our novels.

Join us at
www.avonbooks.com

AVON

An Imprint of HarperCollins*Publishers*
www.avonromance.com